The Age of Privilege

By

Donna Wootton

AOS Publishing, 2024
Copyright © 2024

Donna Wootton

All rights reserved under International
and Pan-American copyright conventions

ISBN: 978-1-990496-42-4

Cover Design: Chanelle Poupart

Visit AOS Publishing's website:
www.aospublishing.com

Prologue

When the very handsome Christopher Mann leaned across the counter in her father's shop and kissed her, she didn't tell anyone. Dawn Wright did, however, take his advice and invest in gold. Over the course of the remaining decades in the twentieth and twenty-first centuries, the value of gold rose: doubled, quadrupled, reached heights that even that kiss couldn't have foretold. Christopher married his high school sweetheart while Dawn Wright grew wealthy. This is her story.

The Twentieth Century

The guidance counsellor suggested she enroll in engineering, not a usual recommendation for a girl born in 1945, and not one that Dawn liked very much, but she didn't tell Mr. Bargeman that. What she did say was that she'd bought gold and had to take care of it.

"Gold?"

"Yeah."

"What kind of gold?"

"Bricks."

"Not jewelry?"

"No, like they give you in banks." Mr. Bargeman looked confused. Dawn then realized that he only understood gold in terms of decoration, not in terms of finance. What did she expect? He wasn't even a teacher. He was simply the guidance counsellor. Dawn explained, "You buy it by the ounce."

Bargeman shook his head like he understood.

"What do you invest in?"

Again, Bargeman shook his head. "Me? I don't think about that."

"Right now, I'm thinking about getting rich."

"You think buying gold is going to make you rich?"

"Have you seen my marks in math?"

Bargeman looked down at her file that listed the results of her progress from grades nine to eleven. "Impressive. I can understand how you can score one hundred percent in algebra, but how did you get that mark in English?"

"By writing a perfect essay."

Bargeman looked at her over the tops of his eyeglasses.

"I wrote a perfect geometry exam too."

Again, he looked down at her grades. "But your mark is only ninety-six percent."

"Because Hardy unfairly deducted marks for drawing diagrams that he said were too large."

Bargeman nodded. "Hardy did that?"

"Yes," Dawn said. "So, I complained to the principal. You see, I always get asked to put my homework on the board with the boys. Hardy runs his class like that."

"Mr. Hardy?"

"He gets us to show the correct answers while he helps the dumb girls in the front row who don't understand."

"They're not all dumb, Dawn."

"But he likes those girls, and he thinks that I'm the one who's disruptive because he thinks I'm flirting. That's what he told Mr. Creighton."

"Mr. Hardy told the principal that you flirt?"

"Yes, but what I'm simply doing is having fun with math."

"So, you might enjoy engineering?"

Dawn bristled. "No, I'm going into business to study accounting."

The Age of Privilege

At university in her third year Dawn met Paul Lewis when he was preparing his application for law school. After she told him her story about the guidance counsellor, Paul said, "You're still a flirt."

She leaned her weight on her forearms and stretched across his bare chest to plant a kiss on his cheek. "Aren't you glad I am?"

"Yep," he said.

"You don't look glad."

"Post coitum omne animal triste."

"Latin?"

"Yes, handy for the law."

"What does it mean?" His eyes opened wide. She liked his blue eyes. They were the colour of the sea with the sun sparkling on the vast expanse of water.

"Can't you guess? You said I don't look glad. But I'm content. Great sex. I'm even happy. You make me happy. I don't want to insult you but it's in an animal's nature to be sad after fucking. *Post coitum.*"

"Ah, *triste.* I get it."

"You didn't study Latin in high school?"

"Are you kidding?" Dawn sat up and brushed her fingers through her auburn hair. "I took sciences and math. The only language I studied was English."

"You mean you studied English literature?"

"Had to keep my grades up. Needed the marks for the bursaries and scholarships I used to pay for my education. Unlike some, I'm not from money."

"What are you from?"

She wrinkled her nose at him like a rabbit. "My Dad owns his own business, a stationery store in town. "

"Respectable."

"But hardly profitable," Dawn said.

"Okay, he makes money, just not a lot of money."

"I guess that's how you could put it."

"But he's alive?" Paul asked.

"Isn't yours?"

"No, he passed away before I started university. Heart attack. Sudden. Though he wasn't all that healthy, so we shouldn't have been surprised."

"Still, it must have been a shock?"

"Yes, I wanted to delay leaving home, but Mother wouldn't hear of it. She insisted I go into residence rather than commute. She wanted me to enjoy college life." He reached over and patted her skull with his palm. "I like your hair. It feels like silk."

"Like having girls in your dorm?" Dawn felt the warmth of his hand given like a benevolence. His hands weren't large. They were long. His fingers were long.

Paul looked over at her and laughed. "I want you to meet her. Will you?"

"Your Mom?" This was a gesture of friendship. "Sure, if you want. But first, speaking of English, let's define 'flirt'. As in, you flirted with me, right? I remember you staring at me. How could I forget your blue eyes following me? Maybe flirting isn't about words. Maybe it's about the silent conversation you had when you stared at me. You said a lot with that look."

"Like what?"

"Like, you're interested."

"Maybe."

"Yes, maybe that's really what flirtation is. So, I wasn't flirting in math class."

"Is this still troubling you, Dawn? All these years later?'

"Yes, it is. A girl just can't have any fun without getting a reputation."

"So, you were studious?"

"I was. I was a serious student. But I was a teenager."

"A serious teenager?"

"Yes, not a genius, but studious enough to earn the grades that set me apart from most of the other teenage students."

"You'll go far. That's my prediction."

Dawn grinned at Paul. She liked his approval and felt she could count on his eternal support.

———

Barbara Simpson watched the apartment window from the street. She knew it well, having been there over the past two years on many occasions with Paul, the man she thought she'd marry. Now she felt betrayed, humiliated, scorned. It was as if she'd never been in his life. Who was this intruder, the 'other' woman? She would make it her mission to find out.

Striding along the sidewalk she made her way between the brown brick buildings to the inner courtyard. The windows adorning these walls were mullioned, small panes between narrow strips of wood in cement casements that opened like French windows. Barbara threw a stone and waited. Her cousin, the Dean of Humanities, stuck his head through the narrow crack and said with indulgence, "Barbara, dear. What gets you up so early? Or are you just getting home?"

"I wish," Barbara said.

"Have you been spurned, darling?"

"Yes, in so many words." Gordon had first-class degrees from Oxford and Cambridge. Why did he call her 'darling'? Didn't he know better? What was the point of such an esteemed education if you still behaved like a twit? She wasn't his darling. She wasn't anybody's darling, not even Paul's. "I need your help." Bottom line. Had she reached the bottom, she wondered.

"You always do."

It was true. She only came to him when she needed his help. His was the lone calming voice left to her. "I haven't been with anyone." Why was she admitting this? Did she *have to excuse herself? She felt guilty for all the wrong reasons.*

"You should visit me sometime for drinks."

"That's why I'm here. Can I come in?" Did she have to beg?

"The coffee is brewing."

Barbara entered the creaky building hoping she wasn't disturbing the sleep of students. On entering Gordon's suite, she smelled the aroma of coffee. His room was stuffy, and she noted that he'd left the narrow window open. If this was her little apartment, she'd leave it open all night to let in the fresh air. Her cousin didn't indulge in healthy lifestyle practices. She entertained the thought that he was as stuffy as his room. Just look at the place. His desk was piled with papers and books. Gordon had never married but it was rumoured he'd had many liaisons. So, not conventional, Barbara conceded. He never divulged personal details yet was all too willing to let her reveal her personal problems. He took a philosophical approach with her and began the morning's confession with, "Tell me what's new in Barbara's world."

That's all she needed. Someone to listen. Someone to confirm her deepest suspicions.

Old Mill Towers, where Paul's mother lived, was situated on the banks of the Humber River. Soon the subway would expand west so the building would have its own station. They'd taken a taxi and the valet opened the door for Dawn to exit. She couldn't help but be impressed. Paul paid the driver, tipped him, and greeted the valet. He placed his hands under Dawn's elbow and led her into the lobby. In the elevator he pressed the button for the fifteenth floor. Dawn felt the floor underneath her rise. She wasn't used to high rise buildings and didn't quite trust that the elevator rise was safe, but she didn't share her doubts with Paul. She didn't want to appear provincial.

Within minutes after introducing his mother as Morgan Lewis, his mother asked them what they would like to drink. "Wine?" Paul asked, turning to Dawn.

Paul's mother invited Dawn to sit and explained, "This twenty-three-storey concrete and glass tower is designed by the architect Raymond Mandel. He fled Poland with his family. And he got his degree in Architecture from the University of Toronto, where you both go."

"That's a *nonsequitor.*"

"Paul, spare us your smart-ass comments."

Dawn sipped the chilled white wine that Paul served.

"What do you think of my son wanting to become a lawyer?"

"Practising law is an art, the art of the word."

"He always could argue circles around us."

Dawn grinned. It occurred to Dawn that Morgan was a Welsh name given to both girls and boys and that Mrs. Lewis could pass for either if she cut her hair short. She was tall and chunky, so Dawn guessed that Paul must have inherited his thinness from his father, until she saw the wedding photo on the side table beside the sofa with a younger Morgan as a wartime bride beside a strapping male. Later she would learn that Paul had inherited his physique from his paternal grandmother. Both his sisters took after their mother, which was a shame as far as Dawn was concerned, because the grandmother was a knockout, but the mother wasn't anything special. Dawn felt a frisson of conceit thinking that.

"She's small, isn't she?" Morgan said, turning to her son.

"She has a name, and she is sitting across from you."

"Umm," Morgan said, looking directly at Dawn. "How old are you Dawn, if you don't mind me asking?"

"I was born in 1945, same year as Paul." Following a *nonsequitor* with a riddle Dawn felt she was playing a game of chess. She looked at Paul. Was this why he wanted her to meet his mother? She asked personal questions after having just been introduced.

"Really? You look so young. I took you for a teenager."

"Well, Mother, Dawn is older than me by half a year. Her birthday is soon."

"April first."

Morgan tilted her head and barked out a laugh. "April Fool's Day. Good for you, my dear."

Dawn shrugged wondering how Paul's mother could think Dawn had anything to do with her own birth date, or conception. Who gets a choice about when to be born? But she liked that Morgan had a sense of humour.

"Do you want to have children?"

"Mother!"

"I use birth control."

"Marvelous! That puts my mind at ease. Paul has a bright future ahead of him in law. He's waiting to hear where he's been accepted."

"Yes, I know."

"And what about you, Dawn? What's in the cards for you?"

"I'm graduating from Business School in June."

Morgan threw herself backwards. "You're in Business? Well, isn't that great?"

She turned to her son. "Paul, I approve. At last, you've brought home a decent girl." Morgan didn't wait for her son to close his mouth to speak. "I find so many young girls to be frivolous. Don't you, my dear? You seem so sensible. What will you do with your Business degree? Do you want to work in finance?"

"Yes, I hope to work for a mining company."

"Well, you've come to the right household. My late husband had many clients in mining. Before you go tonight, let me give you some references."

Dawn smiled. She refrained from admitting that she owned gold. Why show her hand? She'd won Paul's mother over. That was a victory.

During the week Dawn found herself mulling over what Morgan had said on Saturday. She'd said when eavesdropping on other women mostly what she heard discussed was trivia. "Never ideas. Always what's personal. Don't you find?" And Dawn had to agree she did. She'd always found what other girls talked about was silly. Dawn knew she was at a disadvantage because she didn't have siblings and her mother, Mary, was strict and religious. Talking to her mother was like talking to a character from the Bible. That's where her ideas originated. That's where she'd met her husband, Peter Wright, at a Bible camp east of Cobourg where her father grew up, and west of Trenton where Mary's family lived. Her father wasn't strict. He was the loving parent. Dawn liked working in his store. Mary was the enforcer. Dawn didn't like working around the house, which was fine by Mary, because she found her daughter aggravating; Dawn seemed oblivious to any chores that needed doing. She always had her head stuck in a book.

The upshot of meeting Paul's mom was that Dawn fell in love. She'd been promiscuous with Paul because she'd found him physically attractive and because it was the sixties and everyone at university wanted to rid themselves of their virginity. Plus, Dawn wanted to defy her mother. She wanted to define herself in opposition to Mary and her Bible. "The duality of the Christian Mary," Dawn said when she was in Paul's arms again *post coitus.*

"Are you complaining about your mother?"

"Yes, and the split personality of Mary: the whore and the virgin. Your mother is so liberated. She believes any woman is both."

"Can be both, you mean?"

"Should be, I say." Dawn rolled over onto her back. "She understands what I've always known about girls who can't do math. They think everything's personal, so they can't think clearly about what's outside themselves. Like numbers."

Paul turned on his side and smiled at her. "I'm so glad you like her. Other girlfriends found my mother cold and uppity. Left over from the class system."

"Not at all. She's very warm. She's probably just misunderstood. She's more complicated than other females so they don't get it."

"But you do. I was right about you." Paul kissed her forehead, which felt damp from their lovemaking. "When do I get to meet your mother?"

"When you put a ring on my finger. That's the only way she'll take you seriously. You'd have to show me enough respect to commit to a permanent relationship before I'd take you anywhere near her. I've never taken my boyfriends home."

Paul smiled broadly. "Then the next step is for you to meet my sisters."

Dawn pushed herself up and looked down at his handsome face on the pillow. "Wait a minute. Is this a test? Do I have to walk the gauntlet of your female relatives before you'll commit?" She grinned. She wasn't sure she was committing herself so quickly. She was still playing word games, wasn't she?

"Something like that."

Dawn relaxed. "The question is, will they like me?"

"I hope once they see how much I love you they will."

"You do? You hope?" What question did she want answered first?

"I do." Paul locked eyes with her. "I do love you. But I must warn you. My elder sister can be difficult. And that's putting it mildly."

Dawn should have paused then; she should have dreaded the implication that she had to walk the gauntlet, like some role reversal. So much for the fairy tale of a knight in shining armour. But instead of taking what Paul said seriously or averting a looming crisis, she rolled on top of him.

———————

Barbara Simpson was going to be a midwife. Her mother had instilled in her the view that childbirth was a normal process, not some potentially dangerous and pathological event. Barbara thought Paul's mother would be sympathetic to her ambitions, which in a way she was, but the older woman asked, "Have you thought of being a doctor?"

"You mean, an obstetrician?" she'd replied. Then Barbara had to explain that midwifery was a specialized and highly trained profession that allowed women an alternative to intervention in hospital settings which were places for sick people and being pregnant wasn't a sickness. While Morgan agreed, she continued to extoll the virtues of rising to the top, of challenging the male dominated field in medicine. Barbara quoted her mother when saying that doctors were just body mechanics and that she wanted to approach women's health in a more holistic manner.

Clearly Barbara hadn't won that argument or won over Paul's mother who continued to look at her suspiciously. Barbara was from a well-off family, an old family, a family of stature. Shouldn't she be more ambitious? What strange notions Morgan had coming from Wales. She was an ardent feminist and once told Barbara that when she was growing up, they called a vagina a 'front bottom'. "Rather chirpy, don't you think?"

Barbara thought it was a deceitful vague moniker.

Dawn, Barbara learned, was in a program dominated by men. She was challenging the status quo. She had Paul wrapped around her little finger, and probably his mother's, too. Paul was a fool, a male Pollyanna, the eternal optimist and ripe for the plucking. Barbara didn't like succumbing to *those in authority. She didn't like that Morgan was in control. Barbara had thought she and Paul were kindred spirits, but he had all those women in his life: Morgan, an influential mother, Pam, an outspoken older sister, and Patti, a younger sister whom Barbara didn't know well because she was away at school, but Paul insisted was sweet. He'd betrayed her for a woman who was no mother substitute. Dawn must be good for something else. This thought ate at her.*

———————————————

Beside Pam Lewis, Dawn felt small. Paul's sister was even bigger than his mother. They were loud together, which filled Dawn with envy. Mother and daughter had a roaring good time talking about everything from sports to sex. "What do you think of the NHL expansion?" Dawn had no opinion. "Mummy played field hockey in Wales; didn't you Mummy? I was born in Wales. Paul was conceived in Wales but born here, in Toronto, weren't you Paul?"

"If you say so."

Pam and Morgan hooted. "Do the math, brother."

Morgan took pity on Dawn and Paul. "I can see Pam is challenging your strength. Paul built you up as a math whizz. I was pregnant when we left Wales and immigrated to Canada."

"Just a year apart. Weren't our parents busy, then?" Pam asked, looking at Paul. Her eyes were larger than Paul's, but not as strikingly blue, so not as intense. Yet the atmosphere around her was fierce.

"Pam," Paul said, "you don't have to talk about our parents' sex life in present company."

"What?" Pam asked, feigning horror. "We know you two are at it. Not some little virgin by your side."

"I was Patti's age when I immigrated," Morgan said, trying to regain control of the conversation. She stood up. "Come, Pam, help me with the food."

Dawn felt shocked, then relieved. She wondered if her face betrayed her reactions and looked over at Paul expecting some empathy, but he wasn't paying attention to her. He was watching his mother and sister retreat to the kitchen.

Paul rose and suggested they help, too. As they followed, they could hear mother and daughter continuing their conversation.

"I'll bet she's busy, too, in Switzerland." Pam looked at the couple then rattled around the utensil drawers. "Hah," she said, picking out a pair of salad tongs.

"At Neuchatel," Paul said, turning to Dawn. "It's in Switzerland."

"Right, you told me." Dawn remembered where Patti was. Now what Dawn also remembered was what else he'd told her about his older sister, Pam. She was bold, in your face bold. Dawn had looked up the name of the private school at the library when she'd learned his younger sister was attending an international school. Paul thought his mother had gone against her strong beliefs in public education and funded her youngest child to go away to school so that she could buy the condo without feeling guilty. She'd sold the big house in Etobicoke and downsized to this two-bedroom apartment which Dawn found anything but small. The rooms were generous and the table they were sitting at could seat eight, more if extra leaves were added.

Pam handed Dawn the salad bowl before sitting across from her. "What Patti really loves, besides the boys, is the skiing."

"She's a great skier, our Patti," Morgan said.

"Do you ski?"

"No, sorry, I don't do many outdoor activities."

"Don't be sorry, my dear," Morgan said.

"Dawn swims," Paul said.

"That's good exercise. I never learned to swim," Morgan said. "The ocean was too cold and there were no recreational pools, in-ground or indoors, above ground or heated. I was amazed to discover so many pools when I immigrated. Of course, all the children learned to swim. I think here, it's a safety issue, don't you? Are you a good swimmer, dear?"

"Better than me."

Pam pulled herself upright. "Not better than you? Good on you, Dawn."

Dawn smiled at Paul. He was such an enthusiast, not competitive in sports like his mother, but full of sports culture. He loved watching games as much as playing them. Yet she shrank in the face of Pam's mockery. Was this rude creature really related to him? Paul was so gracious. Or to Morgan? Morgan was forthright, but she had a sense of decorum.

"Whatever happened to Barbara Simpson?"

"Pam, please," Morgan said.

"I haven't seen her lately."

"No, I guess you haven't."

"Tell your brother where you're living now, Pam. Maybe he knows about it."

Pam finished chewing before speaking. "I was saying to Mummy that I've moved into Rochdale."

"You have?"

Morgan looked from her son to her daughter. "Well, he apparently knows about this place." She looked back at Paul. "Pam says it's a commune. That sounds enlightened."

Paul shook his head. "It's legal."

"Are you going to get all lawyerly on us now?" Pam scooped up some food on her plate with her fork. "You know, Mummy, he'll be intolerable. I don't know why you think this is such a good idea."

"He'll be qualified to take care of us," Morgan said. "But don't change the subject. Is this a hippy place?"

"Yes," Paul said.

"What's wrong with hippies?"

"There's nothing wrong with hippies, Pam. I approve of hippies. Free spirits. Unlike in the old country with its class system. Your father wouldn't have been nearly so successful back there as he was here. Didn't go to the right schools." Morgan turned to Dawn. "You have to understand how important that is. There's lineage up and down that island nation. Families with ancestors going back centuries." Morgan took a sip of water. "Besides, you're only young once. Live the good life but don't get caught up in some cult. If it becomes a cult, leave. Keep your independence. That's why we came here."

"Yes, Mummy."

"You're so obedient," Paul said.

"That's so unlike you to be sarcastic, Paul. Are you showing off for your girlfriend?"

"He doesn't need to show off for me," Dawn said.

"Well, the question still remains, are you marriageable?"

"I warned you, Dawn."

Yes, Dawn thought. And who's Barbara Simpson? An old girlfriend? Dawn told herself not to feel jealous. Barbara was history. And what did Pam mean? Marriageable? Dawn decided to let it go. It was Pam's way of accepting her.

On the first Monday in March, Dawn walked to Bay Street from her residence. She was nervous about the interview she had at ten am. The walk helped her clear her head, but it also made her cheeks red. The temperature was cool, especially since spring was just around the corner. It had been a cold winter, at least outside, Dawn thought. It had been cold outside, but she'd barely noticed since she was indoors so much studying or wrapped up with Paul. True to her word, Morgan had come through with a reference which helped enormously. Dawn felt she was ahead of the game, at least, ahead of her classmates in finding work after graduation. After passing the Art Deco building that housed the Toronto Stock Exchange, she turned into the lobby of the next building and took the elevator to the fourth floor where she met the receptionist who greeted her warmly but then explained, "I'm sorry, I thought you would be male."

"I'm Dawn, spelled Dawn, not Don."

"My grandfather's name is Donn, but it's spelled with a double 'n' at the end."

"That's unusual."

"It is some strange family tradition on my mother's side."

"Please take a seat, Ms Wright. The partners will be with you shortly."

Dawn turned to sit and immediately felt nervous. She swallowed. Whatever calm she'd felt in the elevator vanished upon hearing the plural word, partners. That could only mean she was being interviewed by more than one person. From her seat she could see the receptionist's name plate: Ms Hilary McMahon. Dawn felt reassured that the receptionist was a feminist. Not a Miss or a Mrs. Maybe they'd get along if she got the job. Pam had not been helpful by telling her how chauvinistic the business world could still be, especially in publishing where she worked. According to her, it was still male dominated: the men were the stars, the writers, the movers and shakers. Women like Pam were handmaidens. They competed for the attention of the males; they fought like snarling cats; and they rarely got published.

Hilary lifted her eyebrows and smiled as if alerting Dawn. Sure enough, there was a male in front of her bending to extend his hand. "Good morning, I'm Timothy Rupert." His hand was small, but his fingers were long. His body was long and slim, too.

Dawn followed him into the boardroom where she was greeted by another extended male hand. "This is my partner, Ross Green."

"Hello, please sit." He was shorter than Timothy and much thicker in his physique.

Rupert & Green was new on the block, as Morgan attested, and young, so more likely to hire a female intern. Most of the established firms were still stodgy in their practices.

"Tell us about yourself. What made you go into business?"

Dawn sighed and began by telling them about her upbringing. "My father owned a store and I worked for him on the weekends. It's in a small town, Cobourg."

"I know that town," Ross said. "Had a girlfriend in undergrad who came from there. Maybe you know them?"

When Ross said the name, Dawn said she did know them. "Her father's a lawyer. My father owned the stationery store on the main street. His firm were customers." It was beginning to feel like she was part of the family, and she couldn't have been more at ease, so she explained in detail what jobs she'd done.

Then they checked her curriculum vitae and asked about her university courses. They had many questions. It seemed to Dawn that they knew nothing of her studies. Yet hadn't they received the same education as her? When they offered to tell her about themselves and their business, Dawn understood. They'd met at Harvard. She left feeling a nervous wreck. How could she compete with Harvard? Ross hadn't married the girl from her small town. He'd married a Harvard grad. Was that what Pam meant when she asked Dawn if she was marriageable? What did that even mean? Her question had sounded impertinent, insulting. When she'd spoken to Paul about the matter, they'd concluded that Pam thought Dawn was too independent. Now that seemed like a naive conclusion. It worried her. She wasn't worldly or cosmopolitan. She was from a small town. She was the only girl from her year to go into business at the university level. Sure, plenty of girls had taken commerce. They would get jobs as secretaries. In Dawn's undergrad classes there were only three females. They'd applied to grad school. She felt like she didn't belong with those sophisticated young women and Pam had sussed that out. Pam made her uncomfortable in a way that made Dawn feel she was competing with her sexually. Marriageable? It didn't matter that she wasn't a virgin. That was less of a threat than not being marriageable.

Not belonging to the right social class. Not getting the right education. It was as if Pam, born in Wales, held on to the old-world values despite all her loud protests to the contrary. She seemed conflicted. She was too self-absorbed to be polite.

Later that evening, Paul did everything he could to reassure Dawn "They want someone to work for them, not someone to challenge their partnership. Did you like them?"

"Yes, they were professional. Their office has a nice feel to it. I liked the receptionist."

"Who is?"

"Hilary McMahon. Ms. She emphasized that."

"So, she's liberated?"

"Yes, but why is it that the secretaries are always female?"

"They are at any professional office I've been to."

"Will that ever change, I wonder?" Dawn asked more rhetorically than seriously caring, although in future she would start to care.

"Did they say when they'd let you know?" Paul asked.

"By the end of the week."

"Great. Won't spoil our weekend." Paul opened the newspaper and showed her an obituary. "Sad news. George Vanier died."

Dawn didn't know how to feel. Was she supposed to be sad? Paul said he was sad, but she didn't understand why. She started reading the obituary. "He studied law in Montreal?"

"Yes, he was a lawyer, a soldier, a diplomat. He's been our Governor General since appointed by the Queen in 1959. I greatly admired him."

Dawn returned to the obituary. "Yes, I can see why." She didn't admit to Paul that she hadn't known he was their Governor General. She was hopeless when it came to politics. They didn't talk politics at home. She knew her parents voted conservative, and on that basis, she voted liberal the one time she got to cast a ballot. When they kissed and said their goodbyes, she gave Paul an extra squeeze. He needed some reassurance. They both had to study.

Paul suggested she needed a bicycle. He had one and if she got one, they could get around the city, they could even ride along Bloor Street West all the way to his mother's condo. "But how will we get home?" Dawn asked. They were walking along Bloor Street now to the cycle shop that was west of Spadina. "It would be dark. We'd have to ride in the dark."

"I have a light on my bike."

"I don't like the idea of cycling home in the dark."

"Why not?"

"I was never allowed to ride in the dark. That was the rule when I was growing up. You had to be home by dark."

"So, you can ride a bicycle?"

Dawn laughed. "Of course, I can ride a bicycle. That's how I got around town. I rode to school. I rode to work. I rode to the pool."

"Here I thought I was going to make an outdoors girl out of you." Paul squeezed her hand.

"Well, the pool was outdoors. School and work were indoors."

"You didn't work as a lifeguard?"

"No, I only worked at my father's store on Saturdays. Never after school. That time was for homework."

"Hey, Goldie." Dawn stopped, recognizing the male beside her walking in the opposite direction. "Ron."

"How are you?"

"Paul, this is Ron from Cobourg." Dawn felt an immediate compunction to let him know how she was by declaring she was in a serious relationship, something that had not happened in high school.

Paul extended his hand and shook Ron's. "Nice to meet you."

"How're you doing? Getting near the end, eh? Who would've thought three years could go so fast? Are you graduating or doing a fourth year?"

"Graduating," Dawn said. "I have a job. Start work May first."

"No shit. But I'm not surprised. If anyone makes it, it'll be you, Goldie." Ron looked at her while bobbing his head. "Isn't this a glorious day? Finally, some sunshine."

"We're off to the cycle shop to buy me a bicycle."

"No kidding. Hey, I remember that green bike you used to ride to school. Sorry, Goldie." Ron looked over to Paul. "I used to pull wheelies around her to terrorize her."

"You weren't the only one." Dawn tilted her head. "All you boys did."

Ron laughed.

"What about you? Do you have plans for the future?" Dawn asked.

"Yep. I'm off to teacher's college."

"What do you plan to teach?" Paul asked.

"History. Well, nice bumping into you and meeting you, Paul. Maybe see you back home sometime?"

"Sure. Do you go home often?"

"Yes, see the old gang. I'll tell them I saw you. They'll be interested. You know what it's like?"

"Yes," Dawn said and gave a little wave. Unfortunately, she did know what it was like. They would be more than interested in her, not necessarily out of good will either. More likely those boys would want to hear the dirt on her, would want to know if she was successful, would be interested in spreading gossip. Why did women have a reputation for spreading gossip when boys like Ron were only too eager to, too?

"Goldie?" Paul asked.

"My nickname," Dawn said, continuing to walk along the sidewalk which was getting crowded with students and parents with children.

"How did you earn that nickname? You don't even have blonde hair."

"Then I'd be Blondie."

"Patti gets called Blondie."

"Does she? I look forward to meeting Patti."

"You haven't answered my question."

Dawn's mind was racing the whole time they were talking. Should she tell him? Of course, she should. What good were secrets? "It's because I bought gold." She'd bought it and told everyone back home.

"You bought gold? Like jewelry? Are your bangles valuable?"

"No, my jewelry is costume. I own gold bars."

"You do?"

"I do. I made a big thing about it in high school. I was the only girl in math class in grades twelve and thirteen and I guess I was a bit arrogant about it dishing out advice about how to get rich."

"Are you rich? How much gold do you own?"

"A hundred ounces."

"At thirty-five dollars an ounce that's thousands of dollars. You can pay off your student loan."

"I'm not cashing it in. The point is to keep it as an investment. I plan to purchase more as soon as I start getting a regular paycheck. Why would I rush to pay off my student loan? It isn't much and the interest rate on it is low."

"My little accountant."

"That's how I got the name 'Goldie' among my friends." Were her classmates her friends? Just because they were in the same class in high school? She hadn't kept in touch with any of them. They'd gone their separate ways. It was only by chance that she'd crossed paths with Ron.

"Were your friends jealous?"

"They weren't really my friends."

"Renuntiatio amicitiae."

"Meaning?"

"You've renounced your friends."

"Something like that," Dawn said. Dawn felt the way she suspected she would, if and, when Paul knew what she was doing. She felt defensive, protective, exposed. She even felt vulnerable. Why? Because she was making financial decisions on her own. Because she owned a product with no inherent worth except for its value on the market. Because she had hidden assets that others in her age bracket didn't own. Because she'd applied for a loan based on her father's income. She hadn't needed much, what with all the bursaries and scholarships she'd won. Still, here she was walking along the streets of Toronto with her cover blown. Would her relationship with Paul change? In a moment of self-defense, she returned to her question about Patti, the younger sister.

"She's not at all like Pam."

"That's reassuring."

"I know. Pam's poison, isn't she?"

"Does she have friends?"

"I don't know. I think she's confused about her sexuality."

"Ah," Dawn said and thought Pam's vulgarity was covering up something. She can get attention by causing trouble. By making problems for others. By spoiling things like she must feel things are spoiled for her. "I think there are other reasons she questioned my being marriageable. She's projecting her problems on others, on me."

"Yes, she likes getting attention. I used to think it was because she was the eldest. She likes to keep reminding us that she's important. It isn't just you she puts down."

"No?"

"I won't let her spoil things for us."

There was a party before exams at a fraternity where Paul knew one of the members who was also attending law school in the fall. They'd become good friends. As soon as Dawn entered the crowded room, she thought she recognized someone from another party she'd attended in first year, a party that'd turned into a drunken orgy, a party that she'd fled alone after being groped by this guy who was now standing in front of her smiling, and suddenly Paul was not there. Where had he gone so quickly?

"I remember you," he said.

"Funny, I don't remember you," Dawn said.

He held a beer bottle in his hand which he swayed dangerously close to her breast. "Little Miss Prim. I do remember you. You fled the scene of the party with the engineers. I'm Kurt, by the way."

"Let me guess, you're an engineering student?"

Kurt smiled broadly.

"So, Kurt, why aren't you with your fellow engineers? Why are you here with all these lawyers?"

"I could ask you the same question, doll."

"I'm not a toy."

"Well, tell me your name and I'll show you some respect."

Dawn could smell the booze on his breath. She was squashed in so tightly against him that she couldn't even turn her shoulders. A disadvantage of being short. "You answer my question first."

"I'm here with a girl but I seem to have lost her. Do you want to go upstairs?"

"No, I'm here with my boyfriend and we're engaged." Dawn gulped. She kept her eyes on Kurt hoping Paul wasn't squeezing in somewhere behind her and had overheard. Why did she say that? They weren't engaged. It was questionable that she was even marriageable. Maybe that's why she'd blurted out that she was engaged. To prove she was marriageable. She didn't have a ring on her finger. Kurt could challenge her. Not that he could focus clearly enough to see her ring finger. She wanted to be rid of Kurt the engineer.

"Whoa, so you are graduating with your Mrs." He slurred *missus.*

There was no point in resenting Kurt's comment. How could a boar like him begin to understand? She was right not to have taken Mr. Bargeman's advice and enrolled in engineering. "Here you are."

Dawn looked up into Paul's blue eyes. Rescued! She accepted the glass of white wine he proffered. "Thanks."

"You could get lost in this crowd."

"I did," she said.

"Come with me. I want to introduce you to my friend." Paul took her hand and led her into the kitchen. It, too, was crowded with partiers, but not packed like the living room. "Manfred! This is Dawn."

A slight male with dark hair smiled over at her. "Nice to finally meet you," he said. "I've heard a lot about you from Paul."

Dawn smiled, feeling comfortable at last. She didn't even have to tell these men what she'd just experienced under their roof. Why admit what she hated? She wasn't defeated. She wasn't oppressed. She didn't have to play that game because that was what Kurt and misogynistic men like him wanted. They wanted to talk about it, to tell you what they really thought, but she wouldn't let him, and probably the girl he came with wouldn't let him, so instead he drank beer and propositioned her while she drank wine and chose when to have sex. Did that make her a flirt? Maybe, but if it did, she was happier being a flirt than a victim. Manfred didn't have a girlfriend and he was flirtatious, but Paul wasn't jealous because Paul assumed her honesty and loyalty was attached to him and he was right. In the future the three of them would reap the rewards of their friendship. Later, when they were leaving the party, Paul seemed excited. "I'm glad you got along with Manfred."

"He's the draft dodger?"

"Yes, he's become my best friend."

"That's nice that you have a good friend. Unusual."

"Why do you say that?"

"You know, everyone says guys don't make friends the way girls do, but you have a best friend, and I can't name my best friend. I left my high school friends behind. I haven't made friends in my class, but then, there aren't many girls in my year."

"Maybe that'll change in the future as more females enter business."

"Maybe," Dawn said, remembering the smile on the receptionist's face before the interview. Maybe Hilary wanted a friend in the office? Dawn swallowed. "Wow, I think my ears are clearing."

Paul nodded. "Yeah, it was pretty noisy in there."

"Do you like that music?"

"Show me that you need me," Paul sang. He stepped along the sidewalk keeping time to the music he hummed. "Show me that you love me," he crooned.

"Hey," Dawn laughed. "You can sing. What is that song?"

"That's the music of Brenton Wood. He's an American singer-songwriter."

"So, you can sing and dance."

"There's lots I can do, baby." Then he started humming a Supremes tune. "You like it?"

"I like the Beatles."

"All the girls like the Beatles. My sisters joined the screaming mob when they came to town."

"They did? So did I. My cousins arranged it and I went with them, thinking at the time how crazy they were, but joining in and then screaming too."

"Who are these cousins of yours?"

"The Wright sisters. My Dad's younger brother's kids. I guess you could say they're the closest friends I have. They're crazy and fun."

"That's nice to hear, Dawn. Tell me the names of these cousins of yours."

"Well, there's three of them. The eldest is Isabel. The middle one is Teresa and Gwen is the youngest."

"Sensible names," Paul said. "I never have figured out why my parents named us with alliterative 'p's. It's confusing, don't you think?"

"What was your father's name?"

"William. William Paul Lewis."

"So, you're named after your father."

"Yes, but Pam's the eldest, remember."

"Maybe after Pam and Paul they decided to stick with 'p', so the youngest wouldn't feel left out."

"Maybe."

Dawn started humming and stepped to the rhythm of 'Ain't No River Wide Enough'.

Paul put his arm around her small waist and twirled her down the street.

Barbara Simpson approached Kurt when he was talking to Dawn. With the usual party noise, conversations were loud and Barbara heard Kurt ask Dawn to go upstairs. Her reply came as a shock. They were already engaged! She turned her back to them, tense with rage. Now Barbara was breathing fire, like a female dragon, like a poisonous serpent. "How are you, Barbara?" Paul had asked when she'd saddled up to him earlier, but he'd stood aloof as much as anyone could in the crowded space. He'd treated her like she was some casual acquaintance. "I thought we were still friends?" he'd asked when she'd challenged him. What was the point? Talking to him was impossible. Paul always turned everything positive. She'd thought, at first, he was well mannered. Now she knew differently. He was two-faced. He was out for himself. Dawn had wasted no time getting her claws into him. Barbara overheard Paul interrupt Kurt and lead Dawn away. In fact, Paul was oblivious to what Kurt had attempted and probably would never know because Dawn wouldn't whine to him. What would be the point? He was secure in their relationship.

"I'm Barbara," she said, turning and smiling.

"Kurt."

"Who was that you were just talking to? Your girlfriend? Stolen from you?" Barbara felt the sting of irony in her voice. She was projecting her problems onto this drunk. How low would she stoop? She'd been outwitted.

"Not my girlfriend. A tease."

"Really?" How typical of an arrogant drunk to think the fault lay with the female. She should steer clear of him, but she felt driven to exploit the situation. "What's her name?"

"How do I know? Can't remember. Do you want me to find out?"

"Yes, please," Barbara said, using her own teasing charm, as if she didn't already know. Keep Kurt on the hunt. Get the drunk talking. Let him throw Dawn's reputation into question.

"What about you? You here with anyone?"

Barbara blinked. "No, but I'm not going upstairs with you."

Kurt took a swig. "But you want a favour?"

"I'm not the only one who wants to know her name, am I?"

"Ah," Kurt shrugged. "Girls like her are a dime a dozen."

"You think so? You might be in for a surprise."

"Jeez," Kurt blinked. "I can be the skunk at the garden party but what's your bargain?"

"When are you graduating? Maybe I could help you. I'm well connected."

Kurt leaned his upper torso away from her. "Lady luck, are you?"

Barbara smiled. "Something like that?"

The following morning, on Saturday, April first, Dawn stayed in bed listening to the birds. Some small birds kept up a constant chatter, maybe sparrows. Then the raucous crows drowned out the smaller birds. She raised her eyes and looked out the window. She's forgotten to pull the blinds. She was surprisingly hungry. After eating tons of food and drinking gallons of wine she didn't expect to be ravenous. Stretching her arms above her head and pointing her toes into the sheets she purposefully yawned. Not only did she need food Dawn required oxygen. The residence's cafeteria was on the ground floor, so she didn't have to go outside to eat. She did look forward to meeting up with Paul later.

When she arrived on her new bicycle, he plunked a kiss on her lips. "Happy Birthday."

"Mm," she said, "Thanks."

"How's it been so far?"

"Some stupid pranks at breakfast, but otherwise, slow and delicious. On Saturdays they serve eggs Benedict."

"No shit?"

"And on Sundays, pancakes. I'll be glad when I don't have to eat cafeteria food anymore."

They mounted their bikes and wound their way to Bloor Street. Heading west, they peddled between parked cars and moving vehicles. Dawn felt a great sense of relief when they coasted down the small, curved hill that dipped into the Humber Valley. Crossing the bridge over the Humber River was like entering the country. Suddenly there was greenery. Dawn inhaled deeply. Life was good and it was about to get better.

Dawn and Paul got off their bikes in front of Morgan's condo.

"Your Mom seems happy here."

"She is. The doorman treats her like royalty. He likes her accent."

"Does he?"

They locked their bikes at the side then rode the elevator. Morgan greeted them with cheek kisses and light hugs. They told her how they'd ridden their bikes along Bloor Street.

"When the weather gets warmer, we can take picnics in the park. I'm always surprised that more people don't do that. We usually have the place to ourselves. In Wales, people get out and use public spaces, but not here."

"Most people here have big backyards," Dawn said.

"Well, I know that, dear. We used to have a big backyard, but now I'm in a condo with only a sunroom so I go outside every morning."

"She does," Paul said. "She walks beside the river."

"Up to the bridge and back. My morning constitution. No matter the weather. My late mother and her good friend used to swim in the ocean every morning. They were mad. No one else swam. Well, to be truthful, they didn't swim. They took a dip. They said the freezing cold salt-water cured them of all their ailments. How do you like the bicycle?"

"It's good," Dawn said.

"I'm going to make an outdoors girl of her yet."

"Do you want some coffee or tea?"

"Coffee," Paul said.

"The same," Dawn said.

"Don't be shy. If you want tea, say so. I've had my cups of tea, but I'll make coffee. Why don't you two go into the sunroom."

There was no sun in the sunroom. It faced west. Morgan brought in a tray and Paul stood. "Let me help you with that." There were sandwiches and cakes which Paul served. Morgan poured coffee. "How was the party last night?"

"Loud and crowded," Paul said.

"I met Paul's friend, Manfred."

"Manfred Freundlich, the draft dodger. That American War is criminal, don't you think? Johnson's only escalated everything. I predict it's going to get worse before it gets better. Nobody's going to win this war. It's not like Europe. We knew the enemy. I do like Manfred, though, don't you, Dawn?"

"Yes," Dawn said too quickly, alert because Morgan had spoken her name. At least Morgan wasn't asking her to comment on the politics of the war. She'd spoken about the enemy. Was Morgan simply clarifying that Manfred wasn't the enemy? He was a draft dodger, so not fighting in the war. He wasn't a soldier. Were soldiers the enemy? This was why Dawn steered clear of politics. Paul and his mother could debate about the president and his role, arguments too ambiguous for her mind.

"Capax imperii nisi imperasset," Paul said.

"Unlike Kennedy," Morgan said.

Dawn looked at mother and son. They seemed to understand one another.

"Where are you taking her for dinner, Paul?"

Dawn bristled. Had Morgan forgotten her name? Possibly. Just as she assumed Morgan was on her side. Why was everything so fraught? Dawn inhaled. She needed oxygen. It had been a long ride. She needed to stay calm and take baby steps. Not quite there yet.

"Ed's Warehouse."

"Ah, can't go wrong there."

Dawn wondered if she was supposed to be surprised. There were no secrets with Morgan.

Paul excused himself before they left and went with his mother into her bedroom. At the door before leaving, Morgan pressed a card into her hand and gave her a slight peck on the cheek. Dawn flushed, said, "Thank you," and opened the envelope when she was alone in her room getting ready for going out to dinner. Morgan's script was small: *Dear Dawn, I am very happy Paul brought you into our lives and hope you will remain a part of our family. Happy Birthday and here's to many more.* Her message brought tears to Dawn's eyes. Morgan not only knew her name, but she was also subtle and knew how to be kind and welcoming. Dawn had never been the sentimental type. Yet now she felt the weight of the future, not as a negative premonition, but more an anticipation of events that she knew would unfold, events that she would accept but not necessarily fully control. She'd always been in control, at least, she'd always thought she was in control. Maybe that was just youthful innocence.

Dawn's parents phoned to wish her a happy birthday. "I'm sorry I didn't come home to celebrate," she said to them, excusing her absence. They said they understood and asked how she was celebrating. "A friend is taking me to dinner." They thought that was lovely. Dawn left it at that. Mentioned no names. Didn't say if it was a female or male friend and they didn't ask. Her parents were gracious and trusting. She could imagine their conversation together after talking to her on the phone. They might say that it was nice she had a friend to keep her company; that they didn't want to impose themselves on her time; that she was simply taking a break from her studies to celebrate. They would talk again soon.

The restaurant's name 'Warehouse' belied the space. Yes, there was a former warehouse on King Street, and yes there was a broad set of cement stairs to climb that reminded Dawn of formidable buildings in her hometown like the library and post office, but once inside the large interior was broken up into intimate spaces for dining. Many were eating dessert and shortly left for the show at the theatre next door. They ordered a shrimp cocktail that came in a glass bowl with a stem, two bowls, one holding ice and the other an insert holding the shrimp with the tails sticking over the sides and a dab of sauce in the middle. Paul ordered wine and took a small sip when the waiter poured a taste into his glass. It was red wine to go with the filet mignon. Paul became maudlin from the drinking, eating, atmosphere, and company. He shared with her what his father was like, a quiet man who worked long hours in the lucrative insurance business that specialized in mining operations, who was loyal to his family and supported them in everything they did.

"You miss him?"

Paul stared at her and nodded. "Death is so final, I know that sounds banal, he's dead but with me still in memory. It's like his personality echoes through me."

Dawn felt her eyes water. What kind of a birthday leaves her in tears? "Time is a great healer."

"Yes. *Tempus abire tibi est.*"

"*Tempus* is time."

"You're getting the hang of it."

Dawn shook her head and smiled. Maybe he'd run out of common phrases to translate.

"*Non omnis moriar.*"

"More Latin."

"Get used to it. The law is full of Latin."

"What does it mean?"

"I shall not wholly die."

"I wish I'd met him."

"I wish you had too."

Dawn thought about his sisters and cousins and friends who had known him and attended his funeral. She had not much experience with grief. Her generation didn't, so it was especially poignant that Paul's family did. She was learning how much that loss had changed their lives. His family was not devastated by his passing; they were privileged to live in comfortable circumstances; yet they were grieved.

When they finished the food on their plates, they both sat back and smiled at each other. "Your mother was right, can't go wrong here."

Before dessert arrived, Paul pulled out a small jewelry box. He stared at her with his strong blue eyes and asked, "Dawn, will you marry me?"

She looked from his eyes to the contents of the padded box. "It was my mother's ring," he said leaning into the table and showing her its contents.

"It's beautiful."

"It had been her grandmother's."

"The small female."

Paul laughed. "Yes, she said they'd had to enlarge it, but I think now we'll have to make it smaller again." Paul lifted the diamond ring from its slit and held it between two fingers.

Dawn stretched her ring finger to meet the gold band. It swam on her. They laughed. "Yes," she said. "Paul Lewis, I will happily marry you."

———————————

That Paul was engaged was a personal affront. Barbara had to do something about it. She wouldn't let him off the hook that easily. Give up. Not in her character. If Barbara was anything she was persistent and stubborn and willful. Gordon told her as much when she once again came calling. "Who is that relative of ours on Bay Street?"

"Barbara, dear girl, we have a company of relatives on Bay Street. Don't you know where your trust fund comes from?" Gordon asked.

She admitted she didn't. She admitted she was her mother's daughter, ignorant of her finances, her income, her spending. A privileged white woman out to do good. Midwifery was doing good. She could do good because she could afford to do good. Unlike other healthcare services, midwives weren't covered under OHIP. It didn't matter to Barbara that her chosen profession earned a small salary in comparison to their expertise. By definition, midwives were low risk. That's what Bob Simpson told her when she went to visit him on Bay Street. "Your trust fund, like your chosen profession, is low risk. Sorry, you can't transfer the funds to high risk. Not allowed. Is there something else I can help you with to increase your earnings?"

"Oh, no," Barbara said, recognizing her relative was misinterpreting her visit. Then she asked about Rupert & Green, the firm where she'd seen Dawn Wright go when she'd followed her to work. Bob obliged, eager to share what he thought of upstarts with Harvard educations.

"But do they have a future?"

"Yes," Bob said. "I'll let you know if and when they go public."

Barbara nodded. "What about engineering firms? Don't mining companies need engineering firms?"

"Right," Bob said, shuffling papers. He found one that met her criteria. "I'm glad you're taking an interest, Barbara. I'll divert some funds and have it written up. You'll have to come back to sign the papers."

"No problem."

Gordon invited her for drinks. "What's this I hear about your investments? You're not like your mother, Old Girl."

Barbara thought she was. She knew she was a fraud, but she'd promised Kurt. He was feeding her information she already knew, but he would be telling others. The corporate world was provincial despite the growth in international trade. "I have to be responsible. I'm on my own."

"Indeed, you are. Not dating?" Gordon swilled the ice cubes around the bottom of the crystal glass.

"No." Barbara thought of Kurt. She needed a protector.

"Don't rush into anything is my advice."

"Thank you, Gordon. Are you speaking from experience?"

Gordon smiled. "Beware the rebound."

"Good advice," Barbara said. How to keep Kurt on a string without giving in to Kurt. She was good at managing her situation if she kept a clear head. Be honest, Barbara thought. Tell Kurt she didn't want him to be a quick dalliance on the rebound. "Thank you," Barbara said, smiling at her cousin. He didn't often smile. He didn't have good teeth. Too many gaps. He looked boyish when he

*smiled. Vulnerable. When she left the offices of Simpson &
Bull she took a detour to the address of Rupert & Green.*

The time was right to introduce Paul to her parents: exams over and a ring on her finger. They took the train east and her father met them at the station in his grey Chevrolet Impala. "Peter," he said, extending his hand to Paul after Dawn introduced him as her father, Mr. Wright. He lifted the trunk and stood aside for Paul to put both bags inside. Dawn sat in the front with her dad, but he talked about the university to Paul in the backseat all the way home. She kept her hands folded, covering her ring finger.

Their home was a few blocks from the station near the beach on Lake Ontario and the shops downtown. It was a two storey, red brick house on a corner lot with a long driveway and a single garage at the back. Peter parked near the steps on the front veranda. "Well, here we are."

Dawn smiled at him. They never used the front door. Her mother was waiting inside. "It's a pleasure to meet you," Paul said, bending over to shake her hand. Like Dawn, Mary was short and small boned. She invited them into the living room where she had tea ready and some home-made oatmeal and raisin cookies.

"We're so proud of you, Dawn, getting your degree and landing a job. Congratulations," Peter said.

"Yes, well done," agreed Mary.

"Thanks, Mom and Dad." Dawn felt slightly embarrassed. Her mother never praised her. Dawn had felt nervous about bringing Paul home. He wasn't religious and had a challenging family. What would her mother make of the likes of Pam? And Morgan could be indiscreet. What would she say about birth control and virginity? "I may as well tell you straight away, we're engaged." Dawn extended her left hand.

Mary gasped. Her teacup rattled in her hand. "Oh my, I don't know why I'm surprised. We guessed you must be serious, bringing a boy home to meet us."

Peter rose and stood over her. He took her hand and looked at the ring. "It's beautiful, Dawn." He bent over and kissed her cheek. "I look forward to giving

you away."

"Let me see," Mary asked, leaning into her daughter.

Dawn extended her hand. "It was his maternal grandmother's ring, then his mother's"

"Yes, it looks antique," Mary said.

"And very valuable," Peter added.

"When do you want to get married?"

"At the end of the summer."

"What? So soon?"

"Don't worry, Mom. I'm not pregnant."

Mary's face turned red.

Dawn nearly said sorry. She hadn't meant to be so blunt. "It's just that Paul starts the bar then and I'll be working so it makes sense for us to get an apartment downtown. We just want a small ceremony. Family only."

"Are you sure? But you will get married in the church, won't you?"

"Yes, Mom." Dawn looked sideways at Paul as if to say, see I told you. She took a cookie. "I miss your home-cooking, Mom."

"You do? I'm astonished."

"Well, Dawn always had a sweet tooth, Mary."

Dawn examined her mother's surprised expression. Was she so ungrateful a daughter she never let her mother know what she liked? Dawn supposed she'd always told her mother what she didn't like. Her mother was a saint.

"We'll have to call Reverend Cahill to book it. Tomorrow, when we go to church. You'll come with us, won't you? We'll go together and introduce you."

"Of course, Mom." Then Dawn remembered. Cahill. That was also the name of the lawyer in town with the daughter who dated Ross. "I'd forgotten his name was Cahill."

"Oh, you know the Cahills," Peter said.

"Yes, I remember the lawyer and his daughter. Is she married?"

"Yes, a big church wedding, last year."

"What denomination are you, Paul?" Mary asked.

"My Welsh parents were raised Anglican, but we didn't join a church here."

Dawn looked over at her mother to see her reaction. Mary seemed stoic. Her earlier flushed face was drained, void of all emotion. It was always hard to tell with her what she thought in the moment. Later she would offer an opinion or advice or pass judgment. That was always when things took a turn for the worse, when she passed judgment on someone or some situation. Mary waited until she could control her response. So unlike other mothers who thought they had a right to interfere.

"You're from Wales?" Peter asked.

"I was born here but my big sister, Pam, was born in Wales. My younger sister, Patti, was born in Toronto, too."

"Have you met his family, Dawn?"

"Yes, Dad, I've met his mother and big sister."

"My father passed away a couple of years ago."

"Oh, I'm sorry," Mary said. "And what about the younger girl, Patti, you said her name was?"

"She's at school in France," Paul said. He, too, took a cookie.

"My, my, isn't that something," Peter said. "Well, I have to get back to the store. It's closing time soon."

"Do you want to take your bags to your rooms, Dawn, and go with your father, show Paul the store."

Dawn looked up at Paul. He shook his head. "Sure, I'd like that."

"I put you in the sewing room. Do you think he'll be okay there, Dawn? It's such a small space."

Dawn grinned. "Well, I bet his feet will hang over the end of the trundle bed."

"I'll be fine," Paul said, smirking down at her.

They followed Mary upstairs. Paul carried all the luggage. He poked his head into Dawn's room and said approvingly that he could picture her there. Then they followed Peter out the door and walked hand in hand on the sidewalk to King Street which was the main street. Wright's Stationery was situated near a restaurant called The Dutch Oven.

"Was the town founded by the Dutch?" Paul asked.

"No, not at all," Peter said, taking the couple through the back door.

Paul surveyed the alley before following Dawn inside.

"You know Gwen still works here on Saturdays?"

"Yes," Dawn said, knowing her father was warning her about the reception to expect, and sure enough, as soon as Dawn entered the store, Gwen screamed and ran over to her to give her a hug.

"This is Paul," Dawn said. "We're getting married at the end of the summer." She thrust her hand toward her cousin.

Gwen screamed again and started jumping up and down. Peter went over to the lone customer standing by the shelf near the window to ask if he could help. Gwen started flapping her hands and picked up the telephone. "Mom, Dawn's here and she's engaged." When she hung up, she said, "My Mom knew because Aunt Mary already called her. My sisters are coming down."

"Doesn't news travel fast?" Paul said.

"It's a small town," Dawn said. The customer was looking over her shoulder at them. Dawn guessed that by dinner time everyone would know.

Paul asked Gwen about her work at the store. "I like it here better than the car dealership."

"That your father owns?"

"Yes, Teresa and Isabel like it there well enough, so he has plenty of help."

The front door flew open and two young women raced into the store. The young teenager who had her hands over her mouth Dawn introduced as Teresa. "This is Isabel," Dawn said, "my eldest cousin."

Paul smiled and said, "Hello."

"Show us," Isabel said.

Dawn thrust her hand out and Isabel took her ring finger. "It's beautiful. Is it, like, new?"

"Isabel," Teresa said, "that's rude."

"Actually," Dawn said, "it was his grandmother's ring."

"That's a big diamond," Teresa said.

"We were so surprised," Gwen said. "We never thought you'd get married, especially so soon, right after university. That's something we'd expect Isabel to do. Get her Mrs."

"I'm not there to find a husband. I'm there to get an education," Isabel said.

"Believe me, I'm as surprised as you are. I never expected it to happen so suddenly," Dawn said.

"Well, you know what everyone is saying?"

Dawn looked into Isabel's eyes. They were twinkling. "What?"

"That you have to get married."

"But, if I had to, I'd go to City Hall."

The three cousins laughed. Paul shook his head.

"What do you mean, "is saying"?"

"The rumours have already started, that you have a boyfriend from university, that he's tall and dark haired and handsome." Isabel grinned at Paul.

"How did you meet?" Gwen asked.

"How did you fall in love?" Isabel asked.

Teresa whispered, "He's so handsome."

"When is the wedding?" Isabel asked after slapping Teresa's forearm.

"At the end of the summer, and you're all invited. In fact, you're the only ones invited, except for Paul's family. We want to keep it small. Isabel, will you be my Maid of Honour?"

"Of course."

"Can I be the flower girl?"

"Teresa, you're too old to be a flower girl."

"I know, but I never got to be a flower girl."

Dawn looked over at Paul who was grinning from ear to ear. "Paul has a friend standing up for him. Dad's already excited about giving me away. I think that's as big as the wedding party will be, but we'll have a real party afterwards. Maybe outdoors?"

Paul laughed. "Perfect," he said.

After the service on Sunday Dawn and Paul walked from St. Peter's Church a few blocks south beside the park. The trees along the sidewalk were budding. "It's nice here," Paul said. "You can see the lake." He kissed the top of Dawn's head.

"Lake Ontario," Dawn said. "Where I swam. We can walk along the beach later."

Paul looked overhead. "Look, squirrels."

"Ha," Dawn said smiling.

"But the red squirrel is chasing the black squirrel. That's so unusual because the black squirrel is dominant."

"And much bigger."

"Like us," Paul said. "You're the little red squirrel and I'm the bigger black squirrel."

"Only you're not dominant."

"No, we're equals. Oh, look, here's the red squirrel coming back on its own."

"Scared off the black squirrel."

Now Paul laughed.

"Did you notice people staring at us in church?"

"No," Paul said looking down at her with a serious face.

"They're voyeurs, at least, some of them are. The ones who are asking if we *have* to get married."

"I find that so old fashioned."

"It is, but we're in a small town. There's not much distraction."

Paul sighed. "Let's not tell my mother. She'll call them malicious, then get on her bandwagon to reform them."

They turned east on Perry Street then south on Green Street and walked a block further to The Breakers Motel. "Is this the place where we're spending our honeymoon?"

"Just the first night," Dawn said defensively. At the reception desk Dawn checked the availability for the last weekend in August. The owner offered to show them some rooms. There were ground floor corner rooms with one bed and a sofa bed as well as rooms between those with two double size beds. "Let me show you the corner rooms upstairs."

They liked that room because it had a private balcony with a view of the lake. "This looks more like a honeymoon suite," Paul said.

"All the rooms on the second floor have a walkout to a balcony."

"Well, maybe we could let my mother stay in the other corner room and my sisters in the two rooms in between?"

"You want to book the second floor then?" The owner asked.

Paul looked over at Dawn. "Yes," she said. "But we have to put Manfred up, too."

"He'll be fine downstairs," Paul said.

"Any other guests coming?" The owner asked. "I can block off some for others to make their own reservations."

"That won't be necessary," Dawn said. "It's a small wedding and the other guests all live in town."

The dead-end road beside the motel led to the beach. Paul wrapped his arm around Dawn's shoulder and pulled her close. "Done," he said. "That was easy."

"Yes, my mom can do the rest."

Paul inhaled. "Smell that? I look forward to coming here to visit your family."

Some gulls squealed overhead "Seagulls," he said.

"No, actually, herring gulls."

"How do you know that?"

"My Dad is a birder."

"Nice."

"The smaller ones are terns," Dawn said.

"Really? I never knew. You're a fountain of information," Paul said.

"What do you think of my cousins?"

"They're hilarious. Who's the middle one again?"

"Teresa."

"She's like you, small with auburn hair."

"She's physically like me but none of them are like me. They all think I'm too serious."

"Yet you get along."

"Yes, they're family. Funny how I accept them and their silliness."

"They're genuine."

"You're right, Paul. They don't play games with me."

"I don't know why females do. Well, in my experience they do. Since neither of us had brothers, we can't compare."

"I think Isabel's the beauty of the family," Dawn said.

"According to whose standards? Beauty is in the eye of the beholder," Paul said. "In my eyes, you're the beauty of the family."

"Flattery will get you everything."

"You are my everything." Paul squeezed her shoulder.

On the train ride home Dawn sat in the window seat and Paul slouched beside her, sticking his long legs into the aisle. She ruffled his black hair then turned away from him and contemplated the passing scenery. Her mind roved over the past few months. So much had happened to change her future. When asked at Christmas if she had a boyfriend she'd said 'no'. Her cousins always shared stories about their boyfriends. The girls didn't hide themselves from each other. They openly shared, gave opinions and advice, but didn't pass judgement. She'd hidden her experiences from them. They weren't part of her future. Dawn knew that when she was seeing those other boys. None of them were important to her life. Only Paul. She knew right away he was different. He was the one and she'd held her breath while their relationship unfolded, not secure or confident until now that it would become her future. What does the future hold, she wondered?

Dawn and Paul found rental space in the Annex neighbourhood, the first floor of a house on Kendal Avenue, which was an unusual street that went east and west, then north and south in defiance of the normal grid pattern. To add to the confusion north of Dupont Street, a major artery, and past the railway tracks, its name changed. For them it was a convenient location and mostly populated by young people.

On her first day of work Dawn walked to Bloor and Spadina where she caught the Spadina streetcar south, then changed to the College streetcar going east to Bay Street. Hilary greeted her and showed Dawn to her office. Hilary was tall and blonde. She looked great behind the reception desk and even more stunning when standing inside Dawn's office. She had an office. "This is mine?"

"Yes," Hilary said, "so let me show you how to reach me and the others."

Dawn pushed the button and heard the call ring outside the door at Hilary's desk.

"It only rings once, but stays lit, so don't be put off if I don't answer right away. Sorry to get personal so soon, but is that a ring on your finger?"

Dawn smiled. "It is."

"Wow, did this just happen?"

"It did. Do you think the partners will be okay with me getting married?"

"Of course. Congratulations. Who's the lucky guy?" Hilary asked.

"Paul Lewis. He's a law student, at least, will be come September."

"Sounds like a good catch. When's the wedding?"

"The end of August." Dawn suddenly felt defensive. What if she's expected to invite her and the partners and their wives? "It's a very small affair. Just family. I'm working but he's still a student and my parents wanted us to get married in their church."

"Where's that?"

"In Cobourg. St. Peter's Church. My cousin, Isabel, is my Maid of Honour, and Paul's friend is his best man. Paul only has two sisters, and his other relatives live in Wales where we're going to take our honeymoon, but not until next year."

"A delayed honeymoon? That's okay. I live with my boyfriend, but we haven't talked about making it permanent, and he certainly hasn't popped the question yet. Did Paul actually propose?"

"He did. At dinner at Ed's Warehouse. And the ring was his grandmother's, which his mother gave to him to give to me because she's a widow."

"Wow, that is so cool. She must really like you."

"She does. I think. Sometimes it's hard to tell."

"Does she have airs?"

"Not really, but she wasn't born in Canada. They come from Wales. That makes it easy for me. I don't have to get to know an extended family. Paul just met my parents and relatives over the weekend, but they all liked him. In fact, my younger cousins were practically swooning over him. I have three younger cousins. Paul has two sisters. I've only met the eldest." Dawn let that sentence hang. Why share the negative? Why divulge too much information? Keep the romance. Pam wasn't going to spoil her plans, only Dawn feared she could spoil the wedding. At a small wedding anyone could, but especially someone like Pam. There was no point worrying about what her family would think of the likes of Pam. Maybe her mother would be too preoccupied to notice. Mary would be nervous making sure everything goes according to plan. That was another reason Dawn thought it best to keep her wedding small.

"I think any relationship is a challenge, so you need others on your side. It's hard being someone's best friend, trusted confidante, and lover. Lord knows we keep trying. I'm here for you."

"Thanks, Hilary."

"Well, listen, I look forward to meeting Paul. There's a file on your desk you're supposed to look over. Timothy will be in soon to speak to you about it. They never get here until ten-thirty because they go to the gym to play squash every morning."

"That sounds healthy."

"These guys are so cool and easygoing. You're going to love it here."

Dawn smiled at Hilary's back. Would she love it? Was she 'easygoing' enough? Already she was feeling too rigid. How had she sounded to Hilary? Straight out of university and engaged to be married? She hadn't told her parents that Paul and she were living together already. They'd never find out because they never came to the city, the 'big city', they called it. Too big. Too noisy. Too many people. The one time her dad came to the city they drove together with Uncle Joe and Isabel. The wives stayed home. "It's a landmark," her uncle said. He'd been, and knew where to park. The discount retail store was an entire block long, stretching from Bathurst Street to Markham. Now the area was called Mirvish Village. She and Paul shopped there to outfit their flat because it seemed the right thing to do, since they'd gotten engaged at Ed's Warehouse. Sometimes Paul's sense of humour outshone his romantic tendencies.

Dawn opened the file. It was on Agnico Mines, a silver producer in Cobalt. She knew all about them, so when Timothy called her into his office, she felt confident with their discussion.

"You're a quick learner."

Dawn smiled. Let him think that, she thought. Why say she'd studied that mining operation in one of her courses?

"So, you're okay with visiting their head office?"

"Yes, is there a problem?"

"Is there a problem with our young lady knocking on the door of a mining company? Never." Timothy laughed.

"I'm sure I can handle myself."

"We're sure you can, too. That's why we hired you. I suspect you'll come off as small but mighty."

Now it was Dawn's turn to laugh.

"I bet I hear back that you are as fierce as your red hair makes you out to be."

"My, you think they'll get that personal?"

"Yes, indeed I do. The guys always get personal but in a male way. They welcome men into their club. It'll be a challenge to welcome you into their club."

"I don't aspire to be part of their club. I simply expect to be treated as an equal. If they must mind their manners, so much the better."

"That's the spirit. Great to have you on board," Timothy said, closing the file. "What do you do for exercise?"

"I swim."

"Were you on the Varsity team?"

"No, I'm not competitive, or big enough, but I've kept up my membership so I can keep swimming there. Hilary said you and Ross play squash every morning?"

"Yes, at a new club on Adelaide Street. That's all they have. Squash courts. When do you like to swim?"

"I used to swim after class three times a week."

"Keep up the routine. We are happy to see you leave in time to get in a swim before your evening routine. Got it?"

Dawn shrugged her shoulders. "Sure."

"Great. Very important to stay well rounded. We don't want any nerds here. We are confident you can handle the load and a personal life. You got the marks. You're a quick learner. Up for the challenge."

Dawn left feeling confident she'd made the right choice; at least, her soon-to-be mother-in-law had. As she walked the city streets to the streetcar stop, she ruminated on what Hilary had said. Was it too much to expect one person to be all three things: best friend, trusted confidante, and lover? Paul was not only her lover; he was a confidante. Yet he wasn't her only confidante. Or was he? She needed to be wary about making him her best friend, or only friend. How could she expect one person to provide what used to be provided by an entire village? Certainly, her parents were joined at the hip. They had each other, but they also had a small town behind them with family and church. A community. She pictured the main street where her father's store was located. When Paul asked if the town was founded by the Dutch, she'd felt the smallness of everything. All familiar. With Paul she was entering unknown territory. She needed to be alert. When she'd said she was going to keep her maiden name, Aunt Muriel had said, "How modern." Pam had said, "A woman with three names: Dawn Wright Lewis." She'd had to correct Pam. "I'll still be Dawn Wright." She'd found out later what, "a woman with three names" meant. Artists, early feminists, women who still needed the support of their husbands. Well, that wasn't her, Dawn thought as she boarded the streetcar.

Barbara Simpson made friends with Bob Simpson's secretary who, conveniently, was pregnant. She waited months before broaching the subject of the role of secretaries in firms. Nancy said she wished she had the brains to be a midwife or work in the medical field. "I feel so comfortable having you by my side through this."

"I'm glad your doctor agreed. You're a healthy, young woman."

"It's demanding being in an office with mostly men. Don't get me wrong, your family is generous. In fact, one of the best firms to work for. I'm lucky that way."

"Do you know other women who work as secretaries?"

"No, my two best high school friends became teachers."

Barbara was not deterred. "So, you don't know anyone else at the other firms?"

Unsuspecting, Nancy asked, "Is there someone you want to know?"

"Yes, actually." Barbara explained. Nancy wanted to know more. She liked the gossip: the spurned Barbara, the former boyfriend, the ambitious accountant.

"I do eat lunch with a group of gals in the food court. I'll ask for you."

Barbara smiled.

Gordon called Barbara and invited her for drinks. She didn't know whether to be thrilled, flattered, or wary. Usually, she called him. She was the one with problems.

He immediately put her at ease with light conversation about a student of his who tried to defend his paper by saying how much he liked the topic. "Really, can you believe the immaturity of some of today's crop? Sit, please." He sat opposite her in a chair covered with a crocheted throw that some student had made for him. "Now what's this I hear about you making friends with Bob's secretary?"

"More than friends, Gordon, I referred her to a midwife."

"Your supervising midwife?"

"Yes. She's highly qualified and Nancy is committed to a home delivery. Her doctor supports her in this decision."

"Well, be that as it may, you did take advantage of the situation when you went to Bob's office and saw that this girl was pregnant."

"Woman. Soon-to-be mother." How did her cousin get away with calling them 'girls'? Did no one at the university admonish him? An administrator? A student?

"Bob says there's more going on than the girl's pregnancy. He doesn't quite trust what else you're up to, my dear."

"Up to?"

"Yes, something about meeting the secretaries at the food court for lunch and spying on your old boyfriend's girlfriend."

"That's absurd. They're engaged to be married."

"Ouch!"

Yes, it still hurt.

"Does your mother know?"

"Gordon," Barbara said, shifting in her seat and putting down her drink. What an affront! These men in her life were out to humiliate her.

"If you're going to behave like an adolescent, Barbara, you'll be treated as a thirteen-year-old."

"I thought you were loyal to me?" She thought he was like a big brother. Maybe this was how big brothers behaved. Big Brother watching over her.

"Come to my drinks party next week. You might be smitten by an academic."

"That's very kind of you, Gordon. Are you suggesting one might be smitten by me?"

"Yes, you've got your pluck back."

Barbara laughed. "You are behaving like a big brother. I'd be honoured to come to your 'drinks party'."

In 1967 Montreal was a city of three million people. It hosted Expo67, touted as the greatest show on earth celebrating Canada's centenary. On a Friday in June, Dawn and Paul took the train to that cosmopolitan city in the province of Quebec to visit the fair with Paul's sister, Patti, who had flown straight from Switzerland to take a job as a hostess. Most hostesses had had to start before the fair opened in April to receive training, which meant they interrupted their studies to work for the summer. Younger than these girls who were mostly university students, Patti had accepted her rejection, but was thrilled to receive a call late in the season. The fair was proving to be popular, a huge success for a small country. She was fully bilingual and took only a week's training before her assignment at Canada's pavilion, Man and his World.

On the train Paul started singing, "Canada, we love you. Now we are twenty million. Canada, proud and free."

Bopping in her seat, Dawn hummed along.

"North, south, east, west. There'll be happy times."

She joined in, "It's the hundredth anniversary of confederation. Everybody sings together."

Other passengers joined them and soon the whole car was singing together.

Laughing, Dawn said, "See what you've started."

At the train station they found their way to the Metro. It was a spanking new subway system, cleaner and quieter than Toronto's. Dawn didn't like riding the subway at home. She preferred taking the streetcar to work because she could look out the window at the world passing by while reviewing files. Paul cycled to work. He'd gotten an internship with a government agency at Queen's Park. He was happy to lock up his bike on the rack provided outside rather than park underground or walk from the subway. "This feels like a toy train," Dawn said, "not like an underground subway."

"It's a rubber-tired track," Paul said. *"Protos heuretes."*

"Dare I ask?"

"A new technology."

They rode to Longueil on the yellow line. It connected the city centre with the expo site and La Ronde, the fairgrounds. They walked to Patti's apartment each carrying their weekend bags. Her apartment was a low-rise, four storeys, and she was on the top floor in a one bedroom with a roommate, a girl who worked at La Ronde.

Patti buzzed them up. When the elevator door opened, she was there to greet them.

"This is Dawn," Paul said after giving his sister a big hug.

Patti took Dawn's bag and ushered them inside. "Congratulations you two. Are you okay sleeping on the pullout couch?"

"Of course," Paul said. "Thanks for putting us up. Have you lost weight?"

"Yes," Patti said. "We don't cook much. I've gotten into the habit of having yogurt for lunch. Do you know yogurt?"

"No," Dawn confessed. Patti was nearly as tall as Paul and practically as thin. She had her blonde hair tied in a ponytail. Even the roots were blonde, and her eyes were as blue as Paul's.

"We had it for dessert at Neuchatel, so when I saw that it's available here, I started buying it. It comes in different flavours with fruit at the bottom. I know I should eat more for lunch, but we don't get much time and I like to tour the pavilions whenever I get a chance. I've got you passes for tomorrow to the American pavilion."

"That's the geodesic dome."

"Yes, Paul." Patti turned to Dawn. "Are you sure you want to put up with this guy for the rest of your life?"

"Heh," Paul said.

"Show me your ring. Is it Mummy's?"

"Yes," Paul said.

"Oh," Patti said, giving Dawn a big hug. "Sorry I don't have any food. Maybe just a can of potatoes."

"A can?" Paul asked.

"Yeah, the corner store sells everything in cans, including cheese. And they sell beer and wine."

"You're kidding?"

"No, Dawn. I'm not. It didn't come as a surprise to me after living in Europe."

"Well, I'm from a small town where you have to submit your order in writing."

"I know. Isn't that backwards? So, do you want to get something to eat here, or go straight to Expo and buy something at the concession stands? I find them expensive," Patti said.

"We'll treat," Paul said. "We're both working."

"Aren't there any restaurants there?"

"Yes, great ones."

"It's a beautiful night. Let's do that," Dawn said. "What about your roommate? Can we treat her too?"

"No, she's working. She mostly gets evening shifts. While I work only the day shift, always the same hours;

that's why we can share a one bedroom. But we better make a reservation, otherwise we'll be standing in line for at least a half an hour." Patti phoned La Toundra at the Canadian pavilion. "They know me there," she said, raising her eyebrows.

Dawn liked Patti. She was friendly and straightforward, honest and fun. Her hair was shiny. So was Paul's, but his was black. Pam's hair was a mousy brown. Pam seemed to have missed out on all the attractive family traits. Dawn couldn't help but wonder what their children would inherit. Paul's height? Patti's blonde locks? Pam's brain?

On the ride back into the city they joined in singing French Canadian songs with a group of school children. Their goodwill and camaraderie showered Dawn in happiness. Sure enough, at the large restaurant the female hostess named Ayu knew Patti and showed them to a table beside the sea-green walls that were covered in Arctic motifs of the tundra. The seats were upholstered in sealskin. "This is amazing," Dawn said. What a world had unfolded for her with Paul and his sister. Her head was reeling from the sights and the crowds they'd meandered through to get here. Every pavilion was unique, and she wished they were staying longer. She could understand why Patti wanted to spend her lunch hour visiting places.

Patti ordered an appetizer she said they could share. It came immediately. The plate had a selection of Inuk tidbits: smoked Arctic char and grilled whale meat. Before ordering their main course, Patti told them about the cook who was going to attend chef school next year. She made recommendations on what to order for the mains.

"Tell me how you two met?"

Patti was looking at Dawn, waiting for an answer. Dawn looked at Paul, expecting him to answer. Paul and Patti may have been adult siblings, but they behaved together like children. It wouldn't have surprised Dawn if they started kicking each other under the table.

"Well?"

"Your brother started flirting with me at university when we were in a café with some other students. We didn't know each other, and our classmates didn't know each other, but Paul kept looking over at me staring. He couldn't keep his eyes off me."

"Then we couldn't keep our hands off each other."

"Paul!"

Patti laughed until she choked. Finally, she regained her composure. "I knew you'd tell me a different version from Mummy and Pam. What's with Pam, anyway? She's living in some group home."

"It's not exactly a group home, Patti. It's experimental. They're all radicals."

"For sure Pam sounds radical. She still doesn't have a boyfriend. She's never had a serious boyfriend," Patti said, turning her attention to Dawn.

"Well, I didn't either until I met your brother."

"Pam said you were loose."

"She what?"

The diners at the neighbouring table paused. It was an awkward moment. Dawn turned her eyes away from their gaze and said, "Don't worry about it, Paul. She could be jealous."

"That's an understatement," Patti said.

"Jesus," Paul said.

Dawn balked. It wasn't like Paul to swear. She hoped he wouldn't lose himself anytime he was around her parents. They were strict when it came to swearing.

Patti giggled. "Wait until she comes here. She may think she's experimenting with radical ideas, but Toronto is still prim and proper compared to Montreal."

They shared some personal sentiments on what they thought about the waitresses, the other diners, and the Expo uniforms. *"Sotto voce,"* Paul said, patting his hand in small, rhythmic gestures to catch his sister's attention. Patti sat back and gave him a look of disapproval.

"It's certainly modern here," Dawn said, changing the subject.

"I like that the pavilion's called Katimavik, the Inuit word for 'Gathering Place'. And on Notre Dame Island. Great mish mash of languages."

"But no Latin," Dawn said teasing.

"Cena parata est."

"What?"

"Dinner's ready."

Dawn turned and smiled at the waiter. "Impressive," she said looking at her dish of broiled quail on rice.

By the time they'd finished eating the pavilion was closed so they wandered outside and walked around The People Tree, dazzled by the orange and red lights.

On the long weekend in July, Dawn and Paul borrowed Morgan's car and drove north to Gravenhurst. Manfred had bought a cottage on an island in Lake Muskoka and was meeting them at Campbell's Point. They continued north on Highway 169 outside the town and easily found the turn off. Neither one of them had ever been to the Muskokas, Dawn having grown up in eastern Ontario and Paul having spent his summer vacations with his family at the beaches on Lake Huron, never felt the need to explore the Muskokas.

When they reached the top of the wooden stairs, Manfred waved to them from the dock. "You okay with those bags?" Manfred yelled before Paul descended the stairs.

"Yes, thanks, I'm fine." Dawn carried their weekend bags while Paul hauled the groceries.

Manfred took the bags from Dawn and loaded them in his outboard motorboat. Paul handed him the bags of groceries. "I'll store everything under my seat here, at the back. You two can sit on the front seat.

Paul got in first and extended his hand to help Dawn. The front seat was simply a wooden bench.

"Hello, are you the new owner of the cottage on Jeanneret Bay?"

The three of them looked over to the boat on the opposite side of the dock. Two females sat behind the windscreen of an outboard motorboat painted red. "I'm Karyn, spelled with a 'y'," the one behind the wheel said.

"And I'm Caitlyn spelled with a 'c'," the other said, "and a 'y'."

"Hello, nice to meet you. I'm Manfred spelt with a 'Man' and yes, I am the new owner. My friends are visiting me for the weekend. Paul and Dawn."

Dawn had her back to the sun and raised her sunglasses to get a clearer look at the women in the boat. Paul simply nodded and bent to pick up a bag.

"Welcome to cottage life," Karyn said. "We're in the cottage on the point."

"You must come and visit us," Caitlyn said.

"Well, likewise, ladies. You are welcome to come anytime to visit us."

"Anytime? As in this afternoon?"

When Paul stood, he looked at Dawn and winked. She smiled.

"Sure. Please come this afternoon. In fact, why don't you come for lunch?" Manfred gestured to the bags he had at his feet.

"Thanks," Karyn said with a big smile. "See you at noon." She roared away. Caitlyn waved.

"Now I get why you bought a cottage," Paul said. He watched the receding motor- boat standing with legs akimbo and hands at his waist.

Manfred laughed and, stepping into his boat, handed them life jackets. "You don't have to put them on," he said, "but keep them at your feet." He jumped out to untie the tether after Paul and Dawn were settled. Then he stepped back into the boat before pushing away from the dock.

Dawn turned her head to let the wind blow her hair away from her face and watched the scenery as they sped over the water. With its tall jack pines and granite outcrops, northern Ontario had a different look from where she grew up. She found the shoreline stunning and marveled at the cottages dotted along the water, some with wooden boathouses. Manfred's dock was a simple wooden structure, and it was an easy climb over the rocky path to reach the cottage which had a screened in porch built around the outside. "This is delightful," Dawn said following Manfred down a narrow hall past the kitchen.

"Here's your room," Manfred said, depositing their bags on a double bed.

"I like this," Dawn said, surveying their small quarters. Besides the bed the only other furniture was a small dresser with three drawers. The wall panels were made from pine boards. As if a wave had crashed over her head, she felt a deep longing for her childhood. She'd missed this growing up, although she'd often heard others speak about going to cottages. Paul was next to her, his upright stance casual. She felt the intimacy between them, both new to this shared experience, but for different reasons.

Dawn inhaled the fresh pine smell. "I've always wanted to visit this part of Ontario to see the scenery that was painted by the Group of Seven." She smiled at her host. The men left and she opened their bags. She placed their few items in two of the drawers. When she returned to the kitchen, she gave Paul a squeeze from behind. "Aren't we lucky?"

"Yes," Paul said, turning his head to smile down at her with his twinkling blue eyes. "Thanks, Manfred, for inviting us."

"My pleasure," Manfred said, turning away from the refrigerator where he was unloading the groceries. "I guess we should get lunch ready for the girls."

"Karyn and Caitlyn," Paul said. "Do you think they're twins?"

"Yes," Dawn said.

"Maybe," Manfred said.

"Let's make a bet," Paul said. "One for twins. One for sisters. I'll bet cousins."

"What's the prize?" Manfred asked.

"The prize goes to you no matter who wins," Paul said. "I think you get to choose."

"Guys," Dawn said reproachfully.

Manfred and Paul laughed at her but took the preparations for lunch seriously. Dawn suspected their host was out to impress. She was setting the table in the screened-in porch when she heard the roar of an outboard slow down. "They're here," she called. She watched Manfred disappear through the thin trees then went inside to help Paul in the kitchen. They carried dishes outside and greeted the two females.

"This is a great idea, eating on the porch. Like eating outside without the bugs," Caitlyn said. "I hate spiders."

"Aren't there always spiders around the dock?" Paul asked.

"Yes," Caitlyn said drolly.

"Sit, please," Manfred said, indicating to his guests. Paul and Dawn sat across from the guests and Manfred sat at the head of the table beside Karyn.

"What made you buy a cottage?" Karyn asked, turning to Manfred.

"My mother, who's from Rochester, was sent to summer camp here, and I've always wanted to visit and, when I did, I just decided on the spur of the moment to buy this place."

"So, you're American?"

"Yes, but not from Rochester. Just outside New York."

"You're a draft dodger?" Caitlyn asked.

"That's right."

"We won't tell Dad." Caitlyn looked over at Karyn.

"Maybe you should," Manfred said. "If and when I meet him, I'm sure we'll talk politics."

"He's a lawyer," Karyn said, "and a really good debater."

"Paul and Manfred are going to be lawyers," Dawn said.

"I'm working at Queen's Park for the summer," Paul said.

"And I'm working at Christie, Crombie & Dent for the summer," Manfred said, "before studying at the bar in the fall."

Karyn and Caitlyn sputtered. "That's our dads' firm."

"No kidding?" Manfred said. "I haven't met the partners. I'm downstairs among the files."

"Isn't that a coincidence," Paul said. Later he would challenge Manfred, insisting that he knew about the connection.

"So, are you sisters?" Dawn asked.

"No, cousins. I'm Karyn Dent and she's Caitlyn Christie."

Manfred and Dawn looked over at Paul.

"What?" Karyn asked.

"Nothing," Manfred said grinning. "What a coincidence?"

"Not really," Karyn said. "You'll be surprised to learn how small the Ontario WASP community is. And now you're part of it."

"WASP?" Manfred asked.

"White Anglo- Saxon Protestant," Dawn said.

"Canada's a lot smaller than the States."

"It is," Paul said. "And the population is a lot smaller than Britain's even though the land mass is huge."

"Paul's family is from Wales," Dawn said.

"But I was born in Toronto," Paul said quickly.

"Please," Manfred said, "fill your plates. Choose what you want."

Dawn picked up a bowl and offered it to Karyn who said to serve herself. "No," Dawn said. "Guests first." She felt herself drawn to Karyn who had a mischievous twinkle in her eyes. After taking a helping she offered the bowl to Manfred. Dawn thought that was a smart move. Didn't return the bowl to Dawn or offer it to her cousin who was also a guest.

"Our parents are hosting the extended family tonight for my grandmother's birthday," Karyn said. "You'll probably hear us. Sound carries across the water."

"It does," Manfred said. "I've noticed that."

"Maybe you heard us last night," Caitlyn said.

"We were out on the dock until late," Karyn said.

Manfred nodded his head. Dawn looked from Karyn to Caitlyn. She could imagine what they were talking about sitting together at night keeping an eye on the newcomer down the lake.

"How many are staying at your cottage?" Paul asked.

"Um, the usual," Caitlyn said. "Both our parents, us, and this weekend, our grandparents. How many more are coming?" she said, turning to Karyn.

"Your guess is as good as mine."

A roar from a motorboat wafted up from the lake. "Probably a group arriving now." The engine sound cut and was replaced with voices.

"What about you, Manfred? Are you planning to come up every weekend?"

"Yes, all summer." He smiled at Karyn. "Have to whip this place into shape."

"It has been neglected for years," Karyn said.

The cousins excused themselves after two hours, saying they didn't want to overstay their welcome.

"We'll see you again," Caitlyn said. "Thanks so much for lunch. It's great meeting you, Dawn and Paul, and we look forward to having you as our neighbour, Manfred."

He walked the cousins to their boat and Paul and Dawn went to their room to change into their bathing suits. "Well, what do you think?" Dawn asked.

"I think Manfred's struck it lucky."

"But which one do you think he'll like best?"

"Dawn, I won the last bet. Are you going to challenge me again?"

"Oh, silly, just talk to me."

"Let's cut Manfred some slack. He's only just over his last relationship."

Hand in hand they walked down to the dock and dove into the water screaming in delight. Dawn came up for air and rolled over to float on her back thinking since she didn't know the depth of the lake she should head back to the dock. The lake water was cool and clear which she found refreshing. She raised her head and saw Paul thrashing about. What was he doing? He disappeared then surfaced like a torpedo. He saw her and waved then swam to her side. "Find any deep-sea treasures?"

"No, just wanted to check how deep it is."

"Did you make it to the bottom?"

"No." He swam past her, and she rolled over to join him on the dock. Rising out of the lake like a sea-queen, Dawn pulled herself up. Drops of lake water patterned the wooden planks and her wet feet left prints on the slats. Standing beside him, she shook her head and body spraying droplets over Paul. He reached for a towel and stood. "Let me pat you dry," he said leaning over her.

Later that evening the three of them returned to the dock after dinner to watch the sunset.

"It's so peaceful here," Dawn said.

Manfred looked east, away from the setting sun. "No noise from our neighbours."

"What's that sound?" Paul asked.

They listened to the haunting calls that seemed far away. "The loons," Manfred said. "I can't believe I'm identifying for you Canadians the sound of the loons."

"We don't have those on Lake Ontario," Dawn said, feeling slightly defensive.

"Or Lake Huron," Paul said.

"Not on the Great Lakes," Manfred said, "but found on smaller lakes. Keep watch. We might see them floating by."

Silently they watched. Manfred pointed. Dawn studied the lake until she saw the profile of the floating birds. "If we come down to the dock in the morning, we might see them again."

They stayed until it grew dark and the stars came out.

Barbara Simpson learned all she could about Hilary: a privileged beauty, a graduate of private schools who hadn't gone to university, a popular girl with the boys who wasn't engaged or married but lived with someone, a sailor and member of all the right clubs, a socialite whose mother was a drunk.

Her cousin was right. She met a student of his at the drinks party. Just as Gordon had predicted she became infatuated with an academic. He was an architecture student who was working at a firm in the city over the summer. They went to Montreal together and toured pavilions. He kept her entertained with detailed descriptions which she found fascinating, and wore her out with long waits in line which she didn't mind until they returned home, and he spent endless hours at his office. He would no sooner be available when she would be called to a birthing. The frustrations of both their situations soon cooled their passion but Barbara went into denial. She refused to admit to a second failure.

Nancy's baby was born at home with Barbara in attendance under the supervision of her supervising midwife. Her labour took five hours, a short and safe time. She was so pleased with Barbara's role in helping her have a healthy baby born at home that she gave her baby the middle name "Simpson". Michael Simpson Grady weighed eight pounds, four ounces, a healthy weight and a good size for a first baby. "Maybe the first and last," Nancy said. Barbara's reassurances that what she'd experienced was the best of normal left her feeling that, while she absolutely adored, in fact loved to bits, her baby, delivery was not easy. "Nothing could prepare you for it."

Barbara visited Nancy and Mikey within days bringing supplies for the infant and presents from the firm. Barbara's mother, Honor Simpson, added heaps to the package, so thrilled that her daughter's first delivery was a success and with a woman who was practically part of the family. "Nancy loves working for the firm," Barbara told her mother. "So much so she's going to return to work and never again take maternity leave. Her husband is over-the-moon with a boy."

"See, darling, it's all worked out for the best. I'll let Bob know so he stops this silliness about you interfering. Really, these men have no idea what it takes to bring a baby into the world and raise a child."

Honor wasn't so helpful with the architecture student. "Consider this, Barbara. It's understandable when a midwife or a doctor is called to work at all hours, but an architect. Why do they have to put in such ridiculous hours? And who gets paid? The partners."

"The same with law firms and accounting firms. It's the partners making the money."

"Yes, Barbara, but think what's at stake for them?"

"Buildings fall under the same degree of responsibility. Don't they?"

Honor wasn't sure and Barbara stumbled along in her less than satisfying affair.

The partners, Ross Green and Timothy Rupert, wanted to host a Jack & Jill party for Dawn and Paul. Hilary was in charge of organizing the event at the RCYC. Dawn had no idea what the acronym stood for and suggested to Hilary that the invitation spell out the venue, the Royal Canadian Yacht Club located on a trio of islands in the Toronto Islands. "I'll also include the ferry schedule," Hilary said, "so everyone knows how to get there." She wanted a list of family and friends to invite.

Dawn thought to include her cousins. She knew they'd jump at the chance to travel into the city for such an event. Their mother, Muriel, along with Isabel, were hosting a bridal shower in Cobourg. Dawn was expected to go to Eaton's and pick out items like linens and cutlery that she wanted for her new home. "What new home?" Dawn had asked her cousin. "I already have a fully-furnished flat."

Isabel had suggested she remain discreet about that and go along with her relatives because their parents' friends in town were very excited about her good news. "You know, they love any opportunity to get together and talk about their adult children. Or brag as in your case. How will I ever compete?"

"Please," Dawn had said. "Whatever you do your parents will be proud of you."

At the RCYC Dawn was relieved to find a large beautifully-decorated box for the Jack & Jill. All the guests deposited cheques through the slot at the top. "Money for our honeymoon," Dawn said to Paul. "Hilary organized that, too."

"The perfect secretary. And you don't even have to flirt with her."

"Do you flirt with the secretaries?" Dawn asked.

"Of course. They're always asking me about you. And Manfred. When we went to lunch, he came to Queen's Park, and I introduced him as my 'Best Man'. Now he's referred to by that."

"I'm sure they're more interested in Manfred than me."

"I haven't told them about Karyn. Why spoil their fantasy life?"

"Why indeed? I'm glad office politics aren't like that at my firm."

Paul nodded. "You picked the perfect place."

"Your family did have a hand in helping me."

"Mother usually likes to take credit but not with you. She gives you the benefit of the doubt."

"I'm glad I have her full support."

Manfred took the ferry across with Karyn and Caitlyn and their respective parents. "How did the partners get invited?" Paul said when he saw them arrive en masse.

"Again, Hilary's doing," Dawn said. "Don't worry, your cohorts are invited, too."

"I know. They talk of nothing else but the razzle-dazzle and glitz and glam of my Jack & Jill party. Won't they be disappointed to see Manfred here with his extended family."

"Come, let me introduce you," Dawn said, leading him over to Hilary who was wearing a sleeveless, mini-skirted dress that was white with brown trim along the hem and neck. "That's a very fashionable outfit," Dawn said.

"I wanted to test the waters. Do you think Ross and Tim will let us wear these short skirts to the office?"

"The secretaries do at Queen's Park," Paul said.

"You mean the ones you flirt with?"

"That's what secretaries are for," Paul said.

"Whoa," Hilary said.

"Sorry, Hilary. I didn't mean to give you the wrong impression of me on our first meeting."

"You're joking, right Paul," Dawn asked.

Paul shook his head. His face was red.

"I like your pink dress," Hilary said. "The right colour for the bride-to-be."

"Thanks," Dawn said looking down at her printed, flared skirt that hung to her knees. The top of the dress was a solid pink shade.

"Are the partners members here?" Paul asked.

Dawn could see that Paul was impressed by Hilary.

"No, I am," Hilary said. "So is my boyfriend, Stuart. He's around here somewhere."

"I don't know everyone here," Dawn said, taking Paul's hand. It was the perfect firm. It wasn't old Toronto. It was new and young and fresh. Yet it did help to have Hilary's connections.

"I'll introduce you," Hilary said. "The ones you don't recognize are probably your clients."

They spent the next half hour making small talk with executives from mining companies and accounting firms, with engineers and lawyers. The disruption of her giggling cousins' arrival gave Dawn an opportunity to disengage from the formal crowd. Paul seemed happy to continue to be in their company. He would hopefully make a good lawyer, Dawn thought. He seemed to like the business of networking, or schmoozing. Standing tall and upright, he remained in one spot and let others find him.

"Are we late?" Isabel asked.

"I don't think you can be late for an event like this," Dawn said.

"It sure is swanky," Teresa said.

"Come, I want you to meet Paul's family." Dawn scanned the room until she saw the tall head of Pam who stood out not just because of her height, but also because she was wearing a brilliant, red-patterned jumpsuit. "Mrs. Lewis, Pam, these are my cousins."

"Oh please, call me Morgan." She gave each girl a hug. "I'm sorry Patti can't be here."

"We're going to Expo," Isabel said.

"That's super," Dawn said. "You'll love the pavilions and monorail."

"And the rides," Teresa said.

"When are you going? I'll let Patti know and you can go see her at the Canada Pavilion."

"I've seen pictures," Gwen said. "It's so weird. An upside-down pyramid."

"Dawn said your parents aren't coming today?"

"No, Morgan," Isabel said. "Our father didn't believe it would be a mixed shower. He and my uncle, Dawn's dad, have never attended anything like this, and Mom and Aunt Mary are hosting their own bridal shower."

Dawn smiled at Isabel, thinking how well she'd find her way in the world.

The clinking of glass drew their attention. "Welcome everyone. I want to introduce you to the hosts of our party, Ross Green and his wife Denise, and Timothy Rupert."

The partners called Dawn and Paul up and proceeded to sing the praises of the young couple, especially their employee, Dawn, "The brightest little redhead on the planet as far as I'm concerned," Ross said.

"We're hoping to get to know Paul better in the years ahead. They make a handsome couple and I want you to raise your glasses to give a toast in their honour. To a wonderful wedding. Dawn and Paul."

Servers with trays of champagne had distributed bubbly to the mingling guests and now everyone raised their glasses, "To Dawn and Paul."

The clinking sound left Dawn feeling child-like, vulnerable, insecure. Despite all the goodwill in the room, her parents were absent. Understandably so, but still, she was bereft of their physical company. "Okay?" Paul asked quietly.

"Yes," she said, shaking her head. They'd gotten to know each other so well they could sense one another's thoughts. Later, after the ferry ride to the mainland and the goodbyes to the parting guests, they spoke to one another about the evening as they always did. They talked and eventually Dawn shared her one moment of sadness.

"A melancholy," Paul said.

"Maybe." Dawn wondered. Was that word too extreme? She remembered her mind had briefly slowed down. There was a sense of distance. He was the man with an art for the word, but she wondered if there was another word for her emotion.

After the wedding rehearsal Dawn stayed in her old bedroom at her parents' house. "Keeping up appearances," she said to Paul. He was the only one staying at the Breakers Motel on Friday night. He'd told Manfred to skip the rehearsal as there was hardly anything to practice about standing beside him at the front of the church. Besides, Manfred's relationship with Karyn was now hot and furious, so why drag them away from the big city. She was attending the wedding ceremony with him and one night in the small town was as much as Paul wanted to ask of them. They were both very cosmopolitan. Paul did suggest they bring their bathing suits.

Before going downstairs to join her parents, Dawn paused in front of her gown that was hanging on the closet door. It came from the local dress shop that Isabel insisted they patronize. When Dawn suggested at the Jack & Jill that they should have chosen to wear fashionable minis, Isabel said that would have shocked the town. At the rehearsal Isabel wore a lovely whirl-skirted mini in a patterned print. She and her sisters had decorated every pew with big bows. When Dawn asked why they were going to so much trouble, Isabel said they had to make it look festive for the town. "But it's only us," Dawn had said.

"Are you kidding me? The whole town will show up. All your dad's customers, all your old high school friends, everyone from the church. People want to see you get married."

"Even though we didn't invite them to the reception?"

"People go to weddings even if they're not going to the reception. It's common practice here. Be prepared," Isabel said.

"I know you think it's just us, but your mother has asked her family too."

"From Trenton?"

"Yes, they're staying at the Breakers," Gwen said.

Dawn then realized her wedding night would not be a private affair. Good thing she wasn't a virgin fraught with the fear of the unknown. Later she kept that to herself while seated in her parents' living room after her mother asked her if she was nervous.

"Nervous? No, why would I be nervous? I get nervous when I have to meet new clients, especially ones that have assets worth millions. They can be intimidating."

"We like Paul," Peter said.

"We look forward to meeting his family," Mary said.

Dawn immediately thought if anyone was intimidating it was Morgan. What would her mother think of Morgan? Such opposites. What if Morgan spilled the beans that she'd been on birth control? Mary never talked to her daughter about birth control, or sex, or even menstruation. Dawn had learned about all that from her Aunt Muriel and cousins. They were always talking about female intimacies. Usually, they laughed about those things. The life of a female was hilarious to them.

"We're very proud of you," Peter said. "We always have been."

"Even when I was getting into trouble in high school?"

"Dawn, you didn't get into trouble like other girls do. I'm so relieved you didn't have to get married like so many of them here in town."

Dawn looked at her mother in disbelief. "Are teenagers still getting pregnant here?"

"Well, yes. Some of them have no morals."

Dawn thought but didn't say, haven't they heard of birth control? With the ever-present judgement of immorality linked to sex young women didn't have a chance. The subject was fraught with outdated attitudes.

"I did sometimes wonder if you would survive high school," Peter said. "I remember you fighting with the teachers and the principal."

"I didn't fight with the principal. He stood up for me."

"You've got a good head on you."

"You know your father and I sometimes talked about whether we should ask you to do our books, to take over my role in the store, since you were so good with figures, but then we thought, no, leave you to your studies, because you were good in other subjects too."

Dawn smiled at her parents remembering how they were always talking together. Every day her mother took lunch to the shop and ate with her husband in the back room. She kept the accounts and did the taxes. They had a close relationship. It was something Dawn insisted Paul and she do, talk. He could be glib and dismissive, but she would challenge him and make him sit down and talk to her, really talk. Her parents might not be modern in their views, but they were good role models on how to stay together. It wasn't just about sex.

"You know, Dawn, we would have paid for a big wedding," Peter said. "You've never cost us much. But we respect your wishes."

"Speaking of, Isabel said the wedding will be bigger than I thought. She said the pews will be full of people from town."

Mary crossed her hands on her lap.

"It's what your mother wants," Peter said.

Dawn felt embarrassed. Why deprive her mother of what she most wanted? Her mother didn't raise a stink when Dawn traipsed off to university. Her parents raised no objection about her choice. Isabel was going to Trent, the new university in Peterborough, close enough that she could commute rather than live in residence. Maybe that was to save money? After all, Aunt Muriel and Uncle Joe had three girls to educate. Of course, he made lots of money from the car dealership.

"I didn't mean that," Dawn said. "Is Grandma coming?"

"No, she's too frail," Mary said. "It would be nice if you went to visit her in the nursing home. She asked after you. She still has her wits about her. But everyone else from Trenton is coming. My sister and her husband and their children and grandchildren and my grand old uncle. There's twelve of them, so, of course, we invited them to the meal."

Dawn smiled. "That makes twenty-eight?"

"Yes," Mary said.

"Well, that adds up to a party in my books," Dawn said.

"The DJ is Teresa's boyfriend."

"She has a boyfriend?"

"No one serious," Mary said. "At least that's what she's told her mother. She reminds me of you, Dawn. I think of any of the girls she'll be the one to leave town."

Dawn stared at her mother. Mary had an expression that looked not so much suspicious as cautious. Was this the great dare? To up and leave town? Maybe even go abroad? Dawn thought of Hilary. She had traveled abroad with her live-in boyfriend. They'd visited all the major art galleries in Europe including the Picasso Gallery in Barcelona. Paul had not seemed interested when Dawn told him. He was determined to take her to Wales. Hilary was full of stories about Picasso and his many wives. She'd said a young Gilot replaced Dora Maar as his mistress because Gilot had been trying for some time to get beyond the barrier called virginity. Dawn didn't share that with Paul. Now Dawn gave her head a quick shake to bring herself back to the present.

"I want to say, Dawn," Peter said with a note of seriousness. "I look forward to giving you away. I don't mean that we want to get rid of you. It's just that a father always thinks about the well-being of his little girl and feels protective of her because the world can be a challenging place. You haven't been any trouble, really. Joe and I talk about this a lot because he'll have many challenges ahead of him and none of his daughters has the smarts like you, so he worries what kind of men he'll have as sons-in-law. Paul is not someone I can see myself ever being close to. He seems a very intelligent young man and so fit and active. I'm none of those things, but he's been really respectful of us. He has good manners, and we can see that he truly loves you. In fact, he adores you just like I do."

Dawn's eyes smarted. Was she going to cry? She held on but stood and went over to her father and gave him a big hug. Then she felt embarrassed. Should she give her mother a hug? Mary was not the hugging type, not very tactile, not a kisser. In fact, right now, Dawn saw that her mother was retreating. It was quite awkward. She was every inch the Christian wife, at least the fundamental kind, nothing Old Testament about her. No rage. She had become one with her upholstered chair. Her face looked strained and held a martyred expression. At that moment Dawn knew that her father's physical needs were tolerated by his wife, not enjoyed. No play. It made Dawn sad but not for long. Mary clapped her hands, something she did to get herself motivated, and Dawn snapped out of her reverie.

———————

"'Until death do us part." Those words hung in the air and in Dawn's head while she kissed Paul then turned to see that, indeed, the church was full of witnesses. Arm in arm, she and Paul walked down the aisle smiling at the well-wishers. Outside they were greeted by a group throwing confetti. Dawn's hairdresser, Marilyn, was among them. Dawn had spent over two hours in her salon prior to the big event. In that time, they'd learned more about each other's love lives than Dawn cared to share with anyone else. What was it about preening that forced intimacy? Marilyn had praised her auburn hair for its virtues: soft, brilliant, pliable. Marilyn was new to hairdressing and flattered to be asked to work with the wedding party.

The interior of the church was very familiar to Dawn from growing up here. It was a beautiful space which reminded her of the cathedrals they'd visited in England. Her eyes rose to take in the balcony which was usually empty but today had a few onlookers gazing down at them. Dawn raised her free arm and moved a few fingers to give them a little wave. Her eyes travelled to the high ceilings, reaching to the heavens, Dawn thought. She accepted the comfort of all that was familiar. The bells in the bell tower were pealing announcing to the entire town that the wedding ceremony was over. It was complete. No doubters fled the scene. No naysayers challenged their union. There was purpose here.

Paul shook the hands of people who introduced themselves. Females whispered messages into Dawn's ear, 'You look beautiful,' 'He's so handsome,' 'May your lives be filled with joy.' Dawn felt joy. She was full of head-spinning astonishment at all these happy people. Even her mother was smiling. Yes, she had done the right thing by her by marrying in her church. This was her crowd, her flock. This was how she did her mother proud.

Hand in hand the couple ran across King Street, the main street, the road that was the first highway along the lake, and gathered with the wedding party and relatives in Victoria Park for the photo shoot. The sun dropped light shadows on the assembled group. First the photographer snapped a picture of the four in the wedding party together, then the couple with their parents, and so it continued until the photographer insisted on having the newly married couple pose in more than a dozen different takes.

When they got into Manfred's car to drive to the Legion Hall, Karyn turned to look at them in the back seat. "You two really are the handsomest couple. I love your hair, Dawn. What beautiful curls. You should keep it long."

"No," Dawn said adamantly. "I'm not going to spend two hours every day getting my hair ready."

Karyn laughed and turned back to Manfred. "Darling boy, when are you going to make an honest woman of me?"

"You want a permanent relationship?"

"She wants you to marry her," Paul said.

"You're spoiling my surprise proposal," Manfred said. "Is this the place?"

"Yes," Dawn said. It looked plain on the outside, but the staff had decorated the inside with white crepe streamers and corrugated silver bells. The table sparkled with polished cutlery and gleaming glassware. In the middle sat a tall, iced wedding cake. Some children immediately started running around the dance floor. Dawn looked at her mother's relatives and felt a frisson of shame. Maybe she should have had a big wedding? Maybe she should have asked one of the grandchildren to be a ring bearer? Maybe she should have let her mother invite everyone to the party? Mary sat three seats away from her. The table was arranged in a U. Isabel sat beside her, and her father beside Isabel. Her mother was in the first seat kitty corner to her husband. Mary was beaming. She'd had her hair done, too, at the salon earlier in the day. Dawn relaxed. She needn't worry. Her mother always found strength in the comfort of her faith. Her daughter had just given her a church wedding. It was a happy day.

During the meal her cousins, on both sides of the family, banged their glasses wanting the newly-weds to kiss. Dawn looked over at Pam who'd come with a date, someone she'd hidden from the family. Her date was female, a fawn-like creature with freckles. When Paul suggested a game where other couples would kiss, Dawn censored it. What if Pam stood? This was still a small town. After the meal her father reiterated in his speech what he'd said to her last night, bringing tears to a few female eyes. Then they took to the dance floor for the first dance.

"It's A Wonderful Life" by Elvis Presley started. For the next two minutes Peter and Dawn danced what they had choreographed the night before. They started the upbeat tune with Dawn swaying in her father's arms, then broke apart while he spun and twirled her under his arms and ended with the two of them twisting separately. The room broke out in applause.

The DJ announced that the bride and groom would start off the next dance. Paul shyly approached Dawn. "You didn't warn me that your dad could dance."

Dawn laughed. "He has hidden talents. 'It's A Wonderful Life' is also his favourite movie, which he made me watch with him every Christmas."

Clutching her hand in his Paul led Dawn to the dance floor. It felt damp in hers and she whispered, "Relax." She moved her arm to his shoulder and led him step by step. "My parents are big Elvis fans. I remember when he first appeared on the Ed Sullivan show. I like your choice of song."

"You are my brown-eyed girl," Paul said. After their song The Temptations' 'My Girl' started playing. The DJ announced, "Everyone's invited to join Dawn and Paul on the dance floor."

Cheers went up and soon they were surrounded by dancers and singers. "That's better," Paul said. Dawn laughed. Her new husband had many talents, but dancing wasn't one of them.

Later, at The Breakers Motel, Dawn insisted on changing in the bathroom. "Why?" Paul asked.

"I have a surprise for you."

"It's not like I've never seen you naked."

Dawn winked at him and closed the door. She wondered if her father had ever seen her mother naked. Mary was so prim and proper it could be that he hadn't. What Mary had done was ask everyone at the Bridal Shower to give Dawn a trousseau for her wedding night. Now Dawn changed into silk pajamas and tied a matching silk robe around her. The material was light and cool; it slid over her skin; the pale pink colour highlighted her tan. She made an entrance by first showing a bare foot through the crack in the door, then pulled the door wide open, keeping her eyes on Paul. They sparkled and held hers. When they embraced it felt like it could have been for the first time.

———————

Sunday was a warm day, but cloudy. The air was close, as humid as a July morning. Dawn and Paul each expressed relief that the weather was better yesterday. "A perfect day for a wedding."

When Paul stopped, his feet sank into the sand. "Today is a good day for a swim. Should we wait for the others?"

"Yes. We can put our towels here. You know, I've never been on this part of the beach because it's private. We always went in over there," Dawn said, pointing west.

"Near the pier?"

"Yes. Where it's calmer."

"Good morning."

They turned to greet Karyn and Manfred. "Good morning."

"Perfect day for a swim," Manfred said. "This is an amazing beach."

"Look at this sand," Karyn said, kicking up some grains with her toe. "It's nearly white and the beach is so wide. Dawn, you're wearing a two-piece."

"Yes, it was part of my trousseau." She twirled around on tip toes in the fine sand.

"I like it. Get your midriff tanned. Was the swimming cap a gift, too?"

"Yes," Dawn said, touching the top of her head. The turquoise cap fit snugly and was decorated with two rows of gathered material. When she'd opened it, she vowed that she would never wear it, but it seemed prudent this morning to keep her curls in place.

Paul grabbed her hand and ran with her into the water. The lake was shallow for more than a hundred feet, and after running at least a hundred steps, he let go and plunged. "It's warm."

Dawn immersed herself. "It's always warm at the end of the summer."

Karyn bobbed beside her. "Not like the lake. It only warms up near the rocks, although some cottagers actually do have sandy bays."

"Not even like Lake Ontario in Toronto," Manfred said.

"Wahoo."

The four of them turned to the shore and waved at Morgan, Patti, Pam, and Trudy. They waded into the water together. "The water's warm."

The two couples laughed. "I've just explained," Dawn said, "that by the end of the summer the water is warm here on the beach. It's shallow for a long way out and the sand heats it up."

"Except for the jogger we're the only ones here," Morgan said, turning her head to survey the shore.

"A sleepy town," Dawn said.

"I think I'll take up jogging," Paul said.

"Why?" Dawn asked.

"My dear, you know by now that Paul will do anything that gets him outside."

"You should have become a forest ranger," Patti said.

Paul splashed Patti. That started an assault. Dawn broke away and floated. Soon Patti was at her side coughing and sneezing. "My brother's an idiot. I don't know what you see in him?" She stood. "Look, Mummy's swimming."

Dawn did the breaststroke, displacing the water with her cupped hands and kicking with her feet with every stroke. "I think you can still touch bottom here."

Morgan stood. The water was up to her neck. "Yes, I'm safe. I'm determined to learn to swim properly."

"Paul said you were taking lessons."

Morgan turned. "Yes, but I think I'll swim to shore."

Left alone, Dawn took the opportunity to swim overhand for a distance, then turned herself about and returned to the group. Pam and Trudy were floating on their backs. Paul had Patti on his shoulders. "I'm going in," Karyn said. "Time to sunbathe."

"One, two, three," Paul counted, then launched Patti into the lake.

"Are you coming, Manfred?"

"Yes."

Dawn beckoned to Paul and Patti. Together they waded back to shore.

"Well, my dear," Morgan said, patting the towel spread on the sand beside her. "Come and join me."

Dawn folded herself and sat cross-legged. She shuddered.

"What a perfect celebration your family orchestrated. Can I formally welcome you to our family, even though you're remaining a Wright, not taking our name?"

"Mummy," Pam protested. "'Feint praise."

"You're not taking Paul's name?" Karyn asked.

"Would you take Manfred's if you married him?" Pam asked.

"How bold," Morgan said.

"Would I choose to be Karyn Freundlich instead of Karyn Dent? What do you think?"

"Why does everyone assume we're getting married?" Manfred asked.

"Because love is in the air," Morgan said.

"Mummy, what a romantic you're turning out to be."

"It's taken years of celibacy."

"Mummy, are you bitter?"

"No, first monogamous. Now celibate. I'm ready to break out."

Patti fell back laughing.

"I like your family, Paul," Karyn said. "They're so forthright."

"I suppose that's one term for it."

"Honest," Pam said.

"It must be the European in you," Manfred said. "Definitely not American."

"We're Welsh," Paul said, "not European. Not English, either."

"I understand European," Manfred said. "Karyn, will you marry me?"

"Yes, I don't mind if I do."

"There. That's settled."

"You mean I don't have a chance?" Patti asked.

"You're too young," Morgan said.

"Do you find him attractive?" Karyn asked.

"Yes," Patti said, hugging her knees to her chest.

"Sorry, I don't have a brother."

"This is so perfect," Morgan said. "Like a scene out of Jane Austen. Only updated."

"Do you think so?"

"It's not just modern," Paul said. "It's very much Dawn. Who else would want to go swimming instead of attending a breakfast wedding?"

"What will we do now, for the rest of the day? Are we going to stay here?" Paul asked.

"You should visit your grandmother," Karyn said.

"In Trenton?"

"Why not? It's not far. I can't tell you how happy my Granny was when we had the family at the cottage for her birthday."

"I've never met your Gran," Paul said.

"I haven't seen her in years. Since before I went away to university."

"Then it's settled. To Trenton."

The nursing residence was a one-storey brick building situated near the river and a park. Dawn approached the front desk and waited for the receptionist to finish her phone call. She was told, "Go around the side to the back where you'll find her outside her room. That's where she likes to sit most afternoons."

Dawn hailed the others to accompany her. "Gran," she said approaching the patio.

"Is it Dawn?"

"Yes," she said, sitting down on the empty chair beside her elderly relative. "I've brought someone to meet you."

"You don't say. Who's that?"

"My husband."

"Ah," Gran said, chuckling. "I heard you were getting married. I'm sorry I couldn't come. I don't go too far anymore."

"This is Paul."

Gran lifted her chin and stretched her head to get a closer look. "Paul. Aren't you a handsome fella? You've got blue eyes and dark hair. That's a winning combo. Where you from?"

"My family is Welsh."

"That so?"

"But I was born in Toronto."

"That so?"

"That makes me a true-blood Canadian."

Gran nodded.

"And these are our friends, Karyn and Manfred. Manfred was our best man."

"Glad to meet you. I hear Isabel was your bridesmaid?"

"Yes, she was. She took charge."

"That's our Isabel. Wish I'd been there. Will you have tea with me?"

"Of course, that would be nice."

Gran instructed them on where to find the kettle and fixings inside. They stayed for over an hour. On the drive back to Toronto, Dawn thanked Karyn for suggesting the visit. "You never know for how long she'll be around."

"Too true. Interesting guest Pam brought. Had you met Trudy before?"

"No," Paul said.

"No," Dawn reiterated.

"We've had our suspicions about my elder sister."

"Not a good choice of words," Karyn said.

"It's hard to admit to. We need to be supportive. Like your mother."

"Yes," Paul said. He ruffled the hair on the top of his wife's head.

Barbara Simpson supported Nancy in finding help to allow her to go back to work. She knew that Paul and Dawn were now married, in a church no less, in a small town, a town she'd never heard of. Hilary had not gone to the ceremony or reception. It had been a small affair. No glamour after the build-up of an engagement party. Nancy had introduced Barbara to Hilary in the food court. Like comrades in arms, they had talked in detail about the marriage of Hilary's boss to the lawyer, Paul Lewis.

"Barbara knows him," Nancy said.

Hilary raised her eyebrows.

"We dated," Barbara explained.

"I'm sure he dated plenty," Hilary said.

"No, he didn't," Barbara said, "but she did."

Hilary laughed. "Really? You must tell me more sometime. She's so conservative."

"Only in her studies," Barbara hinted.

Barbara couldn't plan to meet Nancy on a regular basis. Babies had a way of intruding. Still, when she did, Nancy updated her. Paul and Dawn had delayed their honeymoon to Wales. When Barbara had suggested travelling to Wales early on in her relationship with Paul, Morgan had nixed the idea, telling her that she wouldn't like the small towns or countryside. Barbara now understood that Morgan hadn't wanted her to meet the Welsh relatives, to be part of her extended family, to become Paul's wife. What an interfering bitch! The old hag now had a whore for a daughter-in-law. Barbara had plenty to say on the matter, although she chose her words carefully with Hilary, who was still loyal to Dawn. Hilary had her own personal problems, which Dawn knew *about because she felt safe confiding in her. She was a sympathetic ear. "Maybe she's too good to be true," Barbara said, the closest she came to passing judgement on her rival.*

Hilary liked to hear about the architect. Her advice was the complete opposite to Honor's. Barbara appreciated that. Gordon was nonjudgmental. "Barbara, life can be a bitch. Suck it up."

Barbara raised her glass. "To your health, Gordon. That's everything. Bottom line. I've learned that much."

"You're probably right. Maybe I should start exercising."

"Maybe you should. Paul has taken up running."

Gordon set down his crystal glass. "Now how do you know that, my dear? Don't tell me you're still carrying the torch?"

Barbara denied she was.

By June of 1968 Dawn had paid off her student loan and purchased one hundred more ounces of gold. The value of an ounce had risen 22.54%, from $35.50, the original price of her purchase, to $43.50. She was confident it would continue to rise, even if it did fluctuate from time to time. She could handle the risk.

Paul finished law school and was grateful that he had attended when he did, as Osgoode Hall Law School was moving from downtown Toronto to York University next year. "That would have been a long commute."

"Especially by bicycle."

Now they were ready for their honeymoon in Wales, only they decided to start in London, England. They took a room in a terraced house facing Bloomsbury Square. On waking, Dawn pulled the curtains apart, unlocked the two doors onto the Juliette balcony, and inhaled deeply. Paul sat up in bed. "Listen to that," he said.

"To what?" Dawn asked. There were many pleasing noises coming from the streets of the great city: the roar of traffic travelling on the wrong side of the road, the bustle of pedestrians walking to work, the clatter of trains - all distant sounds. Across the street it was peaceful and quiet in the square.

"That bird. What is that bird?" He stood beside her and studied the trees in the square. "I think that's their robin," he said, leaning into her shoulder and pointing. "There, it's smaller than our robin."

"Sorry, I can't see anything."

"I'm pretty sure that's its call." They listened. Paul whistled in imitation, a string of ten syllables.

"I hear it."

"It's the size of a sparrow with an orange, russet breast."

They waited. "There," Paul said again pointing.

"Yes, it is small. Good, we have twenty-twenty vision."

"Breakfast?"

They dressed and went to the dining room in the basement. The waiter seated them at a small table with a white linen tablecloth set with silverware. "My, this is formal," Paul said.

"We're guests," Dawn said. They asked for coffee and agreed to the full English breakfast.

"Let me guess," an elderly gentleman beside them said. "You're from Australia?"

"No, wrong colony," Paul said.

"Canada then?"

"Yes," Dawn said. "We're here on our honeymoon."

"Congratulations. You've picked a good place. Do you know the history of the square?"

"Yes, Bloomsbury Group," Paul said.

"I know there was a duel fought here," Dawn said.

"There was?" Paul asked.

"Yes, in 1694," the gentleman said. "The economist and financier, John Law, fought Edward 'Beau' Wilson, killing him. Law was convicted and sentenced to death, but he escaped."

"He cheated the law," Paul said.

Dawn smiled at the gentleman. "My husband's a lawyer. I'm in business and know about the Mississippi Company."

"Right. How long are you here?"

"Just today. Leaving tomorrow. We take the train to Wales from Paddington Station."

"I have relatives in Wales," Paul said.

"You've a lovely day for sightseeing. Enjoy your visit."

"Thank you. We will." Paul leaned back to let the waiter serve his breakfast.

"I can't eat all this," Dawn said, looking at her plate of eggs, sausage, bacon, beans, fried tomato, and toast.

"I can," Paul said, reaching for the condiment tray. "Look, real marmalade."

"You sound like Paddington Bear."

"Funny. I always liked the Spectacled Bear from Peru. Which reminds me, we must check out St. Paul's Cathedral."

"We will," Dawn said, watching Paul eat. Clearly, he was famished. She was feeling the jet lag.

Paul looked at her without stopping his eating. "What is it, Dawn?"

"I'm not used to this kind of travel."

"I warned you about the changes in time zones."

"Yes, I know you did, but I hadn't realized how grinding travel can be."

"You're not sorry you came?"

Dawn smiled. "No, of course not. Maybe I'll eat a big dinner?"

Paul laughed. "We'll find you a pub."

Dawn was flabbergasted by the name of the area in Swansea where Paul's relatives lived: Cwmbwrla. "That's seven consonants."

"My mother warned me they would put on a show for us," Paul said in the taxi ride to the address on Fern Street where the Lewis family lived. "However, that said, their idea of hospitality differs greatly from ours."

"Forewarned is forearmed."

"Let me explain. They've never had much after the war. Like everyone else here they paid for the war after the fact."

"Is that why your parents emigrated?"

"Yes, partly. Now the Welsh are quite prosperous. Not rolling in it, mind, but comfortable." The taxi stopped and they got out. The driver lifted their luggage and left it on the sidewalk. Dawn barely understood what he said and hoped Paul's family wouldn't have such a strong accent. Or maybe the driver was speaking Welsh. "You didn't tip him."

"You don't tip the same here as back home."

Two black-haired beauties burst out the door of the terraced row house. "Hello."

Dawn gulped, stunned by how much they resembled Paul. Would she have girls who looked like them? She could only hope. She returned their embraces.

"This is Megan," Paul said. "And Moira."

Behind them a woman called from the doorstep. "Look how tall you've grown. Come here, lad."

Paul picked up their suitcase and sprinted to the woman.

Megan and Moira each took one of Dawn's arms and led her to their mother.

"This is Dawn, Auntie Rose."

Paul turned to shake his uncle's hand who then gave Dawn a squeeze. "Lovely wee lass."

"My Uncle Josh."

"Come in, you lot."

They were led into the parlour that had plates of food on the side table: scotch eggs, finger sandwiches, small meat pies, pickles, tomatoes, squares, sliced cake, sponges. Dawn smiled at Paul. Paul disappeared to take their suitcase upstairs. "You're in my room," Megan said.

"Sorry, we didn't mean to inconvenience you," Dawn said.

"Stop that, girl. No inconvenience. Megan's sleeping in Moira's room tonight. The girls are thrilled to have their big cousin here."

"And to meet his new bride," Megan said.

"We have a gift for you," Moira said, handing Dawn a box wrapped in shiny paper.

Paul returned and they opened the gift. It was a crochet tablecloth.

"Rose made it."

"Thought it would be easy to pack," Auntie Rose said.

"We last saw each other when we came to Toronto for the funeral," Josh said.

"We heard all about the wedding from Morgan and she sent a wee album."

"Yes, she said," Dawn said. "Told me I didn't need to bring our big wedding album."

Paul told them about earning a law degree. Then Dawn shared what kind of work she did. Moira and Morgan told them about their plans for school next year. They had attended the neighbourhood primary school that was behind their house. "Which is why we moved here," Uncle Josh said. "Couldn't afford the public fees."

"What in Canada are called private schools."

"Yes, I understand," Dawn said.

"For the past few years, we've had to take a bus to school."

"Are you still in school?" Dawn asked.

"Holidays don't start until the end of July."

"It's different here," Paul said, turning to Dawn.

They were served tea, then spent three hours eating and talking. "Let's go for a walk," Uncle Josh finally said. "We need to stretch our legs."

They walked together down Fern Street and turned into the laneway that led to the school grounds. Crowds of families were out together. Dawn remembered what Morgan had said about people using the parks. She found it all very jolly. Uncle Josh said they would go to Mumbles Pier tomorrow for a Sunday roast.

"And visit the arcade," Moira said.

Paul suggested they hire a car. They were together in the cramped bathroom, 'loo' as it was called by his Welsh relatives, who insisted that was a less crude word than toilet. Paul was shaving and Dawn was helping him by wiping down the mirror. There was much about watching him shave that appealed to her: first the ritual of slathering white foam over his jaw and chin, then the scrape of his razor over his bristles, always the scent of his maleness. Steam from the running hot water tap kept her busy and enraptured. "I know how to drive a stick shift," she said.

"Mmm. Do you want to drive?" His mouth was twisted to one side as he spoke.

"No, I'm not confident about driving on the opposite side of the road, especially with all the roundabouts."

Paul shook his razor and held it under the tap. "We can pick it up in Swansea and return it in London when we catch our return flight. Think about it. We can drive through the Brecon Beacons and Black Mountains on our way to Hereford and through the Cotswolds on our way to London."

Paul's enthusiasm won her over. He took the wheel and steered them through the narrow streets, around the ring roads, and onto a major highway which still struck Dawn as small. "Everything's so close," she said. "I keep thinking we're going to bump into a brick wall or another vehicle."

Paul laughed. He changed gears as if he was racing a motor car. After an hour they found themselves in the Brecon Beacons. Dawn began to relax. The hills were red sandstone, unique, and very old. "Maybe someday we'll come back and hike."

"I'd like that," Dawn shouted over the revving engine. She meant it. She could see herself walking outdoors here. They'd been gone nearly a week and finally she was over jet lag. She was enjoying her honeymoon alone with Paul in the countryside. He got off the highway and took a secondary road.

The Black Mountains were hills, hardly the size of mountains. They were old and worn down. Covered in green grass with lines of trees that served as a boundary, they could hardly be called a forest. Sheep grazed nearby. A few times they had to stop to let them cross the road. "I liked the lamb roast we had," she said.

"Don't you feel sorry for eating it now you see them here?"

"Crossing the road? No," Dawn said, "since we eat beef all the time, and turkey and chicken."

"Those animals aren't as cute as these lambs," Paul said. He stuck his head out the driver's window and said, "Bah."

"Oh stop, Paul."

When they arrived in Hereford, they found a restaurant for lunch. It was a tea shop that served sandwiches with a salad of only lettuce leaves with a mayonnaise style dressing. "The tea is really good here. I wonder why it's so much better than ours?"

"Well, I'd say they invented it, but they didn't. They just think they did."

Paul wanted to see the Magna Carta and Dawn wanted to see the Mappa Mundi. They entered the cathedral and started with the Mappa Mundi. It held numerous pictures of Biblical and classical events. The author, Richard of

Haldingham, had drafted it for educational purposes. It also held geographical features and pictures of plants, people, and animals. It was drawn on a single large sheet of parchment or vellum. "I remember reading about it in history class in high school."

Dawn examined the letters at intervals around the circumference. MORS indicated that all within the circle of its design was subject to mortality. "Latin," Dawn said pointing. "Death."

Paul started reading the Latin aloud, *"Sane Orbis."* When he had to turn his head upside down to read the print on the bottom, Dawn asked him to please stop thinking how she shouldn't have encouraged him.

"Mea culpe."

Shaking her head, she turned away from Paul and examined the top circle that depicted the Garden of Eden. "My mother would like to see this."

"I don't know. Maybe your father. He's the one who's more intellectually curious."

"I suppose you're right. Although she's always had a soft spot for Noah's Ark, and look at this depiction. She read me that story when I was a child so many times. 'Here come the animals two by two.' I remember drawing them in Sunday school."

After nearly an hour of looking, they went into the room with the Chained Library. "I knew nothing about this," Dawn said.

"Me, neither." After half an hour of perusal, Paul suggested they find some refreshment. Dawn purchased a booklet on the exhibit, then they found the Cathedral Café in the Bishop's Cloister. "Can you believe the time?" Paul asked.

"Why, what time is it?"

Paul showed her his watch.

"Maybe we should check into our B&B before we visit the Magna Carta?"

"I'd rather just stay here until we're finished."

At the exhibit Paul read aloud that the Cathedral held the only existing copy. "The Great Charter of Liberties, or Magna Carta, agreed between King John and his barons at Runnymede in 1215, is one of the most famous documents in history. *Habeas corpus.*" Paul turned to Dawn. "That's a very important Latin term."

"I know," Dawn said. "Credit me with some knowledge from my history lessons."

Paul explained, "It was distributed throughout the kingdom with a letter from the king requiring the terms of the charter to be broadcast."

"That makes sense because most people were illiterate then."

Paul looked down on Dawn. "No free man shall be arrested, imprisoned, dispossessed, outlawed, exiled or in any way victimized, or attacked except by the lawful judgement of his peers or by the law of the land."

Dawn listened without disassembling. This was her husband's domain.

"Rebellious barons demanded the king agree to the Magna Carta, which states that the sovereign is subject to the rule of law."

Dawn nodded. "Even a king cannot do whatever he pleases."

"Or queen. We have grown up with a queen."

Dawn smiled. "Long may she reign."

They left at five o'clock, closing time. Returning to their car, they drove a short distance and checked in at their B&B. Once settled and rested, they wandered the town until suppertime. Then they found a pub that was in a Tudor building.

"I think this is the best one we've visited," Dawn said, looking up at the ceiling. "How did they manage to build that structure?" She found the recesses of dark wood comforting.

"Your usual?"

"Yes."

He stood and Dawn watched Paul make his way to the bar through a crowd who were standing and drinking. She still found it imponderable how the locals remained upright while conversing and eating. She read the menu on the chalkboard and decided to try the local lamb. Can't have too much of a good thing, she thought. She placed her hands on the surface of the thick wooden table. It was polished to a watery gleam. Then and there she decided that when she and Paul bought a house they would purchase a long dining room table, one that stood as a welcome to family.

Afterwards, they walked along the River Wye. Paul smiled down at Dawn and squeezed her hand. "Thank you for agreeing to come to Wales for our honeymoon."

"You're welcome. Thank you for introducing me to your homeland. It's been special. Much better than a tropical island."

Their bed that night was a four-poster antique. Paul held Dawn's hand as she climbed on top of the high mattress. The tenderness in his eyes when he looked at her melted her heart. As he climbed in beside her she was assailed by a great feeling of love for this man of great physical strength who could show such devotion and tenderness.

On the plane ride home Dawn sat in the window seat, letting Paul take the aisle where he could stretch out his long legs. It had been a strange honeymoon, full of wonders. She'd gotten to know Paul on a whole different level. He was a more creative person than she was. She was linear by comparison. His love for her was full of the love he had for his roots, his family, his knowledge. What was love without that imagination? She had so many doubts by comparison with her roots and family and education. He could shame her with his depth. How surprising it all was for her to learn that. And reassuring. She could trust him implicitly. Could she trust herself to be as full as he was in his love? She would try. They had a bond that she would honour. Her mother had been right in insisting that she have a formal wedding. It hadn't changed her skepticism of formal religion or altered her lack of faith, but it had publicly sealed her bond to this amazing man. She was getting to know his faults, but she reminded herself to always remember what she'd learned on this very special honeymoon. Nobody was without faults. She needed to keep a perspective on their human connection.

How quickly Dawn's trust was challenged! Hilary was full of the news of Barbara Simpson. Yes, Dawn had heard the name. Yes, she was an old girlfriend of Paul's. This was worse than Pam's tittle tattle. Or obscene tongue. The woman was maligning her role as a mother, a professional, a wife.

"What else?" Dawn asked.

Hilary threw up her arms. "I'm sorry, Dawn. When I was first introduced to her, I didn't recognize what a sociopath she was. It just all sounded like gossip. Girl gossip. Adolescent girl gossip."

"How long have you known her?"

Hilary shrugged. "Maybe a year."

"That long?"

"Sorry, Dawn. My mistake."

"What's motivating her?"

"My guess? I think your honeymoon put her over the edge."

On the walk home from the streetcar Dawn felt like she was being followed. This was not the kind of imagination she wanted to cultivate. Paranoia. This was the dark side. This was a nightmare. Paul was in the apartment when she arrived oblivious to her nervous state, not even sensing the disaster ahead when she said that they needed to talk. He was willing to begin but she wanted to wait until after they'd eaten. Why give themselves indigestion? Why progress into a danger zone when they were both tired from a demanding day, the first day returning to work after their wondrous honeymoon?

"Paul, Hilary told me something horrible today about Barbara Simpson."

Paul looked taken aback. "Barbara Simpson?"

"Yes, your old girlfriend."

"I know who she is, but what of her, 'old' being the operative word here."

Dawn paused. How lawyerly of him. How removed from the imaginative creature he'd been on honeymoon in London and Wales. How dismissive, before she'd even begun. "She's been spreading rumours."

"Hilary or Barbara?"

"Hilary told me what Barbara's been saying."

"What do you want me to do about it?"

"Well," Dawn started. What did she want him to do about it? Stop it. Defend her. Take action. "Could you take some legal action?"

"Like a gag order?" Paul cocked his head which seemed a mockery of her, of his profession, of the entire situation.

"If that will stop her."

Paul leaned forward. "Let me tell you something, Dawn. The law can take action but consider. Is it worth it? It could be costly, and let me tell you, Barbara Simpson comes from money. Old money. She has an inherited sense of entitlement. Legal action is public. It reaches the courts if challenged. Is she really doing us harm?"

"No, I suppose not." Dawn felt meek. "This has been going on for over a year. Hilary thinks Barbara got angry when she heard about our honeymoon." "Come to think of it, she wanted to travel to Wales with me and meet my family. My mother discouraged it."

"See."

"That's still not harmful."

"I guess what I'm saying is, while she isn't doing us harm, she's harming me."

"How? How is she harming you?"

"By slandering my character."

"Is she slandering? That's a hard one to prove. Or is she simply getting your goat? I suspect she's jealous." Paul's blue eyes held hers.

"But why?"

"You have me." Paul smiled.

Dawn thought her husband was being arrogant, but she didn't say so. Should she have? Was he joking? He wasn't one given to irony. "I'm beginning to understand why your mother didn't like her."

"She's probably insanely jealous. If you give her a voice, she'll keep it up. If you challenge her in court, there'll be a blowback. There always is. That's what you have to understand about the law. It's constructed by humans and humans behave erratically. The law is set. It isn't fair. Is that how you feel?"

Dawn nodded. How did he know? "But what if she doesn't stop?"

"Then we will have to address it again. If she's doing harm or exhibiting malicious intent, we'll consider what to do. Yet, keep in mind, it's easier to do harm than good. Doing good requires strength. We're strong, Dawn. Aren't we?"

Now Dawn smiled. "Yes. Yes, Paul, we are." Still, Dawn thought she would ask Hilary to monitor the situation. While she didn't want to meet this old flame face to face as Hilary suggested, Dawn did want Hilary to keep her apprised of any more negative comments. She had a right to a peaceful existence free of interference. She'd confirmed that much with Paul before putting the topic to rest.

In 1972 Dawn and Paul bought a large house on Grenadier Heights in the area known as Swansea. It had been a village from 1926 until 1966 when it was incorporated into the City of Toronto for Canada's Centennial. Their three storey brick house was on the east side of the street and had the great advantage of looking out on the unspoiled nature of High Park during the changing seasons. Morgan approved, saying, "Now you'll be permanently established in the west end close to me." She had joined them once when they toured houses that were for sale. This one was her favourite. "Look at that view," she'd said. "There's no better view anywhere else in Toronto." She'd bounded down the ravine in the backyard, extolling the virtue of having trees but warning them how much care they'd need. Before they'd gotten back into the car, she'd approached a truck on the street and spoke to the workmen. "I got their card," she'd said, handing it over. "You'll have to hire gardeners. They do your neighbours' yards, not just planting and pruning, but raking leaves and trimming dead branches. They know someone who'll cut down trees if necessary."

"Do we want to take down trees?" Paul had asked.

"Only if they're dead."

The value of an ounce of gold had risen to $63.84. Dawn owned five hundred ounces. She'd stopped buying in 1971, after the price took a big jump. Besides, they were saving for a down payment on a house. The purchase price was forty thousand dollars. It was more than they could afford, but given her assets, the bank approved a second mortgage of five thousand dollars. She made the case to Paul that they could pay off the second mortgage in a few years and hold onto the gold, which would continue to increase in value. Paul said she should have been the lawyer she argued such a good case.

On their first morning in the house Paul rose early and went for a jog. It would become a daily ritual. He jogged down Grenadier Heights to Ellis Avenue, up the hill on Ellis to Morningside Avenue, down the hill to Ellis Park Road, along the road to High Park, into the park around Grenadier Pond to the south end, along the bottom of the pond on the Queensway, then up Ellis to his street where he stopped jogging and walked to his back door as a cool down.

Meanwhile Dawn got up, made coffee, and wandered into the dining room. From the Mennonites who had an excellent reputation as wood carvers, they had purchased a dining set made in rosewood, a richly hued hardwood, brown with darker veining. On top of the table sat a box marked 'photos'. She found a knife and cut the tape. Inside were the albums from their wedding, their honeymoon, and vacations. Before storing them in the bottom drawer of the two-drawer credenza, she flipped through the pages, and enjoyed a visual trip down memory lane. There were photos taken at Manfred and Karyn's wedding where Paul stood as best man. The reception was held at the Boulevard Club on the shores of Lake Ontario. Other wedding photos showed Isabel and Glen. She became Mrs. McAndrew. At a family picnic in the park Patti was photographed in a flimsy dress with a long skirt. She was a 'flower child'. Pam and Trudy were also at the picnic, Pam looking very masculine. Morgan looked robust. So was the man beside her, a male friend named Chris who was no longer on the scene.

The back door opened. "In here," she called.

"Look at Miss Chatelaine."

Dawn tilted her head at Paul who was looking at her like he was a boy, exuberance beaming from his face. "I'm not going to live this down." She had been featured in a current issue of the popular Canadian magazine called 'Chatelaine' in an article about women working in the corporate world.

"I'm proud of you. Need a shower."

"How was your run?"

"Terrific."

Their house became the centre of family get-togethers, so it was only fitting that everyone gathered at their house at noon for the final playoff between Canada versus Russia in the World Cup. Paul barbecued ribs. Dawn baked potatoes. His sisters made salads and Morgan dessert. The game started at one pm when they were still eating, so they picked up their plates, and carried everything up two flights of stairs. They'd converted the room on the third floor into a TV room. Usually they didn't allow food upstairs, only in the kitchen or the formal dining room, but this was an exception. This was the eighth game in an eight-game series. It was the first competition between the Soviet national team and the Canadian team represented by professional players of the National Hockey League, known as Team Canada. The Soviets had become the dominant team in international competitions and had long ruled the sport, so for Team Canada to make it to the critical end game was a nail-biting experience. It was so important that the country enjoyed a 'half day' holiday with many high school and university students sent home, while younger students watched at school in libraries. In Montreal's Central Station, five thousand fans gathered around ten TV sets to watch the game.

There was much moaning every time Team Canada got a penalty, and they took a number of early penalties in the first half. The communal moan deteriorated into curses when the Soviets took the lead. Dawn offered to gather their dirty plates and take them downstairs to the kitchen, where she rinsed them. She put the dessert on a tray with plates and cutlery and started upstairs wondering what she'd missed when she heard loud cheering. "Did we score?" Dawn asked.

The Lewis family was in an uproar of exuberance, but by the end of the first period, the Soviet team was in the lead two to one. By the end of the second period, they were ahead five to three. Everyone took a bathroom break. The house had three bathrooms: one ensuite, one full bathroom on the second floor, and a powder room on the main floor.

They were all back in their seats for the third period, when there was a ruckus in the crowd watching the game in Moscow over a protest with the goal signal light. There was a ruckus among the Lewis family too. Dawn thought Pam might break her chair with her pounding. Morgan seemed to have tears in her eyes. Patti was out of her chair sitting cross-legged in front of the screen. She'd been doing yoga for years now and was very flexible. Paul was standing, obviously too excited to sit. Then, with only thirty-four seconds left to play, Paul Henderson made a wild stab for the puck and fell on the ice, then got in another shot and scored. The players erupted in victory. Dawn watched her family hugging and jumping, listened to them screaming and cheering, and felt like a sedentary spectator of a great moment in the sport of hockey. Her father phoned. They, too, had been watching the game and wanted to share their congratulations with Paul's family.

At least the two families had something in common, Dawn thought.

Dawn's doctor gave her a referral to an obstetrician. She received the call at work and wrote down the date: Thursday, March twentieth, 1975. She suspected they'd gotten pregnant after the New Year's party at Karyn and Manfred's home. They'd bought a place in Moore Park near her parents and an easy commute to downtown.

Dawn said to Hilary that she hoped the baby would be born on Paul's birthday.

"That seems sentimental of you," Hilary said.

"I don't think of myself as sentimental, but it would be ideal."

"Why?"

"I wouldn't be rushed then."

"How long will you take?"

"I'm not going to stop work, Hilary."

"Yes, but you'll take some maternity leave?"

"No, I can manage work and having a baby. It's not like I'm going to be sick."

"Let me understand you correctly. You're not taking any maternity leave?"

Dawn measured her response. Hilary was a good friend, loyal to the firm and her, familiar with her family and other friends, a confidant and sounding board. "The way I see it, I am paving the way for other women. We get discriminated against because we bear children and leave work. There's a lawyer at Paul's firm who delivered a baby in the morning and had files delivered to her hospital room that afternoon."

"Did the secretary make the delivery?"

Dawn laughed. "Great pun, Hilary."

"I'll help you anyway I can."

"You're worth your weight in gold. It takes a village to raise a child."

"Speaking of gold, it's down."

"I saw, but at nearly two hundred dollars, it had to crash. It'll go up again." Dawn was thinking at $139.29, her stockpile of five hundred ounces netted her $69,645. By comparison, the value of their house had only gone up three percent. Manfred and Karyn said they wanted to get into the real estate market before they started having children too. Karyn knew her parents would help them with childcare.

Dawn's parents were very excited by the news. To become grandparents was their greatest wish. They'd tried for years before Dawn was conceived and wished they'd had more. Dawn reassured them that she planned on having at least three, mostly because Paul was keen and supportive. He'd grown up with siblings and thought three children was an ideal family size. Mary and Peter could only reiterate that she had married the ideal husband. Dawn wasn't too sure about that but stayed silent on the subject. Paul was not advancing in his job like his friend, Manfred. While Paul was intelligent and good natured, he wasn't cutting it as competitive enough to be offered a promotion. It seemed the only thing he was competitive about was sports.

Isabel already had a baby girl. Gwen now worked full time at the store and Teresa was away at Humber College in the north end of Toronto studying to become a Law Clerk, a program Paul helped her choose, so, even Dawn's relatives thought Paul made an ideal husband. "He's always supported women's work," Dawn said. She'd remembered what her mother had said about Teresa; she would be the one to leave home. Isabel and Glen lived in Oshawa where he was from and where his parents still lived. Lots of people living in Cobourg commuted to Oshawa, a point Uncle Joe made that fell on deaf ears. Isabel had to ask her mother to explain to her father that her husband didn't want to commute. Teresa had pointed out that more and more people were commuting to Toronto on the VIA train, but that wasn't an option for her because of where her campus was located. Of course, her father was willing to provide Teresa with a car, but Teresa said she didn't like driving long distances on the two-lane highway.

Mary offered to come and stay the first week after the baby was born. Dawn said she was grateful for her mother's help, especially since she would still be working, "Only from home."

"But aren't you taking maternity leave?"

"No, work isn't too hectic at that time of the year, so I'll just carry on."

"But you'll want to be with your baby."

"I will be with the baby, at least until the Nanny arrives."

"Nanny?"

"Yes, Paul's cousin, Megan, wants to come after she finishes Nanny school."

"There's a school for nannies? In Wales?"

"No, at Bath in England. Their motto is 'Strength in Adversity', which Paul finds a little over the top. I'm hoping our baby won't be so challenging to warrant such an attitude."

"Your baby will be easy to care for if she's anything like you. You never cried."

Dawn let the gender reference go.

When they made the announcement to Morgan, she said she would be available to care for the baby. Paul told his mother that that wouldn't be necessary. She was thrilled to learn that they had hired her niece, Megan. "Isn't she expensive? She's at that posh school."

"Yes, she is, but she wants to live in Canada, and we can give her a good start."

"My mother wants to come for the first week when I come home from the hospital," Dawn said.

"That's only right that you have your mother with you."

"She's reliable," Dawn said. Then she thought that didn't sound kind or generous. "What I mean is, I'll need lots of help to keep working."

"But you'll be on maternity leave?" Morgan said.

"No, I'm going to continue working."

"Dawn, you're entitled to maternity leave."

"I know, but I want to keep working."

"Of course, you do, dear." Morgan turned to her son. "Paul, talk some sense into her."

"I'm afraid I'm the one who told her about the junior partner at work who took no time off."

"That's senseless. Women fought hard for the right to have maternity leave."

"Yes, they did, but they caved when they let it fall under unemployment insurance. I'm employed."

"Well, it's typical of you to have solved your problem and have your plans in place before asking any of us for help."

Dawn bit her tongue. How was having a baby a problem? Who made it a problem? Who better to solve the problem?

"You know who this reminds me of?" Morgan asked, turning to Paul.

Paul looked at Dawn before answering. "Mother, she's history."

"You think so."

"Do you know something you should be telling us?"

"Well, she's a practicing midwife."

"Dawn's not using a midwife."

Then Dawn realized who they were talking about. After all these years how had this old girlfriend invaded their lives? Dawn inhaled deeply, exhaled slowly, and let the thought go.

Morgan wasn't the only one who objected to Dawn's plan. A secretary named Angela at one of the mining companies Dawn visited regularly questioned her extensively when Dawn explained to her what she wanted to happen with the files after the birth of her first child. "Your first?" Angela had asked.

Dawn could feel the utter distrust in Angela's voice. Her first? Dawn knew she'd already said too much. It was none of Angela's business how many children she had or how many pregnancies she'd had or if she was even the natural mother. Angela had often questioned Dawn's authority. She should have known better than to explain too much, yet she'd felt proud. Pride comes before the fall. That was something her parents often said. Or warned. They were right.

She was bound to fail with Angela on this count. Dawn had stood her ground on other occasions. When Angela had questioned Dawn's authority on tax advice she'd simply said, "That's why they're paying me the big bucks." When Angela had asked if there wasn't more documentation Dawn had referred her to Hilary. Then Hilary had asked who the interfering witch was. Dawn knew she was lucky to have Hilary, who always treated her with respect and deference. Unlike Angela and others who continued to question the outside authority of other females. This kind of distrust made it harder for her to do her job than the male partners. It wasn't just that they had the status of being partners. They were male. They were men. They were the bosses. Dawn was a female foolish enough to have a baby and a working life in the corporate world, in the competitive world of business, in the world that took control. Women like Angela never let women like Dawn forget that.

———————————

Barbara Simpson learned that Dawn was having a baby from Nancy, who was told by Hilary. "And she's not taking any time off."

"What do you mean, she's not taking any time off?"

"Just that, no maternity leave. A few days. Maybe a week at most. Hilary has to keep her up-to-date on her files."

"What kind of a mother doesn't want to be with her baby?" Barbara asked. Over the years in her role as a midwife, Barbara had delivered hundreds of babies, each one a joy, a happy miracle. Vita, gloriosa vita. *If she was with Paul, she'd quote that Latin phrase.* How well she could remember those times when they shared ideas about life. They were soulmates. Still were, yet providence had silenced her, or tried to keep her in the shadows of his life. His marriage to that woman was a folly. This lack of maternal care cemented Barbara's long standing belief that she was usurped by a harpy, a woman so uncaring as to leave an infant; whereas she, Barbara, had had beautiful babies to fill her life with warmth. They came at all hours, those babies. The call came and she attended, sacrificed her personal life for newborns. Both her partners lost patience with the demands of her calling. They fled to the hills, literally, the architect to a country life with an American girl from the Appalachian Mountains and the last one to the Scottish Highlands to uncover his roots. Barbara's mother consoled. "Someday your time will come."

Not soon enough, Barbara thought. "Not everyone's destined to be a mother."

"Well," Honor said, "it would make me a grandmother."

"Not everyone's destined to be a grandmother, Mother."

"Why have you turned to destiny, Barbara? I thought all it took was good planning."

"Mother, you know that not all babies are planned and, furthermore, that all plans don't materialize. I've seen too many frustrated mothers to believe conception is simply willed." Barbara refrained from reminding her mother how not all had gone as planned for her.

On Wednesday, September seventeenth, Dawn was at work when she started to feel cramps in her lower abdomen. She shuffled her position on her chair to give herself some relief so she could continue working. Her denim dress stuck under her bottom, which had widened with the pregnancy. She'd found two dresses on the regular clothes rack that she wore on alternate days. They were stylish with flared skirts: the denim one was copious with large side pockets and the pale green cotton one was gathered under the bodice. At home she wore maternity slacks that had an elastic insert for her tummy. "Huh," she exhaled.

Hilary appeared at her door. "Are you alright?"

Dawn faked a smile. "Yes." Was she really so loud to be heard outside her office? Then she grimaced.

"What is it?"

"I think I have indigestion."

"Maybe you're going into labour?"

"I'm not due for another two weeks."

"I came early. My mother always says how pleased she was to get rid of me. She's been saying that all my life."

Dawn nodded. She'd met Hilary's mother on many occasions. She was a woman of one-line slingers that left others with their mouths hanging open. Still, she had status, so everyone tolerated her warped sense of humour and piercing criticisms. Pushing her chair away from the desk, Dawn bent over double.

"C'mon. I'll call the doctor."

While Hilary was on the phone to the doctor, Dawn phoned Paul's office and left him a message. Hilary led Dawn to the elevator and outside where she hailed a taxi.

Inside the cab Hilary held Dawn's hand. Dawn breathed deeply. "It's gone."

"Let's time when the pain returns."

The taxi whisked them to the back door of the hospital. The pain had returned. Hilary helped Dawn out of the backseat and paid the driver. They walked slowly through the automatic doors. At the small reception desk Dawn explained who she was and what was happening.

"Can we see your Health Card?"

Dawn handed over her purse and the receptionist removed her Health Card.

"Are you in labour?"

"Yes."

"Who is your doctor?"

"Allyson Jokay, the obstetrician," Dawn said.

"I've called her," Hilary said.

"Please take a seat. We'll be with you shortly."

Hilary guided Dawn to the end of the row of seats and stood in front of her. "Why do they call it labour?"

"It's compulsory," Dawn said, "and painful. Very appropriate." She inhaled deeply, trying to take control of her breath.

Hilary held her hand. "That's my girl."

Dawn wondered why she'd suddenly become a 'girl'? Was she going to have a girl?

A gowned orderly pushed a wheelchair beside Dawn and offered her his arm to guide her into the seat. "I'm afraid you can't come with us," he said.

"I can't?" Hilary asked.

"Family members only."

"Don't worry. I've called Paul. Thanks, Hilary."

The orderly took Dawn to the maternity ward and registered her at the desk. Then he wheeled her into a room. Dawn stood, saying she didn't want to lie down yet. She started pacing. The contractions were coming faster now. Paul arrived out of breath. He hugged her and held Dawn's arm under the elbow. Then he helped her onto the bed. He wiped her forehead and pushed back her hair. She rolled over in pain and he timed her contraction.

The obstetrician came within fifteen minutes. "Let me see, Dawn."

Paul held her hand while the obstetrician placed her feet into the stirrups.

Dr. Jokay examined her. "You seem to be in a hurry. It's good I got here when I did, otherwise I'd have missed all the excitement."

She left the room with Paul and they both returned fully gowned with a nurse who placed the bed in position to wheel into the hall. Now Dawn was moaning. "Breathe."

Dawn did as she was taught to do in prenatal classes. Paul held her hand and walked quickly beside her down the hall and into the operating room. He coached her through the quick delivery. By the end Dawn was sweating and collapsed onto the bed.

"It's a boy."

Paul squeezed his wife's hand. "You were great, Dawn."

Dawn laughed, joyful at having delivered a baby, relieved that it was over so quickly, and perplexed about how she had done. It all seemed so out of her control. They placed the swaddled newborn beside her. She looked down at his tiny face. He was over seven ounces, a good size for an early baby. "Hello, Billy," she said, then looked up at Paul. They had chosen to call him William after Paul's father. Paul planted a kiss on her damp forehead.

That night the family came, first Morgan, then Patti, then Pam. They brought flowers for Dawn which they put in vases on the window ledge and around her room. It was a semi-private room, all that was available. The other bed was empty, so the family took advantage and spread out. They were all pleased that his name was William. Patti wanted to know about her labour. "Imagine how big he would have been if you'd gone full term?" Morgan said.

"As big as Paul," Patti said.

"Sometimes boys and second babies are big," Morgan said.

"Will there be a second?"

"Whoa, Patti," Paul said. "One at a time."

"Unless it's twins," said Pam.

"Are there twins in your family?" Dawn asked.

"Yes," Morgan answered curtly.

"Now you tell me," Dawn said.

"I'd like twins."

"For heaven's sakes, Patti, where is this coming from?"

"I think you might like to have twins," Dawn said, looking from Morgan to Patti. "One labour. Two babies."

"I don't think it works like that," Morgan said.

The next day Mary and Peter drove in from Cobourg. "I can come back as soon as you're ready to go home," Mary said. She'd knitted Billy blue booties and a matching sweater.

"How did you get them done so soon?" Dawn asked.

"She has a collection of knitted booties."

Dawn laughed. That was so like her mother. "Do you sell them at the church bazaar?"

"Of course, I do."

Peter had a box of cigars for Paul. "Dad, he doesn't smoke."

"He might want to when he's up in the middle of the night. Besides, we sell them at the store. They're popular again."

That night Paul returned, and Karyn and Manfred came to visit. Now there was a woman in the other bed who was sleeping, so they pulled the curtain and whispered. Paul and Manfred left to go outside and smoke cigars. "I don't believe those guys," Dawn said.

"It's become a macho thing," Karyn said. "There's even a smoking room at the club."

"Really?" Dawn said how well Karyn had timed things. She'd hosted a baby shower the previous Saturday. "I spent Sunday putting things away in drawers."

"When will you be going home?"

"Probably not for a week. Since he came early, they want us to stay."

"That's sensible."

"It is. He's nursing, which is good. They said sometimes babies who come early have more trouble getting started."

"He's really cute."

"Aren't they all? Don't they look the same?"

"Swaddled in little bassinets? Yes, they do, until you look closer. Then you perceive differences. Caitlyn says, 'Congratulations.'"

"How's she doing?"

"She might surprise us with an announcement this summer. She can't believe you're going to have someone living in to help."

"You told her about Paul's cousin, Megan?"

Later, after everyone had gone, the nurse brought Billy to her to feed. Dawn guided her breast to his mouth around which he snapped his lips and sucked. She felt the ping of extraction through her breast. The whole time he fed she studied him, her little miracle. His feeding comforted her as much as it nourished him. They bonded.

On Friday Hilary brought her a file. "Just the one?" Dawn asked.

"This is all you need to finish before the weekend," Hilary said. "Can the partners come and visit?"

"Of course," Dawn said.

"Good, I'll tell them. Timothy wants to visit before he goes home tonight."

"I guess Timothy's never going to be a father."

Hilary shrugged. "No, that's not going to happen. Too bad. He loves kids."

"He's a sweetie."

After Hilary left Gina in the bed beside Dawn asked what the woman had brought to Dawn.

"Just some files from work."

"You have to work?"

Dawn looked over at Gina. She'd arrived in the middle of the night making a great deal of noise that woke Dawn. She hadn't spoken to Dawn and seemed to fall immediately asleep, so Dawn got out of bed and walked down to the nursery. Billy was sleeping and the nurses were placing a newborn in a bassinet. Dawn studied the tiny faces and imagined what they would look like when older. Sometimes the names influenced her imagination as much as much as their features.

Gina's Italian family had visited at nine am: mother, grandmother, grandfather, sisters, and cousins. Mostly women. One elderly gentleman. The men were at work.

"I don't have to work," Dawn said. "I choose to. I don't want to put my career on hold."

"Tony would never let me go back to work," Gina said.

Dawn kept silent, recognizing it was a common sentiment. She was the one in the minority. Why fight this battle in hospital? Other hormones were kicking in, the ones that lulled her into total acceptance.

Dawn left the hospital through the same doors she'd entered, only this time she was accompanied by her mother and had her son in her arms. The attendant pushed the wheelchair to the back door of her father's car. Mary lifted Billy up while Dawn slid onto the seat. "Hi, Dad."

Peter smiled at her and asked, "Is he sleeping?"

Dawn nodded and Peter waited for his wife to settle in beside him. "All set," he said. They drove around the back street then down University Avenue to Lakeshore Boulevard. At the house he parked in the driveway. Again, Mary lifted the infant from her daughter's arms and waited for Dawn to get out of the car before handing him back. Dawn directed her father to take the key from her handbag. They entered the house through the front door. Peter carried Mary's suitcase across the threshold. "Shall I put this in the spare room?" he asked.

"Yes, please." Mary turned to Dawn. "I'll make us a cup of tea."

"That would be nice," Dawn said. She took a seat in the front room and put Billy on her lap where she unwrapped him. Her father came downstairs and peered down at his grandson. "What a little miracle."

When Mary returned, Dawn said, "I think he's messed his diaper."

"That'll happen often for the first few weeks, especially since he's a boy."

"Why do you say that? You only had a girl."

"I had a little brother."

Dawn felt embarrassed. Her mother's youngest brother had died overseas in the war. "Sorry."

"No need. I remember how often we had to do the laundry. He soiled everything. Not only diapers, but blankets and outfits. It's good your machine is on the main floor of the kitchen. I expect that will be a daily chore while I'm here. Do you want me to take him?"

"No." Dawn excused herself and went upstairs to the nursery. After removing his diaper, she placed it in the hamper along with his clothes that had somehow also become soiled. He blinked. She cooed at him. "Look at the trouble you're causing. Not even in the door and we have to change you."

When she went downstairs Dawn asked, "Dad, are you sure you won't stay the night?"

"Yes, I'll drive home after supper. It'll still be light."

"Paul's making ribs. He likes to barbecue." In fact, the only cooking Paul did was on the barbecue. He helped with the washing up, but somehow the distribution of domestic chores didn't include cooking meals. Up to now Dawn had let it go, recognizing that he did most of the outdoor jobs and she didn't want to go outside in the dark, cold, winter mornings to shovel snow. Paul seemed to like shovelling snow. He'd greet all the neighbours, other men on the block who were performing the same task.

"Can I hold the baby?"

"Of course, Dad." Gently, Dawn handed Billy over to him. The baby was fast asleep.

Mary returned with a tray of tea fixings and treats she'd baked. She set three cups on three saucers and poured a small amount of milk before pouring the tea into the cups.

When she handed Dawn her cup she said, "Teresa wants to come to visit on the weekend."

"Lovely," Dawn said. "I look forward to seeing her. How long do you think Gwen will stay working full time for you?" Dawn asked her father. Mary had said to her that she was confident about staying to help with Billy knowing Gwen could help her father. "In fact, she could run the store," she'd said.

"Forever," Mary said without judgement. "She'll never leave home."

"You don't think so?"

"No, she's got it too good. Joe and Muriel take her on vacation with them."

"She always was a bit shy." Dawn sighed. She wondered if Gwen was filling a dual role, being a good daughter and a helpful niece. "I'm going upstairs to change. Are you okay with him, Dad?"

"Yes. I couldn't be happier."

When Paul got home, Peter backed his car out of the driveway to let Paul park in the garage. Paul came in through the door that led into the kitchen. He seemed breathless. "Everything good?"

"Yes," Dawn said, giving him a kiss.

"Where is he?"

"In the front room with his Granddad. He's been changed twice, and I just nursed him."

"I'll start the barbecue after I change." Paul greeted his in-laws, poked his son, ran upstairs, took off his suit, and changed into his jogging clothes. These were his casual clothes for around the house. He darted outside to light the fire and made a great deal of noise banging open the fridge. Mary went into the kitchen to help him with all the fixings.

They ate in the kitchen, taking turns holding Billy. After the meal, Dawn said the baby needed to be put down. Peter said he should be going, but he'd be back next week. Mary excused herself, saying she should go to bed early because she expected she'd be up at the break of dawn. Dawn and Paul found themselves alone. "Finally," Paul said, "I have you to myself."

Dawn laughed. "Until someone starts crying again."

"I have to tell you that I have a big case starting tomorrow."

"Which means?"

"It means long days. I'm glad your mother is here. My mother says she'll help until Megan arrives."

"What's the case?" Dawn was glad to hear that Paul was being given a 'big case'. He'd been languishing at work for months, in fact, during the whole time she was pregnant. Still, he'd been especially helpful with domestic chores, even doing the laundry, and attending prenatal classes. Dawn felt she was overdoing the praise she'd heaped on him, which she mostly did to make him feel better about his stalled legal career.

"Disability. For a vet."

"As in a veteran of the war?"

"Yes."

"Funny, my mother reminded me today she had a younger brother who died in the war."

"Did she?"

"Yes. They never talked much about him. I know Gran has his medals, but I don't know where he fought or where he's buried. They never said."

"Our forgotten heroes."

"We do remember them on Remembrance Day."

"Well, we do, but most families are like yours. They don't keep the details alive."

"Too painful. I was thinking that we were born in an age of privilege. After the war. We haven't experienced loss or hardship the way our parents have. I wonder what the future holds for Billy and his generation. Do you think he'll be as lucky as us?"

"No, I don't. There're too many inequities in the world. Is that him crying?"

"Yes," Dawn said, leaving the room.

On Tuesday, September thirtieth, Paul turned thirty. Instead of leaving the house early for his usual run, he started the day doing laundry for his newborn son. Dawn couldn't help but laugh while nursing Billy. She was sitting in the rocking chair in the nursery watching her husband gather the soiled items from the laundry hamper. He was dressed in the latest running fashion, a cool shirt made of holes which he'd heard about from another runner who'd made the original item from a child's hockey net. That caught Paul's attention. His shorts were red with white stripes. He owned a jacket and matching long pants coloured blue with multiple white stripes down the arms and legs. The weather was borderline. Should he wear long pants? It had been a dry summer and he'd gotten used to wearing shorts. "Someday I'll have to run the Boston Marathon," he said before racing downstairs with the load.

Dawn kissed Billy's forehead. "Did you hear that? Your daddy's going to run a marathon. Maybe he'll take you." She switched him over to her other breast. He felt heavier this morning. "Tomorrow you'll be two weeks old. I think you've put on weight." After nursing she changed him and returned him to his cot. His eyelids fluttered. She watched him fall asleep before going downstairs. The washing machine was running, and the coffee was made. Paul came in through the back door, dripping in sweat. "Happy Birthday, dear."

"I'll be late tonight," Paul said. "Going for a drink with some coworkers."

"It is a special milestone," Dawn said. "Three decades." They'd marked their special birthdays by purchasing a new car. It was a Ford Granada, one of the many models designed in the wake of the oil embargo that forced the western world to rethink its gas consumption.

Paul joined her for breakfast dressed in a business suit. "Will you be okay until my mother gets here?"

"Of course. Silly."

"I'll be happy when Megan arrives.'"

"Just in time for your birthday party."

On the following Saturday, Paul drove to the airport in the middle of the afternoon to pick up his cousin. Megan drooled over the sedan. "A new car?" she asked after they loaded her luggage into the trunk. "So shiny. I like the colour."

"Dawn's choice. Green. She's the one who'll be driving it to work."

"And spacious," Megan said when they were seated.

"Plenty of headroom," Paul said, "for tall people like us."

Megan laughed but turned nervous when they reached the highway. "I wonder if I'll get used to driving on the wrong side of the road."

When they arrived home, Megan marveled at the size of their house. "I don't know anyone who lives in a house as big as this." Paul showed her to her room beside the nursery. Billy was sleeping, but she couldn't resist peeking inside his room. Downstairs she told Dawn that he had a room fit for a prince.

"Well, he's being treated like a prince having you as his nanny. How are you feeling? Tired?"

"No, I'm too excited to feel tired."

Dawn offered her a cup of tea and looked her up and down. Megan's hair was dark and thick. Her complexion was pale and luminous. She'd matured since Dawn had first met her in 1968. "You've grown into a beautiful woman, Megan."

"Aw, thanks. Everything is so big here. I remember thinking that when we came for Uncle William's funeral. Only we were so sad then I didn't really take it in, but there is so much space here. And look at the view you have over the city. I'm so excited to be in Canada."

"We're very happy to have you. Are you up for this party tonight?"

"Of course. Should I give Paul his present now or take it to the party?"

"Take it with us."

"I can't wait to see Aunt Morgan and my cousins."

They dissuaded Megan from wearing her nanny uniform, saying it was too formal for a family party. She fit into her role smoothly. Dawn thought packing up Billy to leave the house for the first time would have been way more challenging without her. Besides family, Manfred and Karyn were invited. Karyn announced that she was expecting in March.

"A toast," Morgan said, raising her glass.

"Mummy, the nursing mother and pregnant lady aren't drinking," Pam said.

"Neither am I," Patti said.

"What? Now you're a teetotaler as well as a vegetarian?"

"More for us," Pam said, turning to Trudy, who took her glass without a smile.

Paul raised his glass. "Congratulations, you two."

Patti sat beside Megan who was watching over Billy in his portable cot.

"You'll have to let me know how it goes with live-in help," Karyn said.

Dawn said it was already feeling liberating. "You can't believe all the fussing that goes into just getting a baby out the door."

"I'll probably take time off," Karyn said. "I admire what you're doing, but I just don't think I have the energy. I'm already feeling tired."

"Don't feel you have to apologize. Every woman has to make her own decision."

"My mother's pressuring me. She says they'll pay for someone to come on a daily basis when I'm ready to return to work. You're lucky you have such a liberated mother-in-law."

"Yes," Dawn said, "I am, but my mother is hardly in the same camp. She's pressuring us to baptize Billy. I was baptized."

"I suppose I was, too," Karyn said.

"She's aghast that I'm working from home, but she did admit that the idea of having someone live in is very modern. Hilary is very competent, and I trust she'll be very supportive."

"What's with Hilary?" Karyn asked. "She's more than competent. She's a bright woman. Why is she just a secretary?"

"She's a good secretary. We need good secretaries."

"I know, Dawn, but I just mean, why isn't she more ambitious? We need nurses. We need teachers. We need legal secretaries. It's just that she comes from such a good family. It's not like she couldn't afford to go to university."

"I think her family's part of the problem. You've met her mother. She's always putting Hilary down. Hilary spends a lot of time taking care of herself."

"She is beautiful."

They ate buffet style. Afterwards, Dawn nursed Billy in Morgan's bedroom just to get him away from the ruckus and be quiet together. Megan joined her and promptly fell asleep on the bed. Dawn debated whether or not to wake her for the cake. "Megan," she said gently.

Megan blinked and sat up. "Oh, sorry. Did I fall asleep?"

"You're suffering from jet-lag. Do you want to sleep or get up?"

Megan looked down at Billy. "He's asleep. He's such a contented baby. Not all babies are as quiet as he is."

Dawn smiled.

"I want to sing 'Happy Birthday' to Paul," Megan said. "He's my big, handsome cousin."

Dawn laughed. "Let's not spoil him."

———

Barbara Simpson disapproved of everything Dawn was doing. "I know Megan," she told Nancy. "His Welsh cousin. They all came over for the funeral."

"What funeral?"

"Paul's dad. Megan's the dark beauty. Imagine becoming a babysitter? A professional babysitter?"

"It's better than hiring an immigrant worker who's a stranger."

"Yes, of course. It was different for you. You had domestic and infant help after staying home to nurse."

"Dawn's nursing. She's being Supermom."

"I don't think so. She's being selfish."

"And she gets paid handsomely because she's well qualified."

"Really?" Barbara asked disapprovingly. Did Megan get paid more than Barbara did? Barbara always said she loved her job. She helped women in their time of need, in their misery of pain, in their life-giving act. Although she'd never been pregnant or given birth, she could feel their pain. She could exalt in their triumph. And she would triumph!

Honor held a party for her daughter's thirtieth birthday. Gordon told Barbara not to mind Bob when he insinuated that she was turning into an old maid. "Does he know how many women are now over thirty when they have their first babies?"

"He knows the price of gold," Gordon said, "speaking of, did you know your rival is a big investor in the gilded metal?"

"No, and how would you know?"

"Bob. There's a club of them, all that glitters, not to be confused with those that wear the brassy stuff. Don't you hate that look, thick chains around the neck, heavy amulets loading the arms, wide loops through their ears?"

"Not my style, but what else is gold good for?"

"That's the sixty-four million- dollar question. What is it good for?"

Dawn woke from her reverie at the sound of the front door opening. Megan was home. Dawn waited until she heard Megan in the hallway on the second floor. "In here," she said quietly.

Megan poked her head around the door to the master bedroom. "He's asleep."

"Yes. I came in here to nurse him, and we both fell asleep." Dawn laughed. "Come in."

Megan entered and gently pulled the door closed. "Is Paul watching the hockey game?"

"Yes." Dawn patted the window cushion. "Can you hear him?"

"Yes, he seems excited."

"The whole family gets excited when they watch a game. He knows all the players and their stats. He could be an announcer."

"They're playing the Chicago Black Hawks at Maple Leaf Gardens," Megan said.

"You're a fan, too?"

"We Welsh are fans of all sports. Believe me, hockey fans are quiet compared to our football fans. I played field hockey in school."

"Did you? So did Morgan."

"Yes, she was a champion, according to my dad."

"I'm sure Paul will take you to a game. Sometimes he gets tickets through work."

Megan's eyes lit up. "I'd like that."

"How was Charlotte Oakley?" Pam had arranged for Megan to meet Charlotte, who worked for her new boss caring for her young children. Pam had a new job with a new publishing house that was boldly entering the fickle world of book publishing. She liked the women at the helm who were risk takers and feminists.

"Charlotte's great. She's from Scotland. I can hardly understand her, but we had a ball."

"You don't have an accent anymore?"

"No, they weaned us off our accents at nanny school. Proper Queen's English for proper nannies. We need to be understood by the educated elite. And you should see the mansion where Charlotte lives. Your house would fit into the front hall."

"Where do they live?"

"I forget the name of the street. It's a corner house and huge. She said the area is called Lower Forest Hill. The living room has camel hair wallpaper, and the dining room seats twenty comfortably. The kitchen has a double range, but Charlotte said that they hardly ever use it because they buy take-out from the shops in Forest Hill Village."

"Take-out?"

"Not like the take-out you get from Swiss Chalet, or that we get back home from the Fish 'n' Chip shops, but real meals. And they have an inground pool that's as big as the one at the community centre. Well, maybe not quite that big, but bigger than most people have in their backyards. So, Charlotte has had to supervise pool parties. They're closing the pool tomorrow. Charlotte's a good swimmer, but she said the girl is disobedient until her mother comes on the scene. Then she smartens up. Charlotte has to use a whistle to call time-outs because it can be very dangerous keeping your eye on them. Charlotte isn't trained like me, but she does have her life-guard qualifications which, she thinks, is why they hired her. She doesn't get paid nearly as much as I do."

Dawn smiled. "Don't worry. We knew we could get someone for less. There's a problem here with childcare, especially infant care. We encourage women to go back to work, but unless you're earning a good income, it's unaffordable."

Megan looked out the window. "The view from here is super."

"Yes, that's why I like sitting here, especially at night when you can see the lights clearly."

Megan looked down and picked up the book that Dawn had left on the window seat. "What's this, *Our Bodies, Ourselves*?"

"Take it," Dawn said. "It's my Bible. It's a book about women's health and sexuality from the Boston Women's Health Collective. Its publication caused a revolution."

Megan flipped through the large book. "Thanks. Doesn't look like the kind of women's health we learned about at nanny school."

"No, probably not. This is an exciting weekend for you. You'll meet Teresa tomorrow. She's agreed to come for Sunday brunch."

"I look forward to that."

Paul poked his head through the door. "Hello, ladies."

"Who won?" Megan asked.

"We did," Paul said, stepping into the room. "Two to one."

Megan raised her fist in triumph. "I told Megan you'd take her to a game sometime."

"For sure. Usually, I get tickets to a corporate box. Very special VIP treatment."

"Wow," Megan said standing. "Do you want me to put him to bed?"

"No, I will," Paul said taking Billy into his arms then walking slowly out of the room.

"Good night," Dawn said softly.

"Dawn," Megan said. She looked down at the cover of the book she was holding then up into Dawn's eyes.

"What is it?"

"Someone stopped me in the street. Someone from Paul's past."

"Not Barbara Simpson?"

"Yes, her. Do you know about her?"

"All I know is she was his girlfriend before me in university and she's been spreading vile rumours about me. She's befriended, well not exactly made friends with, but knows someone who is acquainted with our secretary, Hilary. Barbara has made my life her business."

"Creepy."

"What did she say to you? Where was this anyway?"

"At the Runnymede subway station. She came up to me when I was getting on the train saying she recognized me from the funeral. She sat with me on the train all the way to St. George where I got off to change trains which I did quickly to prevent her from continuing to ride with me. She reminded me that we had spoken at the funeral about visiting Wales. Then she told me that she was a midwife. She laughed and said that was why she was in the west end neighbourhood, to visit a newborn. She kept saying how happy she was giving birth, so I asked her if she had any children, but she doesn't. She said her job is very unpredictable and she couldn't possibly look after a baby when she has to be ready to help others when their time comes. She actually said that, 'when their time comes.' Then she asked a hundred questions about you and Billy."

"And about Paul?"

"No, she didn't ask anything about Paul, but she did ask me to say 'hello' from her. Should I?"

"No, I will," Dawn said.

While getting ready for bed Dawn examined her teeth in front of the mirror in the ensuite bathroom. During pregnancy she'd had gum disease and had visited her dentist, Dr. Julia Lamb, who'd explained to her that hormonal changes can increase the acidity in the mouth. Dawn continued to follow her dentist's advice and brushed with fluoridated toothpaste even though water fluoridation was controlled in the city. She also flossed once a day, a practice that was becoming popular.

"Good, you're still awake," Dawn said, crawling into bed beside Paul.

"This sounds ominous."

"I don't mean to sound menacing."

"Foreboding is the Latin meaning from the root."

"Paul, spare me a wordy explanation, but the menace is back."

"Meaning?" Paul placed his file on the nightstand and turned back to look Dawn in the eye.

"Meaning Barbara Simpson approached Megan on the subway." She held his gaze while he digested her words.

"Megan told you this?"

"Yes, she remembered her from your dad's funeral."

"Megan did?"

"No, sorry, Barbara reminded her who she was."

Paul nodded his head. "I think I need to cross examine Megan."

"It can wait until the morning."

Paul gave her a kiss. "Yes."

On Sunday morning Paul went for a run after bringing Billy to Dawn in bed. Thinking she should let Megan sleep in, Dawn took Billy downstairs. She opened the curtains in the front room and looked out the picture window astonished to see a red fox trotting down her driveway. "Look, Billy," she said, holding him up. She felt an emotional surge, a longing to have her baby with her always, a deep desire to show him the magic of the natural world. The fox had a bushy tail and a solid body. He'd been well fed over the summer. He pranced like a reindeer, and she watched him go down the hill, cross the street, and disappear into the bush around the small pond. Imagining his outdoor life there she summoned up a picture of a den of cubs all barking sharply. How amazing to have been standing inside her house looking out just as the fox appeared before going on her merry way. Dawn identified with the vixen. The animal lived her life adapting to her surroundings, mindless of what else was happening in the larger world. She would carry on feeding, breeding, surviving.

Dawn heard a birdsong she recognized, the cardinal. She scanned the branches of the tree but couldn't find the red body. Billy fussed. Looking down at him, she rocked him in her arms and swayed her hips. Her motion calmed him, and she smiled, a smile she imagined all mothers make at this magical moment. He was comforted in her arms, and she was content.

Teresa Wright arrived at ten o'clock. Paul opened the door to her. He was still in his running suit, for which he apologized. "Found us easily, then?" Not waiting for an answer, he took her coat and asked Teresa how school was going.

"Really well," she said. "I love it. I've made lots of friends and the professors are all great."

"This way," Paul said, leading her to the back of the house. He asked her who was teaching what and nodded his head when he recognized a name. "Would you like a cup of coffee?"

"Yes, please. Am I early?"

"No, we're a bit slow this morning. Excuse me. I need to shower. Megan was out late last night, but Dawn's awake and probably finished feeding Billy. Sit. I'll let the girls know you're here."

Dawn came down first and gave Teresa a hug. "Sorry we kept you waiting. Paul said you're liking your courses. How is everyone? What news on the home front?" Dawn poured herself a cup of coffee and sat at the table with Teresa.

Teresa smiled. "Mom made Aunt Mary promise not to tell, but Isabel is expecting again in March."

"That's wonderful news. Your parents must be thrilled."

"Yes, but someone else is on maternity leave and everyone is complaining about it."

"Not my place to judge, but there are some regulations around the timing of maternity leaves. I can understand taking maternity leave, but it does cause disruptions."

"Aren't you taking maternity leave?"

"No, I'm not. I go back tomorrow. Monday, October thirteenth. Just under four weeks since Billy was born. But I've been working from home. Never stopped working."

"That sounds hard."

"Not really. I've had plenty of support and help. Speaking of, maybe I should wake Megan."

"Paul said she was out last night?"

"Yes, she's made a friend. An Au pair who comes from Scotland. I hope you can be friends, too. It's a bit lonely here for her. Her cousins are older. Patti's been great, but you've met Patti. She isn't exactly your regular person. Although to give her due, Patti said she'd take Megan to yoga classes. They're starting tomorrow night and they're held at the local community centre, so Megan can walk there."

Megan appeared. "Good morning." She stretched, then went over to the table and extended her hand. "Hello. You must be Teresa. I'm Megan Lewis."

"Nice to meet you, Megan."

"Want some coffee?" Dawn asked.

"Yes," Megan said and went to the counter to pour herself a cup. Teresa mouthed to Dawn, 'She's gorgeous.'

Dawn lifted her eyebrows. "A Welsh beauty," she said quietly.

Paul entered the kitchen bringing a rush of cleanliness. He smelled of soap, shampoo, and shaving cream. Rubbing his hands together, he said, "Ready to eat? Billy's fussing, by the way."

Dawn stood. "I'll get him. You two stay and chat. Paul's cooking."

Paul grinned. "Orange juice?"

"Yes, please," Teresa and Megan said in unison.

"Dawn said you were out last night with a friend?"

"Charlotte Oakley," Megan said, "but, I stayed up late reading in bed. Dawn gave me this great book about the historical lack of knowledge women have about their own bodies, and that the lack of this awareness has only one consequence, pregnancy."

"Trust Dawn to have a book like that. I'd like to read it. Dawn is still shocked that teenagers in our town get pregnant."

"In my hometown, too. Lots of unwanted pregnancies. So, this book is about empowering women."

"Which is why I'm serving you two and cooking breakfast," Paul said, handing them each a glass of orange juice.

"This is nice, being served," Teresa said, laughing. "I'll be serving you lawyers soon enough."

"And I'll be serving you tomorrow when Dawn goes back to the office."

Paul turned and strode over to the refrigerator. "I get it. Females are still in the service industry."

"We are. Dawn had a female doctor deliver her baby," Teresa said. "Aunt Mary was very impressed by that. And by Paul being there during the birth."

"See," Megan said. "Women are tackling many areas that were once taboo. Like abortion."

"Aunt Mary wouldn't be impressed by that."

"No one chooses to have an abortion if they're in complete control, so that's why it's important to let women learn about their bodies. Patti must have read this book, too."

"Our flower child turned vegetarian," Paul said from the sink.

"Dawn said you're going to take yoga classes with her?"

"Yes. On Monday nights."

"You'll need it after your first day alone with Billy."

"Paul, your son is an exemplary baby. He's so quiet and affectionate."

"As long as he plays hockey we'll get along."

Teresa and Megan looked at each other and shook their heads.

After breakfast Paul asked Megan about her subway ride. Megan glanced at Dawn who shook her head, so Megan said she'd met Barbara Simpson on the subway.

"And she approached you?" Paul asked.

"Yes, sat down beside me." Megan looked over to Teresa.

"It's fine. Teresa should hear this but keep it hush, will you?"

Teresa nodded to Paul.

"Good practice," he said, "for court work. Did you recognize her?"

"Yes, once she told me her name."

"And did she say anything about Dawn?"

"She asked lots of questions, mostly about the work I was doing. I thought that was because she's a midwife."

"Is she? Nothing negative?"

"No."

"Okay," Paul said cautiously, "if she approaches you again let me know."

"Do you think she's stalking me?"

Paul looked over at Dawn. "No, not you."

Dawn suggested to Paul they leave Teresa and Megan to get to know each other. "I want to talk to you."

Paul followed her upstairs.

Dawn closed the bedroom door behind them and sat in front of her vanity table. Paul sat on the edge of the bed. "I don't think it's a coincidence that Barbara Simpson met Megan on the subway."

"It could be a coincidence."

"I don't think so, Paul. I keep telling you she's been prying into our life. And don't ask me again what I want you to do about it."

"Then what are you telling me to do?"

"Paul," Dawn said trying not to sound exasperated although she was losing patience. "Barbara Simpson is stalking us, your family." Dawn didn't say 'hello' to him from Barbara. What she did say is that he should consult with a lawyer friend he could trust.

"I will," Paul said. "Work out what we think might be her intent."

<hr>

In July the family took their usual week's holiday at the cottage with Manfred, Karyn, and their new baby, Jonathan. Billy was now ten months old, and Dawn decided the time had come to make a complete break. For a couple of months now, she had been weaning Billy off gradually by breastfeeding only in the early morning and late evening. Megan had gone to Wales for a holiday to visit her family. Everything had gone smoothly over the past eight weeks until the first morning on Lake Muskoka. The two women were sitting with their baby boys in the screened- in front porch. It was the only part of the original cottage that remained. The rest had been totally renovated with full amenities making life at the lake very comfortable. The kitchen was large with brand new appliances including a dishwasher. The master bedroom had an ensuite and the main bathroom had a separate shower and deep tub for soaking.

Jonathan was four months old and breastfeeding. As soon as Billy saw Jonathan feeding, he turned his pudgy body around and started to claw at his mother's breasts. "Billy," Dawn said. "You've had your breakfast. You were a good boy and ate all your cereal."

Billy pouted and flung his head against his mother's chest.

"Aw," Karyn said.

"Stop," Dawn said. "That's not helping."

"Sorry. He's just so cute."

Dawn kissed the top of Billy's head. His wisps of hair were pale blonde. Originally, he'd had black hair which had fallen out after a month. "Sorry, mister," she said.

"I have to give you credit for nursing him for so long. It couldn't have been easy when you went back to work."

"I'm lucky the partners are so accommodating. I only had one leakage. Unfortunately, it was during a meeting with a client which had gone on too long. I had to flee the room."

Karyn laughed. "Oh, no. You must have looked a sight."

Dawn turned her head. "Yes, drops were actually dripping from the front of my blouse."

"That's it. I'm staying home for a year."

"They'll let you?"

"Yes, the temp makes a career of filling in for women on maternity leave."

Karyn worked at a small design firm with offices on the Esplanade in the heart of downtown Toronto. There was laughter coming from the dock. She lifted her head to peer through the screen.

"They're having a good time," Karyn said. "Paul's gotten very muscular. Does he work out all the time?"

"As well as his morning run, he's cycling to work. In the spirit of that alderman, John Sewell, who seems to have made the practice fashionable."

"Hasn't he? Don't you ride?"

"Not since I became pregnant. Now Megan rides my bike."

"So, she's coming back?"

"Yes, and I was thinking." Dawn adjusted Billy on her lap and turned her body to face Karyn. "I was thinking, since she is with us and it's working out so well, that I should have a second baby sooner rather than later."

"Sounds like a plan." Karyn moved Jonathan to her other breast.

Dawn watched her slip her nipple into Jonathan's tiny mouth. Like Karyn she loved being a mother and loved to mother, to fuss, to coddle, to nurture, but Dawn also had ambitions which she couldn't forget, a long-held desire to make her mark in the business world. She was managing both so well and wanted to keep the momentum going. "My cousin, Isabel, is expecting her second. She wasted no time."

Karyn looked over at her. "Where are they living?"

"In Oshawa. Glen's from there. He works in the offices at General Motors."

"You know Teresa applied at the firm."

"Christie, Crombie & Dent? No, I didn't."

"Yes, Manfred said she has an interview this week."

"Oh, Paul didn't say."

"I don't think Paul knows. She may have applied at his firm, too."

"No, I don't think so. They're too small. I don't think they're hiring. In fact, they might be downsizing." Another reason Dawn felt she should keep working. What if she became the principal breadwinner?

"Really? Is Paul worried?"

"A little." Dawn didn't share that Paul thought it wasn't the best time to think about a second child. Downsizing could spell the end of his time at the firm. Paul may not seem worried, but she couldn't help but worry. What kind of a position could he get if he was let go? He'd be in competition with fresh grads from law school who seemed brighter with each passing year. Plus, there were always candidates looking to advance their careers.

"How's Pam doing? You know her office is just down the street from mine?"

"Is it? She didn't say, just that it's a totally renovated warehouse."

"They moved after I left."

"So, you haven't been to her office? Well, she loves the place and the work. She says even Jackie Kennedy Onassis works as a consulting editor in New York."

"I read that. At Viking Press."

Dawn smiled. She knew Karyn and Caitlyn were voracious consumers of fashion gossip. They read all the magazines and had copies at the cottage. "How is Caitlyn?"

"My aunt and uncle are mad at her because she's living with her boyfriend and has no intention of getting married. She's bringing him this weekend to the cottage, so that should be interesting." Karyn pulled a face. "I was wondering about Megan because she has a boyfriend."

"Yes, the hockey player. Apparently, his family has a cottage here somewhere."

"They do. We know his older brother. He's a bit wild, but Scott is nice."

"Paul bought season's tickets to Maple Leaf Gardens."

"He did? That's a splurge."

"I know." Dawn kept mum about that added expense. Why air her dirty laundry with Karyn? His decision did seem extravagant to her, but Paul had justified it, saying he always had someone to accompany him, either his mother or sisters, or Megan, or a client, or a partner. Unlike Karyn's father's and uncle's firm, they no longer sponsored a box where Paul worked. Paul's indulgence had caused a heated argument between them. She could see herself becoming a hockey widow. Aunt Muriel identified herself as a golf widow because Uncle Joe played at least three times a week. He said it was good for business. Dawn didn't see how Paul's two tickets were good for business, but he thought they were.

Billy sat up on her lap and pointed. He made a sound imitating the birdsong. "Yes, bird," Dawn said. If Paul thought this gentle child of theirs was going to grow up playing hockey, she thought he might be in for a surprise. Billy seemed more likely to follow in his grandfather's footsteps and be a birdwatcher. So, despite Paul's objection, Dawn thought she should go ahead with a second pregnancy. "But if I do get pregnant," Dawn said resuming her conversation with Karyn, "will Megan still be available? She and Scott seem serious. Tell me more about his family."

"It's not that they aren't a good family. Maybe not as overly protective as some. What I mean is, compared to my parents, they're freethinkers. They don't set curfews. Stuff like that. There's a lot of drinking and revelry that goes on. They're allowed to take the boats out at all hours. Noisy bunch."

Dawn was astonished. "Megan's never said anything about that."

"Scott's not the one who indulges. He's disciplined. Like I said, it's his brother who's the problem. You don't want to introduce him to your sister."

"Or Teresa."

"Exactly." Karyn lowered her voice.

"Morgan says Scott wants to become a professional hockey player."

"Yes, I understand he's a good player."

"Of course, Paul thinks that's great. His whole family likes him."

Karyn laughed. "Isn't that the limit?"

"Yes. Hockey crosses cultures. Or sports."

Again, Karyn lowered her voice. "Manfred told me about the Barbara Simpson situation. All in strictest confidence, of course."

Dawn sighed with relief. She'd hoped he'd confide in Manfred. "Yes, I asked him to seek advice from another lawyer he could trust."

"Manfred said the law is a quagmire in such cases."

"Paul said as much but he didn't say that Manfred gave him that advice. Paul said the lawyer he consulted supports what Paul has thought all along. Best to do nothing. Monitor the situation, but don't rattle her cage."

"A sleeping tiger," Karyn said.

"That's what I think. Not that she makes me nervous. I don't know her. Paul's mother certainly doesn't like her."

"Morgan? Why not?"

"Thinks she's part of the elite. Morgan said the privileged are different here in the new world. In the old world they're visible. They're known. They're in the tabloids. Here they're invisible. They behave with the same sense of privilege, but no one holds them accountable, so they get away with atrocities. That was Morgan's word, atrocities. Morgan is given to exaggeration when she wants to make a point."

Karyn turned her small eyed gaze on Dawn. "That's an interesting observation. She may be right."

"Paul said his mother didn't trust Barbara because she had an unearned sense of entitlement."

"Spoiled, in other words?"

"I suppose," Dawn said. "I really don't trust the situation. She's after something."

"She's after Paul from what I understand."

Dawn shook her head. Was she really being challenged by a homewrecker? A dark cloud of worry descended on part of her brain, somewhere on the outer edges like an advancing front bringing change. She wasn't up to acclimatizing to bad weather. It seemed to her that the arrival of children challenged many marriages nowadays. There was a shift steering the nuclear family off centre. In the higher orders of her mind, Dawn knew she need not worry. She was in a safe zone with Paul. "I guess Paul still thinks he's my Knight in Shining Armour."

Again, Karyn laughed. "Ready to defend you."

"Only his armour isn't so shiny."

"It's outdated, chivalry."

"His armour is rusty."

Karyn messed up her son's scalp. "What do you think? Are you going to grow up to be a knight?"

"Will they still tell them those stories? I wonder."

———————————————

Barbara Simpson attended a birth that got complicated. She called an ambulance. "Sorry," she said to the mother in labour. "You mustn't feel defeated by this. Or that you did anything wrong, but your baby is in a breach position, and we don't want to take any chances. Do you want me to accompany you to the hospital? They'll only let one other person in the ambulance with you."

Barbara stayed until the ambulance had driven off with the mother and expectant father. She decided to visit her own mother who always received her at these difficult times with patience and understanding. Honor took Barbara into her arms and held her until her daughter relaxed. "You must be tired, dear?"

Barbara nodded. "I am."

"What can I get you?"

"Just a cup of tea."

After telling her mother the details of the complicated birth, Barbara said, "Mother, can I confide in you?"

"Yes, what is it?"

"Something personal. It's about Paul Lewis?" Honor nodded. "He married a woman who is an accountant. They have a baby boy. His cousin from Wales is here to take care of their infant while she's back to work."

"Ah, Barbara. I remember you thought you would go to Wales with him. I can see you're still in love with him. Let it go, child. Let him go."

Barbara blinked away her tears. It was the first time she'd given into her emotions over losing him. Could she do her mother's bidding? Could she let him go? She'd tried with others, but the worm inside her head kept nagging that she'd been spurned for another without being given a chance to defend herself.

Early in the morning on Thursday, November eleventh, Dawn got out of bed and went into the ensuite bathroom. She surprised herself by having a very large bowel movement. Usually, it took the first cup of coffee for that relief. She returned to bed where Paul was still fast asleep. As soon as she got under the covers, she felt a cramp which struck her as very odd considering she'd just been to the bathroom. The cramp quickly turned into a deep pain in her abdomen. The pain grew in intensity, and she moaned. Paul lifted his head off the pillow and asked her if she was alright.

Dawn was now in so much pain she couldn't move. When she told him this through gasping breaths he sprang out of bed and dialed 911. She could hear him in the bathroom and then in the room getting dressed. The pain was now numbing her, and she had to struggle to remain conscious. Soon she heard big boots coming up the stairs. Two paramedics slid her onto a stretcher and carried her out of the room. Megan had Billy in her arms who was crying for his 'Mommy'. The attendants pushed her into the back of the ambulance and Paul got in beside her. They took her to St. Joseph's, which was the closest hospital. Inside she was immediately wheeled through the halls, into the elevator, and into a ward where staff took her pulse and other vital signs. She faintly heard Paul talking. Then an intern with very big, dark eyes, leaned over her to say they were going to operate. She saw a large mask cover her face.

When she came to, she was alone on a gurney in a hospital corridor. She heard some activity along the hallway. Still feeling sedated, she couldn't think clearly about where she was or what was happening. It became quiet. Then a nurse was at her side telling her that they were moving her to a room. She nodded and fell asleep as soon as they'd settled her in a hospital bed. When she came to, Paul was sitting beside her. She smiled weakly at him. He rose, bent over her, and kissed her cheek. It was gratifying having him at her side. She could feel the stubble on his face brush against her. He hadn't shaved. He hadn't gone to work. It didn't matter.

"What happened?"

He told her she'd had an ectopic pregnancy, that her blood pressure was so low when she'd arrived, she could have been dead soon, that they'd operated immediately. She wasn't sure what an ectopic pregnancy was although she faintly remembered reading about the term somewhere. Paul told her the fertilized egg got stuck in her Fallopian tube, which they removed. "But you still have the other tube, and you can still conceive again."

That was not what she wanted to hear. She knew her husband was being kind and caring, but she didn't want to think about conception. She didn't want to think about pregnancy or birth. All she could think about was the inside of her body. There was once a tube between her ovary and uterus, and now there wasn't. Was there an empty space?

Paul said that Billy was with Megan, still crying, and asking after his mother. He didn't tell her this to distress her, but to explain why the staff had agreed to let them visit, if she was ready for visitors. Maybe she didn't feel strong enough yet? Maybe she needed to rest? She agreed she did. She was sorry, but the anesthetic was still in her system and making her groggy. When she woke again Paul was gone and she was alone in the room. It was dark outside. The curtains were open. She could hear the roar of traffic. The hospital was beside busy expressways. It wasn't the hospital she was used to. He wasn't her doctor, and it was an intern who had operated. Everything felt different and strange. A nurse entered her room and asked her if she would like something to drink. She nodded and the nurse returned with a glass with a straw in it. She helped Dawn sit up by adjusting the bed to raise her head. The nurse put the straw to Dawn's lips. Dawn said she felt better after drinking.

The next morning Paul returned. He was dressed in his business suit with an overcoat. Dawn asked him if he had to go to work. He said he was driving in rather than cycling because he had had an exhausting night. Paul leaned over her and stroked her forehead saying he was sorry, but Dawn couldn't understand his sentiment because it wasn't his fault. He smelled of fresh air. He wanted to know if she had eaten, and she said they had brought her a breakfast of sorts. It was jello. She wondered if Billy would like jello and said she would like to see him. Paul said he would let Megan know.

Before lunch Megan came with Billy, who reached for her with his outstretched arms. Megan placed him on the bed beside her and Dawn tickled him, telling him that Mommy was better now and that she would be home next week. "Can you be a good boy for me until then?"

Billy hugged her and said he could. Dawn felt the imprint of his small body against her chest, an impression she kept with her all day. It was a nicer feeling than the discomfort down below. They had taken a taxi and Megan said that Billy talked incessantly to the driver telling him about the ambulance that came to his house to take his mommy away and now he was going to see her in hospital.

By lunch time she was sitting up in bed and ate more than she had at breakfast. By Saturday she was standing and could walk slowly down the hall to the end where the window looked out over the lanes of traffic. Pam visited later and told her she was in the Morrow wing. She knew the family name because a woman who worked on the children's magazine they published was from that family. Morgan visited and told her she had never known anyone who'd had an ectopic pregnancy, only women who'd miscarried or had stillbirths. Everyone brought her flowers to cheer her up. On Sunday her parents came from out of town and walked with her through the hallways. They were pleased to see she was doing so well.

Paul took more time off work when she was discharged to drive her home. He admitted to her that he thought they were going to let him go.

"I'm sorry," Dawn said.

"No worries," Paul said. "I'll find something else."

Dawn was worried. Paul was a bit gullible and too trusting. When she'd first met him, she thought he'd make a good lawyer. He seemed to understand the law, he quoted Latin, he was friendly and outgoing. Yet he wasn't like Manfred. He wasn't analytical. He wasn't a fighter. Sometimes, he wasn't even thorough.

The partners told her to take off as much time as she needed. Hilary said she shouldn't worry about her clients because the new intern was happy to work overtime to cover for her. Dawn was not reassured by anything anyone told her. She suffered terrible nightmares and felt tired even when waking. She got up and went out for the first time when she had a follow-up appointment with the young doctor. His name was Dr. Kavoukian. Dawn guessed he was Armenian. He was short and his eyes were big and intense. She felt mesmerized by them as they were the last contact she'd had before going under. She thought about the genocide and what would have happened if his family had been killed. Then he wouldn't have been there for her. She knew this was crazy thinking. Maybe she needed therapy? Or maybe she just needed more time to rest at home?

Paul took her out to dinner at the end of November. He was now unemployed and looking for work. Still, he was optimistic and said they needn't worry. Paul talked to her about their choices. If she didn't want to get pregnant again, they could adopt.

"Paul, I can understand where you're coming from, but I don't want another baby. I mean, I don't want to adopt. I know I rushed this second pregnancy because I thought with Megan under our roof, we could enlarge our family."

"We would be enlarging our family."

"Paul, please understand where I'm coming from. I'm an only child. Having Billy is totally satisfying. I'm not a baby machine. I don't feel my body has betrayed me. I have no desire to adopt. I just want my old self back."

Paul looked hurt. He bent his head and fumbled with his fingers trying to smooth the tablecloth. "You were moaning. I knew you were in terrible pain."

"Yes, I was trying to speak but."

"Your mouth was open but."

"I was trying to tell you my symptoms."

"So, I called an ambulance."

"Yes, you did," Dawn said, reaching her arm out and taking his hand. "You did what you could."

Paul looked into her eyes. "I felt so helpless."

"But you were there to help."

"It's all I could do."

"It's all anyone could have done."

"Well, if that's it for us. One son."

"It's enough, Paul. Count ourselves lucky we live close to a hospital."

Paul smiled and squeezed her hand.

That night she dreamt she was as vibrant as she had been as a girl. In her dreams she was seeing her youth, her beginning, and her wishes. She woke and the dreams faded but left a sensation of loss that permeated her whole being. Mostly she didn't remember dreams. Sometimes Paul shared his with her. They would speculate on what his dreams meant but she seemed a closed book. She decided she would share this night's dreams. Paul listened and agreed with her that she was accepting some sense of loss. He said he was sorry, but again she reassured him it wasn't his fault.

In December she went back to work and decided she was content with one child.

Barbara Simpson took satisfaction in serving as Patti Lewis's midwife. Paul's youngest sister was out of favour with her family because of whom she'd married. Patti didn't remember who Barbara was. She'd been at an elite boarding school abroad when Barbara and Paul were dating. She hadn't even spoken to Patti at her father's funeral.

On her first home visit Barbara admired the wedding photos on the mantelpiece and was immediately drawn to the one personal item in the small room. Their home was in an area called the Junction which had been settled by the Irish at the end of the last century. "Are these your in-laws?"

"Yes," Patti said. "They are Patrick's parents."

"And your family?"

Patti shook her head. "They didn't come."

"Why not?" Barbara dared to ask.

"My mother doesn't approve of Patrick. She thinks I made a bad choice marrying someone who's Catholic."

"Really? Maybe she'll change her mind once the grandchildren arrive?"

"Maybe," Patti said, inhaling deeply. "She's a very liberated woman for her generation but she thinks I've regressed."

"Nonsense, having a home delivery is a very progressive choice."

"I may as well tell you that my mother-in-law doesn't approve either."

"The next time I visit you could invite her to join us."

Patti smiled. "I will."

Barbara smiled thinking how relieved she was to know there would be no interference from Morgan while she was on the scene.

Months later Barbara arrived in plenty of time, having been called when Patti felt the first pangs. She was huge with twins, a double pleasure. She was scared by the prospect of delivering despite having always wanted to be a mother of twins. Barbara saw the first head twist, scrunch up its features, and plop into her hands. "It's a girl," Barbara said looking down at the wet, greyish face. The infant held her fists up on either side of her head. Barbara turned her onto her side and watched the water leak out of her mouth. Her lips turned pink, and Barbara cut the cord. She handed the girl to Patrick, the father. He knew what to do, having been instructed earlier by Barbara. He was helped by his mother. They were gowned and masked as Barbara had instructed.

Barbara turned back to Patti, whose face was beet red. Her yell competed with the baby's howl. Barbara reached inside and eased out the second head. Its cry was loud for such a tiny creature. "Another girl," Barbara announced. She marvelled at how the colour spread to her cheeks, chin, and forehead.

Barbara luxuriated in the praise from Patti's in-laws. The husband, grandfather of the twins, had declined to be present at the birth. He'd waited for the news downstairs. Barbara thought Patti had done very well for herself and wondered what all the fuss was with the Lewis family. Patti didn't confide anymore personal details after that first visit. She was more interested in learning about pregnancy and motherhood. What Barbara did learn was that Morgan hadn't made any contact with her daughter since her marriage to Patrick. Although they both lived in the west end of the city Barbara thought they were confined to their own areas that were self-sufficient with amenities like shops, schools, and churches.

Barbara continued to be helpful and supportive after the birth. She was determined to fill the absent shoes of Morgan. "I couldn't have done this without you," Patti told her.

Barbara was sorry to leave her charge when her work was done. Yet she heeded her mother's advice and stayed clear of keeping up a relationship, as Barbara had done with a few of her clients, like Nancy Grady. She was good friends with Nancy. They still often met for lunch. Despite Honor's advice, Barbara relished hearing news about Dawn. She'd learnt about Dawn's ectopic pregnancy. She understood how painful that was. Yet she failed to feel any empathy for Dawn as she would with her own patients. She'd found out that Dawn didn't plan on getting pregnant again. "You can still get pregnant with one tube."

"I know," Nancy said, "but like me, I think she's had enough of that kind of pain."

Barbara sighed. "It takes kindness, empathy, and patience to endure." Barbara was quoting her mother. "Take support wherever you can," she said.

On the last day of school in June of 1985, Dawn drove to the house on Howard Park to pick up Billy. The large house, bigger than hers, belonged to Megan and Scott, but now Patti lived there with her two children. She was a single mother, not divorced. Morgan complained that her daughter could never get a divorce now since she'd chosen to marry a Catholic, Patrick Sinnott. Not only had she married a Catholic, she converted to Catholicism. "I've lost my flower child," Morgan had complained upon hearing what Patti was doing in 1980. It had seemed then that Patti was prepared to do a complete 180. She'd married Patrick Sinnott in a Catholic Church, a union where they became a loving couple, Patti and Patrick, Mr. and Mrs. Sinnott.

"She even changed her last name," Morgan had wailed.

Patti reminded her mother that she had too.

"But times have changed," Morgan had said.

As Morgan had predicted, the marriage didn't last. Patti had reached out to her brother for legal advice. He and Dawn had visited her at her house in the Junction where they met the twins, Susie and Sam. "There's no need to come into the office," Paul had said. "My services are *pro bono.* That's the least we can do for you after your family abandoned you for four years."

"And I'm here to help in case Paul sounds too intimidating and to give you financial advice," Dawn had said.

"I need all the help I can get. I don't have a job."

"I know, Patti," Dawn had said. She had thought Patti looked very motherly with soft features and full breasts. Her body was thicker, but she'd been so thin as a teenager, adding a bit of weight only enhanced her figure. She hadn't lost her muscle tone. Probably from chasing after twins, Dawn had surmised. Her hair was still shiny and blonde but not styled. "Do you want to work?" Dawn had asked. She'd needed to be forthright. Patti, despite being the one with a year at a private school in Switzerland, was unqualified.

"Not yet," Patti had said. "The girls still need me."

"Yes," Dawn had said, "and if you were to get a job paying for daycare would be so expensive it would take most of what you could earn. Maybe later, when they're in school full time, you could go back to school to train for a career."

"And that is the case we'll make. You'll need a great deal of financial support, Patti. We will pursue no-fault but I must know, have you had marriage counselling to try to reconcile your differences?"

"Only through the church."

"I see."

"Patrick and his parents refuse any other kind of help."

"That's fine," Paul had said. "That's better for your case. I will argue that you weren't raised in the faith and that you have offered to seek lay counselling but was refused. That you have devoted yourself to the raising of your children. That you need full support for years to come to settle the girls and to requalify. How is your financial situation?"

"Patrick's parents have always backed him. They bought this house."

"That puts you in a good fiscal position," Dawn had said.

"But he wants to continue to live here."

Dawn had looked over at Paul who had said, "That could pose a problem, but we'll deal with it. You can't separate from him and live under the same roof."

"No."

"I can't believe you've been so close all these years," Dawn had said, "and we never bumped into you. What a loss. To have missed out on seeing your beautiful girls grow up."

Patti had started to cry.

"I'm sorry. I didn't mean to hurt you. We never knew what to do."

"You know how fierce Mum can be. She was adamant we shouldn't get in touch."

"I know. I was hurt at the time but as stubborn as she was. I thought I was following my heart. We were in love."

"At least she's given me more grandchildren," Morgan had said in consolation when Paul and Dawn told her about the visit.

The twin girls now attended the Montessori School on High Park Gardens where Billy had gone. Megan was married to the hockey player, Scott, who'd been traded to a team in the U.S. She'd offered Patti the use of their large house while they were away. Megan hoped they wouldn't remain in the United States for long. She didn't want her children to be born American citizens.

Now Billy went to the French Immersion school which was walking distance from Megan's house on Howard Park. Megan had totally renovated the three-storey brick house to include a main floor laundry room, a feature she'd always liked about Dawn and Paul's house.

"Hello," Dawn called as she let herself in.

"We're in the kitchen," Morgan said.

Dawn found her mother-in-law and her sister-in-law at the back of the house around the kitchen table. Patti had returned to wearing flower patterned dresses. Morgan was in a track suit of synthetic material. She had walked to Patti's and said she hoped Dawn would give her a ride home. "Don't you look swanky," Morgan said.

"Yes," Dawn admitted looking down at her bold polka dot dress, green with white spots. "It's an Ungaro knock-off. Hilary's good at taking me to shops in Yorkville." She poured herself a cup of tea. She could see the children outside playing. Dawn paid Patti for babysitting Billy before and after school. She used to pay Megan the same amount. She calculated how long she'd been following this routine. It was still cheaper than private school fees.

"I thought tomorrow was the last day of school," Morgan said, "but, Patti says it's a P.D. day."

"Yes, Friday. Billy's coming for the whole day. He seems happy with that arrangement," Dawn said. She always worried that he would miss his classmates, but he never objected to being with the girls.

"They get along well," Morgan said.

"He likes to teach them French," Patti said. She was planning to enroll the twins in French Immersion.

"How's Paul liking his new job?"

"Well enough," Dawn said, "considering this is his third position since becoming a lawyer." His firm had finally caved into the recession that saw Canada's interest rates climb and inflation rates soar more than twelve percent The value of their house had tripled and so had the price of gold. It was valued over three hundred dollars an ounce. They'd agreed to Paul taking a salary cut to work for the government when his firm downsized and offered him an exit package. It was also a bonus that while working for the government he could take holidays anytime during the summer months and over March break when the family could vacation together in warmer climes. Dawn was particularly fond of going south to soak up the sun and swim in the ocean. There was something about saltwater she found particularly healing. She'd stopped going to the university to swim after Billy was born and missed the regular exercise. Then the local public school had built a new wing that included an indoor pool, so she regularly went there in the evenings.

"How's Ernesto?" Dawn asked. Morgan had a new lover. She'd met him at the Unitarian Church which she'd started attending in 1980 in defiance of her daughter who had been somewhat evangelical at the beginning of her conversion. If Morgan was going to seek a spiritual path, she would do so in a liberal religion. Morgan had been raised Christian and liked that the roots of Unitarian Universalism were in Liberal Christianity. She appreciated their intellectual inquiry. Ernesto was from Central America.

"He's teaching me Spanish."

"Is he?"

"Mummy was teaching the children Spanish today," Patti said.

"Won't they confuse Spanish with the French they're learning?" Dawn asked.

"On the contrary, they're both Romance languages. They have a lot in common."

"Except for the pronunciation," Patti said. "The children thought it was hilarious when Mummy showed them how to put the tip of their tongues on the roofs of their mouths." Patti illustrated. "Tch, tch."

"Nya," Morgan said, correcting her daughter. "You're confusing that sound with the double r's, Patti. I doubt I'll ever learn to roll my r's, but the children's tongue and ear will adapt if they're taught early."

"Which is why they're in French Immersion," Dawn said.

"I still think it's a privilege that it's taught in the public-school system. I wonder if that will ever happen in Wales for the Welsh language?' Morgan asked.

"You can only hope, Mummy."

The back door opened, and the three children bolted into the room. All three were wearing blue Osh Kosh ticking striped overalls. "Mommy," Billy yelled. He ran to Dawn and hugged her knees.

"I hear you've been learning Spanish?"

"Si, mi abuela."

"That's grandmother," Morgan said.

"Gracias."

"And that's thank you," Dawn said.

Billy laughed and turned to the girls who joined him in the hilarity.

Dawn ruffled his blonde curls. "I'm very proud of you all."

"Can we have some tea?" Sam asked, rising on her tiptoes and looking at the table.

"No, you can have a glass of milk," Patti said.

"Un verre de lait," Billy said. *"Moi aussi."*

Morgan laughed. "That's my boy. Maybe you'll be a teacher. Or a diplomat."

Billy shook his head. "No, a doctor. To look after Mommy."

Dawn's eyes blinked wide. "Really Billy?"

"You know why?" Morgan said.

Dawn turned to her mother-in-law. "Why?" Morgan simply raised her eyebrows and Dawn understood. Billy had been fascinated by ambulances after her ectopic pregnancy. Now he was older he'd matured from wanting to be an ambulance driver to a doctor. She felt tears smart her eyes. Folding her hands in her lap, she watched her son scramble up to the table to drink his milk. Her little son, full of ambition. Dawn was full of pride. Sometimes she'd felt selfish with her decision to have just one child, but now she felt blessed. And what could be more charitable than bringing a doctor into the world, someone dedicated to helping others.

On the long weekend in August, Dawn drove Billy and Teresa to Cobourg. Paul stayed home because he was in training for a marathon with his running friends. Billy sat in the backseat of their new car: a red, four-door Honda Accord. He was reading an Archie Digest comic book that kept him engaged for most of the trip. His grandpa sold them at his store and promised his grandchildren more Archie comics for the holidays. Billy would be staying the week with his grandparents while Isabel's children were staying with Aunt Muriel and Uncle Joe. Since this was the first time that Billy and his cousins would be away from their parents for an extended period, they'd arranged to make it like an overnight camp experience.

Teresa was wearing a jean skirt and a printed cotton top. Dawn wore a blue striped shirt dress. They both laughed at themselves for dressing up for their families. "Never mind," Dawn said, cranking up the air conditioning. "We'll change for the beach as soon as we get there."

Teresa shivered. "At work I wear a jacket over this."

"Yes, me too. With shoulder pads."

Teresa laughed. "What's with that fashion anyway?"

"Make us look as strong as the men."

"Yeah, power shoulders." Teresa harrumphed like a gorilla.

"How are things at the offices of Christie, Crombie and Dent?"

Teresa turned her head to face Dawn. "Seriously? I've dumped you-know-who."

Dawn nodded her head while keeping her eyes on the road. The speed limit on the Don Valley Expressway was only ninety, but cars tended to weave in and out of traffic changing lanes at random. "That's good since he's married."

"And not likely to ask for a divorce."

Dawn bit her tongue knowing that such men never did. "It's a big firm."

"Yes. Manfred's been great. I think he suspected, but he didn't expose me."

"He's too much a gentleman for that kind of gossip." Dawn knew he knew because Karyn had asked her if she knew.

"It's good I never confided in my sisters," Teresa said. "My parents have enough worries without adding me to their list."

Dawn nodded her head in agreement. "I remember my Dad saying how Uncle Joe confided in him before I got married that he wasn't looking forward to marrying off three daughters."

"He said that?"

"Well, not in so many words, but you get the gist."

"He's only had to pay for one formal wedding. They've accepted that I won't be getting married anytime soon."

"So far, just Isabel," Dawn said. "She seems to be in a secure relationship, but you never know."

"Yes, I feel the same, but try telling them that. Dad's spoken to her about her teacher's pension. It's sponsored by the province, and he thinks she should have some sort of nuptial agreement to protect her assets since she's the one with the secure income. I guess he knows about manufacturing cars, but I always thought working for General Motors was permanent. Of course, he thinks that way because he's in a precarious business selling cars. Forewarning, he'll say something about your Japanese car."

"Dear me. Will he?"

"Remember who Glen works for."

"They're loyal."

"They're playing golf today. Dad says you have to be a good golf player to be a good executive."

Dawn laughed. "I'll tell Paul that. He's in the wrong sport."

"Manfred's become a golf fanatic."

"I know. Karyn says she's a golf widow."

"So's Isabel. That's why my mom took up the game. She spends countless hours and long days at Dalewood. They have an annual fee and must spend their chit every month. Since neither of them are big drinkers, we get treated to meals there."

Dawn recalled the wedding reception there for Isabel and Glen. The clubhouse had a stunning view of the course from the picture windows and the outdoor balcony. "Well, I remember it is a lovely spot. Not something my parents would do, though."

Teresa agreed. "Your parents aren't big spenders."

"Big savers. For what I'm not too sure. Shall we play some music?"

"Sure," Teresa said, reaching for the dial. As soon as she found a station with lyrics she joined in, "I want to know what love is. I want you to show me. I want to feel what love is. I know you can show me. Oh."

Dawn looked in her rearview mirror where she saw Billy staring at the back of the headrest where Teresa was sitting.

The expression on his face was one of utter disgust. He was at that age when he thought such expressions of loving feelings were repulsive. Yet she knew very well what a loving boy he was. He still gave her hugs, and he was not shy about expressing his feelings for Susie and Sam. They hugged and tumbled together like lion cubs.

Dawn took the wide turnpike and continued along the four-lane highway east. They reached Cobourg before noon. After dropping Teresa off at her parents' house, she drove to her childhood home. Billy jumped out of the backseat, picked up his comic book, waited for her to open the trunk to get his suitcase, then raced up the front steps. He rang the doorbell. "Hello, Fella," Peter said in greeting.

After lunch Isabel arrived in her big Buick with her children and sister-in-law, Julie. Teresa had chosen to stay home and sun-bathe in the garden. She was home alone with her mother, no children, no men. A quiet time for just the two of them. Gwen was working at the store. They had plans for the evening, a 'girl' reunion. Aunt Mabel, Uncle Joe, and Glen had offered to babysit the children. He'd driven down earlier in his car. Peter and Mary would take Billy and visit them, leaving their house for the sisters and cousins to party. Patti was going to leave the twins with Morgan and visit Isabel in Oshawa before driving down with her, but the twins got sick.

Isabel had everything packed for the beach: blankets, sun umbrellas, sand toys, inflatable toys, and beach balls. Dawn and Billy got into the back seat with Gwen Junior and Glen Junior. Billy was shy around them. He didn't know them the way he knew his cousins in Toronto. Dawn hoped the coming week would change that for him. Isabel called both her children 'Junior' which Dawn found totally confusing, but somehow, they knew when she was speaking to or about them. They parked at the bottom of Division Street and piled out of the car.

"Can you believe this?" Isabel said. "Has the word gotten out about Cobourg's beach?"

"It's why I asked to come," Julie said. "I've heard how great this beach is compared to anything we have in Oshawa."

"Anything between here and Toronto," Dawn said.

"So, out-of-towners?" Isabel asked waving at Gwen in the middle of the back seat. "C'mon, Junior."

Dawn poked her head inside the car. "Why the cranky face, Gwen?"

"Glen took my shovel and pail."

"Don't worry, he's just helping us with carrying all the gear." Dawn extended Billy's towel. "Do you want to carry this?"

Gwen smiled and shuffled along the seat. Dawn took the girl's hand and walked her to the sandy beach. As soon as her bare feet touched the sand, she quickly picked them up. "Oh dear," Dawn asked, "is the sand too hot?"

Gwen Junior shook her head and giggled.

"Do you want me to carry you?"

Gwen shook her head and kept giggling.

What fun this child is, Dawn thought, but she worried little Gwen might be burning the soles of her feet. Dawn was wearing flip flops and remembered going barefoot at the cottage in Muskoka. There the dry pine needles could get too hot to step on. Often, they went barefoot to the dock and were surprised when they landed on the burning brown needles that littered the dark earth. They would also walk over the lichen and moss on the rocks, which could also scald the soles of their feet if the sun had hit the granite directly for too long.

There was a large patch of sand that was darker, and Dawn directed her charge to walk on the wet packed grains. Gwen let go of her hand and ran to join the others.

When they returned three hours later it was boiling hot inside the car. Dawn rolled down the windows and spread their wet beach towel on the back seat so she and the children could sit there in their wet bathing suits. Isabel drove them to her parents' house. She and Billy stood in the driveway waving goodbye. "See you later."

Billy shouted, "See you later, alligator.'

Dawn looked over at him. "Did you have fun?"

"Yes. Juniors are awesome."

Dawn breathed a sigh of relief.

———————

Dawn woke in her old room. She must have fallen asleep when she came upstairs to change. All the fresh air, hot sun, and laughter at the beach had relaxed her. She stretched her forty-year-old limbs, thinking how quickly she stiffened up nowadays. Her fortieth celebration had been a blast and she was looking forward to Paul's in September. Another milestone. Four decades. She turned her head on the pillow and looked around the room. It was like a time capsule. Nothing had changed. The furniture was the same. The shelves contained all her childhood books. On the wall was the paint-by-number picture she'd done one summer. It showed a clown's face that looked eerily sinister from this angle. Its separate features swam brightly inside the frame: a shining red nose, glaring blue eyes, and a grinning mouth. She could follow the numbers, but she couldn't paint. That was clear. She was never artistic. She couldn't paint. She couldn't sing. She couldn't dance. Not like her cousins. They were talented.

Dawn lifted her arm and looked at her wristwatch. They would be here soon. She stood and changed into a loose blouse and baggy pants, then slipped her feet into her pair of flat espadrilles. Billy's case was open on the chair. On top were a couple of *OWL* magazines. They came from Pam who worked for the publisher of the children's magazines: *OWL* and *Chickadee*. She gave him subscriptions every year for his birthday. When he was young, he got *Chickadee* every month in the mail. It was a magazine for young children, and he'd read them from cover to cover. He would do the experiments, make the crafts, and solve the riddles. Dawn picked up the May issue of *OWL, The Discovery*

Magazine for Children. It had a picture of a beaver on the cover. The April magazine underneath had a picture of a giraffe. Inside the May issue was a photo spread of eight pairs of identical twins. Now she remembered that Susie and Sam had told her what Billy had said to them about the myriad of facts about twins. They were impressed he knew so much. Dawn was impressed, too. He'd learned all those facts from reading the pages of this magazine. Billy was curious about the human body, animals, and birds. Nature in general.

Flipping back to the masthead, Dawn read the list of editors who published the magazines and, underneath, who served on The Young Naturalist Foundation. The bottom paragraph on the list described what the nonprofit foundation did. Dawn thought she should join something like it. Why not? It was time she considered giving back to the community.

Dawn replaced the magazine on the neat pile of reading material. Billy was a very neat boy. At the sound of birdsong, she looked out the window. The maple tree in the front yard was twice as big as it had been when she lived in the house. Some things do change, she thought. Like nature. It was impossible to see what bird was in the tree for all the green foliage, but she guessed she was listening to a robin. On her honeymoon she remembered Paul pointing out the English robin to her on their first morning in London. Now she remembered feeling him standing beside her. He'd come close in an intimate gesture to guide her in naming what nature held. They'd returned on one occasion to hike in Wales, just like they'd promised to do on their honeymoon.

Then busy life had intervened. Maybe they could take Billy on a hiking trip?

She opened her bedroom door. It was quiet in the upstairs hallway. She peeked into the sewing room where her father had set up the trundle bed for Billy for the night, just like he'd done for Paul on their first visit when she'd introduced her parents to him. Such memories made her feel content and blessed. They'd had their struggles: Paul's job changes, her ectopic pregnancy, her constant battles at work when meeting clients. Not everyone trusted a female in a position of authority. She now had a small department under her. The firm trusted her, but it always surprised her how often interns came and left because they didn't like working for a female boss. The new one, Christopher, was ideal. He was an amateur opera singer. He was married. He was talented and self-confident. He constantly entertained them at work and invited them to productions. Hilary had a new boyfriend who refused to go to these concerts, so Dawn and Hilary went together because Paul was often at a hockey game. Christopher had started them off with Tapestry Music Theatre as that company did light opera and musical theatre, ideal entertainment for *nonofficionadoes*. Hilary and Dawn never did progress to the serious stuff.

Dawn went downstairs and searched the rooms which were empty. Her family must have already gone. Then she heard a ruckus in the hallway. Her cousins arrived bearing a pot of chili that Gwen had made, a salad that Teresa had made, a dessert that Aunt Mabel had made. Isabel carried a boombox. "For the party," she said. She lifted the bag in her other hand. "The wine." Three bottles of wine and she brought a six pack of beer.

In the kitchen Gwen plugged in the pot with the chili. "It's already hot," she said. "We're ready to eat."

"Let's eat outside," Teresa said.

"Glen went home with Julie," Isabel said, "so just us."

The backyard hadn't changed either, Dawn thought. There was no deck like her aunt and uncle had built. There was no barbecue to cook food outdoors. All meals still came from her mother's kitchen. There was, at least, a wooden picnic table with benches. In the kitchen Gwen opened a beer and Dawn decided that's what she would like to drink with chili. Teresa opened the red wine and poured two glasses. They raided the kitchen for plates and cutlery, then took their food and drinks outside. The sisters sat across from each other on the benches and Dawn slid in to sit at the end of the table.

"Good chili, Gwen," Dawn said.

"Everything's good when you don't have to cook it," Isabel said. "I am so looking forward to this week when I don't have to cook a single meal." She'd told them at the beach that she and Glen were going to a resort up north for a second honeymoon. "Taking advantage of the first time without Juniors."

"Yes," Dawn said, "it's the first time we'll be on our own without Billy."

"We haven't been able to afford holidays, like you two," Isabel said.

"Aren't you going to go back to teaching?" Dawn asked.

"Are you kidding me?' Isabel said. "I can't even get on the supply list, let alone get a permanent teaching job."

"Do you still like teaching?" Dawn asked. "What I mean is, have you thought of changing careers during these difficult times?"

"No, I like the salary and the holidays. And the security, if and when I can get back in."

"I think," Teresa said, "any job can get repetitive and taxing."

"Have you not found a lawyer yet to marry?" Isabel asked.

Teresa looked over to Dawn.

"What?" Isabel asked, lifting her head. "Tell us."

"There is someone who wants to ask me out, but I haven't encouraged him."

"Are you crazy? Go for it." Isabel shook her head and said, "Men have two motivations in life: hunger and hanky-panky, and they can't tell them apart. If you see a gleam in his eye, make him a sandwich." As her sisters giggled Isabel scooped up a mouthful of salad. "Or make him this salad. Invite him to dinner. The way to a man's heart is through his stomach."

"That is so cliché," Teresa said.

"But true," Gwen said. "Just look at our parents. Dad disappears to work long hours, to play golf all day. Then he comes home and behaves like he's the luckiest man alive just because his wife is feeding him. Well, I do some of the cooking. It isn't just Mom who makes the meals."

Dawn studied Gwen. She was still living at home. She was still working in Dawn's father's stationery store. She was still unmarried. Could it be that she was repressed? Nothing had changed in this small town. They were living in a time warp. Could it be that Gwen was like Pam, but didn't know it? How could she explore her sexuality here?

"What about you, Dawn? You didn't tell us what you and Paul are doing next week?"

"Isabel, Dawn's not going to share her sex life with us," Teresa said. "She's always listened to us, but never divulged what she's up to."

Dawn turned red. It was true. She was circumspect around her relatives, not wanting anything to get back to her mother. Dawn felt more loyal to her mother than to Paul who could care little about what others thought. He was happy. They were sexually active with one another and never jealous or unfaithful.

"Cuz," Isabel laughed. "Are we embarrassing you?"

"Never," Dawn said. "We've taken our holidays. Went to the cottage in Muskoka with Manfred and Karyn and their kids, Jonathan and Anna. Had a week during March Break in Hilton Head where we could cycle. There was a pool where I could swim. Paul is taking a week off later to participate in a marathon."

"He's so athletic," Gwen said. "How'd you end up with such a jock?"

"Love."

The cousins laughed uproariously. "When a man and a woman love each other," Teresa said.

"Isn't that how Mom always started her sex education talks?"

"Yep, started being the operative word. We never did let her get far with that bullshit claim."

"Really, Teresa, I didn't know you were such a feminist," Gwen said.

"Or so horny," Isabel said.

Now it was Gwen's turn to turn red in the face. "Love means far more for a woman than it means to a man."

The eyes of her sisters and cousin turned to Gwen. "It means everything," Teresa mocked.

"Well, it's true that a man cannot fall in love with a woman unless she arouses him sexually," Isabel said. "Men are physical machines."

"I miss you guys and this crazy talk," Dawn said.

"Sex talk."

"Not so loud. The neighbours can hear us."

"Sorry, Dawn. We don't want to get your parents in trouble with their neighbours. Everyone knows they're the respectable ones."

"We're respectable," Isabel said.

"Teresa's right," Gwen said. "The town gossips do compare our families. I think they're just waiting for Teresa to fall off the tracks. Or me."

"You?" Isabel asked. "Say it isn't so."

They stood like a gaggle of geese and took their plates indoors. Gwen scraped and rinsed their dishes in the kitchen sink. Dawn opened more beers. Teresa poured more wine. Isabel set up the boombox outside. They ate dessert listening to the tunes of Madonna singing 'Crazy For You', 'Material Girl', and 'Like A Virgin'.

Dawn studied Gwen again. Was she a virgin? Her cousins often referred to her as the 'unmarried one'. What did that mean?

Barbara Simpson had a new client who was a teaching assistant in the French Immersion programme at Howard Park School. From Judith she learned about the inequities between the teachers' union, which was strong and vocal, and the union representing support staff. Judith was not entitled to the same benefits as those the professional teachers received. One evening she accompanied Judith to a school Open House and met the principal. It was while speaking with him that she saw Dawn enter the classroom with Billy. At first Barbara had a panic attack, but gained her composure when she realized they were not accompanied by Paul. Mother and son would not recognize her.

Afterwards Barbara shared with Judith what the principal had said. Then she asked, "How do you find the students? Are they learning to speak French?"

"Yes, and to write and read it. They weed them out in kindergarten. If they can't handle the programme the school recommends that they return to the main-stream, but they can only recommend. They can't force anyone to leave."

Barbara thought that sounded typical. Everyone had their rights. Aloud she asked about some of the children who'd attended the Open House. From Judith she learned how clever Billy was and that his twin cousins were also in French Immersion.

"I'm delighted to hear that. I delivered them."

"Did you?" The next day Judith shared that tidbit with the classroom teacher, who shared it with the twins' teacher. Who shared it with...

On the morning of Saturday, November ninth, Dawn visited the hairdresser. It was a special day. Her cousin, Teresa, had taken Dawn's and her big sister's advice and had started dating Karl Von Muller at the end of the summer. By the fall she was engaged, and the wedding plans were made. It was a second marriage for him. He was much older and came with children. Her mother was happy to have step-grandchildren, a boy named Keifer and a girl named Kelley, both teenagers. Her father wasn't as keen, but accepted whatever Teresa decided, if it made her happy. Plus, he didn't have to pay for the wedding. He was still confused, though, about plans to give her away at the altar, not at a church.

Paul and Billy went to the outdoor rink at Rennie Park for the first hockey game of the season. In fact, they went early to see Susie and Sam skate. The twins were taking lessons taught by students from the Teachers College. It was the same local programme where Billy had learned to skate.

When Dawn got home, she tripped over hockey gear at the back door. It belonged in the basement. She was tempted to kick the pile over to the stairs but decided to hold her temper. What good would it do her to get riled up? At least they'd made it home in time to get dressed. She bounded upstairs. "I'm home," she said. "Glad you're back. Who won?"

Poking his head out his bedroom door, Billy said his dad told him it wasn't about winning or losing. "It's about playing fairly and being a good sport."

Dawn guessed that meant his team lost. "Do you want me to rub your hair dry?"

"Yes, please."

She could hear the shower running in the master ensuite. Grabbing a towel, she returned to Billy. "Here, mister," she said, and covered his familiar head with the terry cloth. It still filled her with pleasure to nurture him, to play an active role in his upbringing.

They got into the car on schedule and arrived at the Granite Club with plenty of time to spare. Billy made a beeline to Gwen Junior and Glen Junior who were serving as flower girl and ring bearer. Dawn and Paul approached the teenagers. "I'm Dawn Wright, Teresa's cousin," she said, extending her hand. "And this is my husband, Paul Lewis."

"Nice to meet you," Keifer said, shaking Paul's hand. "We're glad you could come."

Kelley smiled at Dawn. "Teresa's told me all about you."

"All good, I hope."

"Yes," Kelley said sincerely. "She says she's indebted to you both."

Dawn and Paul smiled at one another. They'd done well by giving advice that Teresa had followed. Manfred and Karyn joined them. They told the teenagers how pleased they were that they were standing up to witness the marriage between their father and stepmother. Dawn registered the term, 'stepmother'. It seemed such a mature expression for her young cousin who just this past summer had been belting out Madonna songs in Dawn's parents' backyard.

They followed the other guests into the room. Billy joined them. "This is a swish place," he said.

Dawn looked over the room and the guests. It was an opulent room with high ceilings and multiple chandeliers.

Again, Dawn considered her cousin in this grand place. What would it be like to swim here every day instead of at the local school? The guest list mostly included immediate family and lawyers from the firm.

Dawn patted down the front of her jacket. She wore a red suit with a long jacket and tapered skirt that fell just below her knees. Red was a tricky colour for Dawn, but she'd found a shade that did not clash with her hair. Usually, she wore green in the autumn and winter.

They were escorted to their seats on the bride's side, on the left behind her aunt and uncle and cousins. Dawn's parents sat in the aisle seats. Manfred and Karyn sat behind them. She tapped Dawn on the shoulder. Dawn turned and said, "You're not sitting with the partners?"

"We insisted on joining forces with Teresa."

"Was this a political decision?"

"Office politics, yes," Manfred said.

"Who would have guessed that Teresa would be the one to join the moneyed establishment?"

"Paul, I'm surprised at that coming from you," Karyn said.

"From my mother." He smiled. "She did ask me to pass on her and my family's congratulations."

They turned to face front when the music started. Dawn pondered what Paul said. She was surprised to learn what Morgan had said. Wasn't Morgan against Barbara Simpson, who came from the same privileged background? Her mother-in-law's claim sounded more like an excuse than a reason. The last big family explosion happened when

Morgan learned that Patti's midwife had been none other than Barbara Simpson. "How could you?" she'd asked Patti.

"How was I to know?" Patti had cried out in self-defense.

"How was she to know?" Paul had asked when told. Then he'd called for calm and order in the family, claiming once again that no harm was done.

Pam had voiced a different view. She'd said that there were many claims in the publishing world. Writers were often sued for defamation if a third party thought the author had exposed private or personal details, especially in biographies. "But even fictional writers are being sued if someone thinks they've been characterized unfairly. Very hard to prove though. Mostly writers reveal the human condition, so personal idiosyncrasies are used for character building. Petty details could apply to almost anyone."

"But what happens in fiction when homewreckers slander a wife?" Dawn had asked.

"Well, that depends," Pam had said. "Sometimes they get their man. In extreme cases they kill the wife. Good murder mystery plot."

"Dawn, you're safe," Paul had said, and Dawn had thought, My knight in not-so-shining armour.

Now they'd recently learned that Barbara Simpson had been snooping around Billy's school. "Best keep that from Morgan," Dawn had said when she'd learned.

Paul had continued to express doubts. "She'd been public about her inquiries," he'd said. "Not like she's hired a private detective to watch us. I just don't see where her intrusions fit into unlawful practices. Let's not turn this into an *Annus horibilis.*"

Dawn had lost patience with his Latin reference. She hadn't heard much of that cleverness from him in recent months, or even years. He wasn't such a smart aleck now that he no longer worked for a top-notch firm, instead being employed by the government. He was a civil-servant, she'd told him firmly. Not a smart-ass lawyer. She'd been mean in her assessment, and cruel. It wasn't like her. Yet Barbara's intrusion into her son's schooling had driven her to extremes. Was nothing safe from that loathsome woman's claws?

Ever patient, Paul had bowed his head and resting his forearms on his knees had remained mute until she'd finished her tirade. His legs were widely splayed in what Dawn thought of as his male stance. They were together in the front room and Billy was in bed, hopefully asleep. When he'd raised his head, his face was red. "Let's not let rage and revenge drive us. Every person who's been through a trial knows that under the surface lies cruelties, sometimes the worst of humanity. Laws are only in place because we have nothing better, at least in the secular world, and if we're all to get along it's the best we have. Do you understand that? Remember our honeymoon? What we learned? People are complicated."

"I'm a mother."

"You are. And I'm a father. Maybe I'm not as protective as you are, at least not in the same way."

"Sorry," she'd said.

At the reception after the civil ceremony Dawn, Paul, and Billy were seated at a round table with Manfred, Karyn, Isabel, and Glen. At the table beside them sat Gwen, Mary, Peter, Muriel, and Joe. Seven and five at each table respectively, Dawn noted. Odd numbers. She surveyed the room and saw that most tables sat eight. At the head table were Teresa, Karl, Kelley, Keifer, Gwen Junior, and Glen Junior.

They were served lobster bisque, then veal marsala, and Boston lettuce salad with raspberry vinaigrette. Billy objected to everything on his plate and ate a lot of buttered bread. Karyn raised her eyebrows at Dawn. "Our kids would be the same."

Isabel lifted her head. "Yeah, I wonder how Juniors are doing up there?"

Manfred gave her a sideway glance. "Juniors?"

"Our kids," Glen said.

Manfred nodded.

"How's it going, Billy?" Glen asked. "Playing hockey yet?"

"Had our first game today."

"Did you win?"

Billy stuffed more bread into his mouth and nodded no.

"Tonight St. Louis is at Maple Leaf Gardens."

"Do you think the Leafs will win?" Paul asked.

"Let's hope so. I'm going to have to bring Glen Junior up for a game sometime."

"My Dad has tickets," Billy said.

"Yes, I heard," Glen said. "I guess you're missing the game tonight?"

"Don't remind him," Dawn said

"My mother and sister are going."

"They're fans?" Glen asked.

"You're stating the obvious," Paul said.

"You have to know them," Dawn said.

"Next game, we go. Right, Billy?"

Billy nodded his head while chewing. The waitress set down a tray of desserts in the middle of the table and he opened his eyes wide. The adults laughed.

Glen asked Manfred about his law firm. Dawn listened attentively while Manfred answered. He was an admirable man: professional, articulate, modest. He impressed Glen, who concluded that Teresa had made a good 'catch'.

On Monday Dawn stayed home from work and attended the Remembrance Day services at the local Royal Canadian Legion Hall with Billy and Morgan. They'd gone every year since Dawn's ectopic pregnancy. She'd learned she couldn't focus on work on that day of remembrance. It was too acutely personal for her. She recognized her pain didn't match the pain of the public event, but she allowed herself a 'bit of slack', as Hilary had come to describe it. She'd been the one to encourage her to take the day off.

Billy stood between Dawn and his grandma. They wore poppies that he'd gotten from a box one of the veterans had. He was in a wheelchair and wasa veteran from the first World War. Billy said he'd recognized him from when he'd come to the school to talk about his experiences. After the service Morgan went over to shake the elderly gentleman's hand. "Thank you for attending," he said. "You're not from these parts?"

"No, originally from Wales, but I've lived in the west end for decades."

"So, that makes you Canadian?"

"My Grandma is a true Canadian," Billy said. "She likes hockey."

"You know who used to live here?" The veteran asked. "Just down the street. On the south side of Morningside. Gord Brydson. You know him?"

Billy shook his head no.

"He used to play professional hockey for the Chicago Black Hawks in winter and professional golf in summer. Those were in the days when hockey players were paid only for the time they played hockey, just months. Not like nowadays."

Billy grinned and thanked the man. He could hardly wait to tell his dad when he got home from work what he'd learned that day. Paul was impressed and then asked him about the magazine he was reading.

"It's the November issue of *OWL*," Billy said. "Look at this." He opened the magazine that had a dolphin pictured on the cover. He flipped to the pages that showed a boy with brown hair beside a photo of a bald man. "Do you think you'll go bald, Dad?"

Paul picked up the magazine. He read for a minute. "No, I don't. My Dad didn't." He flipped through the magazine. "Look, an article on Halley's Comet by Terry Dickenson."

"Yes," Billy said. "He says the comet isn't to blame for all the bad things that people say it does."

"Pam gets you this magazine, right?"

"Yes."

"It's good, isn't it?" Dawn said, joining them. "Just to let you know, it inspired me to do some good for nature and I have received confirmation that I have been appointed to the board of The Young Naturalist Foundation."

"Congratulations," Paul said, giving her a kiss. "Do you have the time to add this to your schedule?"

"It's our son's future."

"My wife the altruist."

"I thought I needed to start giving back. In my position, it's good to be on boards."

"Pam will approve," Morgan said.

"All in the family," Paul said. "Speaking of keeping things in the family, I'm going with Billy's class tomorrow on a field trip."

"You are?" Dawn asked.

"Cool," Billy said. "Usually, it's the mothers who come."

Dawn looked from her son to her husband, feeling guilty. Maybe she should offer to do the same sometime.

"Where are you going?" Morgan asked.

"To the apple farm."

"Hope it's as nice a day as today," Morgan said. "Well, I must be going. Dinner date."

Later Paul confessed to Dawn that he'd lost his job. She wasn't surprised. Things hadn't been going well for him recently. With a slight shake of her head, she nodded that she understood. They weren't under any financial constraints, so she told him that he needn't feel pressed to find another position, that he needed to look for something that would suit him and be long-term.

That night she lay in bed with her eyes on the ceiling while Paul slept like a baby. She guessed he was probably relieved that he didn't have to go into a toxic environment in the morning. She wondered if he was unlucky in his choice of career, or she was simply lucky. How would he feel if he continued to earn less than her? How would she feel? Afterall, he had a higher education. Then she thought about Patti who still worked at home being a full-time parent and showed no inclination to further her education or get a job. She didn't need the money. She kept herself busy and seemed to enjoy her role. Maybe Paul was more like Patti than Pam, who was ambitious. How would Morgan respond when she learned? Morgan fully supported Patti's choices. It was as if she was making up for years of estrangement. She loved filling the role of a doting grandmother. She enjoyed her freedom to pursue her own interests, "after years of caring for an ailing husband," she'd said to them. Dawn had asked Paul about that. Was his late father a demanding man? How long had he been ailing with ill health? Paul had simply replied that his father seemed typical, not unusual in his lifestyle or his needs. Now Dawn wondered if that would be her future role.

The next day when she came home from work Dawn asked about the trip.

"We identified the different types of apple trees," Billy said eager to share what he'd learned.

"How many types are there?"

Billy listed them. "Ida Red, McIntosh, Russet, Ambrosia, Granny Smith, Golden Delicious, Honeycrisp."

"Which was the apple used to bake this apple pie," Paul said, presenting dessert with a flourish.

"Which you didn't bake," Dawn said, then added thinking she'd sounded mean, "but I see you've cooked dinner. What else did you learn, Billy?"

"How to pick the apples." He demonstrated. "You have to be careful not to damage the bud for next year's crop."

"Billy was the best plucker," Paul said. "He filled his bag first then helped the others."

Dawn felt a wave of pride wash over her. Why be resentful that she wasn't there when she could witness and support such accomplishment. Her son always showed great empathy to others, something she thought he'd learned from helping his younger cousins.

Later Dawn asked Paul if he'd shared with Billy that he'd lost his job.

"No, I didn't want to spoil his day. How would it look if the only reason I was there was because I was unemployed?"

"We'll have to say something at some point."

"Yes, when I get a new position. *Audentes fortuna iuvet.* Fortune favours the bold."

"That's the spirit," Dawn said before realizing that she was hearing her husband quote Latin again. "You should teach Billy Latin."

Paul gave her a hug and kissed her forehead. "Great idea."

That night she slept well, and when she came home from work the next day, Dawn found Paul with Billy reading *Winnie Ille Pu.* "Found it in a used bookstore on the Queensway."

Billy showed her the endpaper with the illustrations depicting the woods where Winnie the Pu lived and pronounced the places for her: *"Arbor Apium, Locus Inondatus, Domus Mea.* That's his house. And I'm in *Domus Mea."*

Dawn laughed and gave her son a hug.

"Do you know Latin like Daddy?"

"No. I'm afraid I don't," Dawn said.

"What did you study?"

"Math and Sciences."

"I'm going to study math and sciences like you."

"Follow in your mother's footsteps," Paul said.

Dawn shook her head while Billy protested, telling him he was going to be a doctor. "Oh, really. Well. Latin will help."

After Billy was put to bed, Dawn approached Paul. He was reading the evening paper in the front room. She sat on the upholstered chair opposite him. "Paul, I was thinking, what about hanging out your own shingle?"

Lowering the paper to his lap, Paul asked, "What do you mean?"

"You know, set up a private practice?"

"I suppose I could." He closed the newspaper. "That's a serious step," he said, looking over at her.

His blue eyes spoke words. I'm listening. "Yes, I realize. It would take some investment." Dawn clutched her fingers in the palm of her hand. She'd thought this through and didn't want to hurry her husband.

"There are a few lawyers with practices on Bloor Street."

"Yes, there are. Some have fancy offices, and partners, but some are small practices on the second floor above shops." She held his gaze, that blue-eyed gaze that had smitten her when they'd first met. Knowing she had to present a steady, firm attitude, one that could be read as showing confidence in him, although she was mostly feeling wary. Paul was no Manfred Freudlich. Recently the two couples had dined together and during the evening's conversation had talked about how hard it now was to get into law school. Of course, it had always been challenging, but they'd concluded that while Manfred would have been accepted, Paul probably wouldn't. That conclusion hadn't seemed to disturb Paul. His amiable nature wasn't prone to being competitive in the workplace.

"Do you really think I should?"

Dawn smiled. "Yes, can't hurt to give it a try." Then she laid out her plan. As was her mien, she had figured out the finances.

In January of 1986 Dawn attended her first board meeting of the foundation. The Director introduced her, "Dawn Wright is a mother and works in finance at Green & Rupert on Bay Street. Welcome, Dawn. We are always happy to have Bay Street meet Nature." This got a chuckle from the members. "Tell us what attracted you to join us."

Dawn thanked the director, then corrected him. "It's Rupert & Green. Bay Street is sticky that way." She smiled. "My sister-in-law works in publishing with your group. She's given my son *Chickadee* and now *OWL* magazines for years. He is ten years old and reads them from cover to cover. He's an avid bird watcher. I am interested in preserving the natural environment for him and all children, and in educating them on the natural world. I would like to make adults more accountable to them and their future. I think I can do that by putting my financial expertise to better use than just watching the bottom line."

It was a long meeting during which she mostly listened and learned. They were a large group of very diverse, highly-talented, and well-connected people. They were also, she noted, very different from the people she met in business. They were more casually dressed; there were as many women as men; they took turns and didn't interrupt. As the meeting broke up, she moved away from her chair to position herself near the exit and thanked each one individually for their support.

When she arrived home her son and husband were sound asleep. In the morning she asked how the evening had gone.

"Dad was late picking me up."

"Sorry," Paul said sheepishly. "Clients kept me and then the traffic."

Dawn raised her eyebrows. His office was in the west end, but a little further west and south than they had at first desired. It was a cost saving measure which meant he had to commute in the opposite direction to driving into the centre of the city, which was fine in the mornings, but could get congested when driving home if there was an event happening downtown, like a hockey game. "Who won?"

"The Leafs," Billy said, raising his arms. *"Gano el juego."*

"Ernesto was there," Paul said. "He's teaching us Spanish."

"I know. You're going to be multilingual, Billy. French, Spanish, Latin."

"And English," Billy said. "Don't forget my mother tongue."

The next morning in the car on the way to school Dawn asked Billy to repeat the Spanish so she could practice what he'd learned. Then she told him about her meeting. "They're going to publish a summer issue of *OWL*. Do you want to do some experiments for summer fun?"

"Can I do them with Susie and Sam? Aunt Pam gets us to do stuff sometimes. We write in all the time."

"What about?

"Oh, you know, what our favourite books are."

"What's yours?"

"The Dog Who Wouldn't Be by Farley Mowat."

"There was a lot of controversy over that title when it was first published."

"I know. How can a dog be a 'who'? Aunt Pam told us. I wrote a story for the contest."

"What contest?"

"On the pandas, Qing Qing and Quan Quan at the zoo."

"Well, good luck with that." Dawn parked the car on the side street beside Howard Park School and watched her son race into the playground. She felt happy for him. He was an exceptional child and she'd had so much support in raising him she could hardly count all the people. Now she could add Morgan's friend, Ernesto, to the list. They continued to live in their separate abodes, but spent time together worshipping, entertaining, traveling, and visiting family. As she drove down Roncesvalles Avenue, Dawn thought about the picnic in the park last summer. She'd offered to host at their comfortable home, but Morgan and Ernesto had insisted they experience a picnic *el aire fresco*. "With the common folk," Morgan had added. And there were masses of people enjoying High Park. Many multi-generational families were having picnics like they were, lots of cyclists either riding solo or in intimidating groups, excited children playing and visiting the animals at the small zoo. Pulling Susi and Sam in an open wagon, Patti only had to cross High Park Avenue then followed a paved road to the picnic tables. Ernesto and Morgan had driven with a carload of gear and food. Dawn, Paul, and Billy had cycled with saddle backpacks.

Ernesto and Paul had played frisbee with the children. "Look at them," Morgan had said, "getting along so well."

"Your boyfriend and your son or the grandchildren?" Patti had asked. She was sitting on the picnic bench recovering from the exertion of her short trip.

"Aren't I lucky to have such beautiful grandchildren?" Morgan had said ignoring her daughter. "I have two daughters and a son and two granddaughters and a grandson."

"You are," Dawn said. She'd emptied all three backpacks and strode over to the bicycles to put the packs over the handlebars.

"You'll never guess who I bumped into?" Morgan said.

"Do tell," Dawn had said as she helped her mother-in-law place the vinyl cloth over the table- top.

"Honor Simpson."

Patti had turned her head to look back at them. "Barbara's mother?"

"Yes. I'm so glad you didn't keep up a friendship with her."

"It was never a friendship. She was my midwife. And she was good."

"Well, she's kept up a friendship with Nancy Grady, which Honor thinks is terribly inappropriate."

"Who's she?" Dawn had asked.

"She's a secretary at their family firm on Bay Street. Simpson & something."

"Really?" Dawn had thought about that situation. She'd connected the dots. It was a memorable day and she'd talked to Paul about it afterwards. Now that he had his own practice, couldn't he do something? And he had. He'd contacted Simpson & Bull and had spoken to Bob Simpson.

The men had agreed that the women were hysterical over nothing. Dawn had felt deflated. Some attitudes never changed.

On a weekend in November Dawn and Paul were invited to dinner with Karyn and Manfred at Teresa and Karl's house. Teresa was nervous and Dawn tried to set her at ease. "We could have brought something," she said. "You didn't have to make everything yourself."

"Yes, I did," Teresa said. "You don't understand the pressure I'm under."

"What pressure?"

"To compete with Kelley."

"Why would you have to compete with your stepdaughter?"

"Because she's won her father's heart through her gourmet cooking."

"Hum," Dawn said, "I think you're taking this too seriously."

"Remember what Isabel said last summer?"

"Yes, I do, but."

"No buts. I followed her advice and now I'm trapped. When courting, Karl was always saying to me how well his daughter cooked, especially for a teenager. Then he would compare what I was making and give it a rating."

"Teresa," Dawn said, "you don't have to compete. You're his wife. Not his daughter. Get a life."

Karyn came into the kitchen. "Hello, you two. Can I help?"

"Yes," Teresa said, relaxing. She handed Karyn two plates with appetizers and two more plates to Dawn. Picking up two more, she led the women into the dining room. "These will satisfy them until we're ready to eat." The three of them went to join the men.

As they walked through the dining room into the living room, Dawn told Karyn about her secretary, Hilary, and another secretary, Nancy Grady.

"Let me get this straight. How do they know each other?"

"Through Barbara Simpson."

"That seems highly inappropriate. Did you speak to Hilary?"

"I did."

Teresa came up behind them. "Hurry up, you two. The canapes will get cold."

"Darling," Karl said, "I was just describing the place in Naples we purchased."

Dawn did a double take. A home in Lawrence Park, a membership at the Granite Club, and now a place in Naples.

"Florida," Paul said, reading his wife's reaction.

"You must go there for the school break," Teresa said.

"In March?"

"Yes, we won't be going until April, and we take possession March first," Karl said.

"There's a swimming pool," Teresa said. "You'll like it."

"Well, thank you." Turning to Paul, Dawn said, "We'll think about it."

"We were thinking of going there," Manfred said. "There's some good golf courses. I think it's going to prove to be a great investment for you two."

Dawn smirked at Paul. Karyn saw her and raised her eyebrows. "We'll enjoy the pool and the beach, won't we, Dawn?"

"Billy and I can rent bicycles," Paul said. "And I'm happy to take Jonathan and Anna with us," he said, turning to Manfred.

Now Dawn smiled and warmed to the idea. Billy got along famously with Jonathan and Anna. Jonathan was only a half year younger than Billy and Anna was the same age as the twins. They attended Baycrest Public School and were enrolled in French Immersion. Karyn and Manfred had moved to a bigger house last year to accommodate their growing family. It was within walking distance of the school. Karyn sang the praises of the neighbourhood that was actively involved in fundraising for the school. It was an easy commute into the city from their house. All pluses.

"That'd be great, Paul. I hear there's good bird-watching, too," Manfred said.

"It's close to Cape Sable where Hurricane Donna hit in 1960."

"Yes," Karl said, "hurricanes are always a concern."

"Nature's vengeance," Dawn said, smiling. Maybe they could make it work. They hadn't traveled to the west coast of Florida. "What made you choose there?"

"Golf," Teresa said. "My parents are very excited about the prospects of visiting, as you can imagine?"

Dawn wondered if Teresa was getting more than she'd bargained for.

"Teresa's taking lessons," Karl said.

Dawn extended her tray of bacon-wrapped dates to Kurt. He took one and she moved onto Paul. He winked at her and said, "Don't mind if I do."

"Take two," she said.

"Did you make all these?" Manfred asked.

"Yes," Teresa said, "but don't suggest I cater the next office party."

"We could ask Kelley," Karl said.

"Give me her contact information," Karyn said. "We're always looking for new ideas."

Teresa shook her head at Karyn as if to say, 'Bad girl.' "Excuse me, dinner will be served in five minutes."

Setting the tray down Karyn followed Teresa into the kitchen and beckoned to Dawn to follow her. In the kitchen the three huddled in conversation. "Tell me again, Dawn. What's this about the secretaries?"

Explaining, Dawn leaned against the counter and watched Teresa. "You know," she said after summing up, "how is it that we still do the cooking?"

"What?" Teresa said, craning her neck to look at her cousin.

"We're in the kitchen. You're cooking. The men are in the living room talking and eating. Something's wrong with this picture."

Karyn laughed. "No, nothing's wrong with it. Nothing's changed." She turned to Dawn. "By the way, where did you get that suit?"

"This," Dawn said looking down at her blue and white checkered skirt topped by a blue jacket with checkered trim. "It's a knockoff of the one the queen wore in China."

"Oh my God," Teresa said. "I thought it looked familiar. Did you see that gorgeous sparkling pink gown she wore?"

"Well, at least you don't have the pillbox hat," Karyn said. "Although, Queen Elizabeth does know how to dress for the occasion."

"Doesn't she?" Dawn said.

"Your dressmaker is superb," Karyn said. "Teresa, let me do that," Karyn said, stepping up to the stove.

"But what is this objection about my cooking?"

"Teresa, I'm not objecting to your cooking. It's just, we lobbied to get men like Paul to help in the kitchen, yet here we are, doing it all."

"Last summer's advice. Remember?"

"I do," Dawn said thinking how they seemed to want it all.

———

In August of 1992 Dawn and Paul decided to celebrate their twenty-fifth wedding anniversary in style by going to New York for the opening of the Broadway production of *Anna Karenina*. Pam and Trudy had moved to New York in 1990. After the recession of the 1980s, the publishing business was hard hit. Then Pam was offered a job with the giant conglomerate, Bertelsmann. To her family's great surprise, she took the position. "What's happened to my Hippie?" Morgan had moaned. "First, I lose my Flower Child to religion, now I lose my Hippie to a global company. Will it never end?"

"What?" Pam had asked her mother. "Will what never end?"

"Takeovers. The world is being taken over by mass movements that will destroy our local culture and economy."

"I will keep your dire warnings in mind." Then Pam had told her family the history of the business. "Originally the Bertelsmann family firm had prospered by printing propaganda for the Nazis during the war. When the war ended, the business collapsed, but the family rebuilt their publishing empire."

Ernesto had come to Morgan's defense. "So, now they will dominate North America, too." Pam had rolled her eyes at the pair as if to say there was no point in arguing with the elderly.

When Dawn and Paul visited Pam at her apartment in New York, she reminded them of this conversation and their predictions. Then she regaled them with stories of her boss who was fun-loving and threw big parties at book openings. "He hosts grand dinners at the Frankfurt Book Fairs. It's the party everyone in the book publishing world wants to attend."

"I don't think you should share this with Mummy," Paul said. "It will only confirm her suspicions."

Pam laughed in agreement. "You don't mind that we're eating after the show? It'll be late, but that's how it's done here. You'll get to meet my boss."

"I can hardly wait," Dawn said. Like a schoolgirl, she was feeling the excitement build inside her. There was glamour ahead.

They took a taxi to Circle in the Square. Dawn purposefully sat in the window seat behind Paul, who sat beside the taxi driver, who spoke with a heavy Bronx accent and kept up a running commentary of the sites of New York. Telling him it was their first visit had prompted his enthusiasm in showing them his world. Considering how often they'd vacationed in Florida and traveled to Britain, Pam wondered why they'd never been here before, but, as Dawn pointed out, they didn't make a habit of visiting big cities. "Except, we began our honeymoon in London," Dawn said.

"Yes, I remember," Pam said. "Mummy said it was the first time you'd been out of the country."

"It was so special in many ways."

"And you delayed your honeymoon?" Trudy said.

"Yes," Dawn said, turning to Trudy and remembering the first time the family had met her, at their wedding. Her parents still had no idea that Pam and Trudy were a couple. When Dawn had told them that they were going to New York to celebrate and to visit Pam and Trudy, Mary thought

Trudy was travelling with them. Then Dawn told her that they lived together.

"Still roommates? At their age?" Mary had asked, astonished.

"New York is expensive," Dawn had said and left it at that.

Dawn had read *Anna Karenina*, a novel she would never have attempted had it not been for the tickets to the play which Pam had suggested and had secured. She had contacts. Dawn was curious to see how they would make the lengthy novel into a musical. Mostly she'd seen musicals with Billy. They'd taken him to *The Three Musketeers* at the Stratford Festival in 1988, which they'd enjoyed so much they'd made a habit of attending regularly. He particularly liked the Gilbert & Sullivan productions: *H.M.S. Pinafore* and *The Pirates of Penzance*. "I am the very model of a modern major general," was a stock response to any criticism levelled at him. And "Things are seldom what they seem," and "Never mind the why and wherefore" became habitual responses to his cousins' queries. The two girls thought their cousin was a font of knowledge.

At the theatre entrance Paul put his arm around her shoulder and they joined the crowd, entering the lobby as a couple. As always, she was grateful for his height on these occasions. He could see the route ahead and lead them in the right direction. In her seat she studied the program and learned about the lead actress, Ann Crumb, who came from a musical family. Despite its tragic plot, it was an exciting musical and the audience gave it a standing ovation. Dawn smiled over at Pam. "I had my doubts, at first, but it worked."

"I think all of New York did, too. Glad you enjoyed it."

Exiting the show was a slow process with crowds of theatregoers blocking the doorways and bigger crowds outside blocking the sidewalk. They joined a dense line waiting for taxis. Glitz and glam, Dawn decided, had its drawbacks. Again, they climbed into a yellow taxi and drove to a restaurant where they met Pam's boss. He was charming and attentive until a celebrity caught his eye. "Excuse me," he said to Dawn and Paul.

Pam and Trudy had already disappeared into the crowd.

"Noisy place," Paul said, "I'm hungry."

"Me, too," Dawn said thinking how she hated eating late because she would get indigestion, then not sleep. Still, they joined the queues at the different buffet tables and dined late into the night. Despite her misgivings, Dawn felt renewed by the sophisticated experience. Lately she'd been experiencing the ill effects of mid-life. It was an experience not shared by her husband which struck her as patently unfair. Females went through so much change and men like her husband seemed to stay the same. He was still athletic. He was still cycling and running. Fortunately, he was also still loyal. She was lucky. So many marriages ended in divorce. Paul's legal practice was dominated by these domestic disputes. He often shared details of the complaints he heard. She wondered why these couples didn't go to marriage counselling and talk things through. "It seems not everyone talks the way we do," Paul had said.

They slept in. Dawn groggily lifted her head off the enormous pillow and looked over at Paul, who was fast asleep. Quietly she got out of bed and went to the bathroom. When she saw her reflection in the mirror, she did a double take. She looked exhausted, and thought in a moment of vanity, that she couldn't let Paul see her looking like a tired hag, so she splashed cold water on her face. Not much of an improvement, she thought. She picked up some of the small lotions on offer. There was one for her face. Before applying it, she wiped her face with a warm face cloth. At least they offered face cloths. She had to pack those when traveling to Britain. Content with her renewed looks, she returned to bed. Paul stirred. Bending over him she whispered, "Happy Anniversary."

He turned his head to her and opened his eyes. "Happy Anniversary."

She sensed his arm under the blanket move, then felt his hand on her hip before sliding over her bum cheek. They kissed. He moved his hand over her breast, then rolled on top of her. Dawn moaned and opened her legs then ran her heels over his buttocks. They were firm. She twisted her fingers in his ears then behind his lobes. She savoured this coupling.

Later they ate breakfast in bed and planned their day: a visit to Times Square, the Empire State Building, The Metropolitan Museum of Modern Art, the Guggenheim Museum. They were dressed and out the door by noon, doubting they would get to see everything, but happy to be walking hand-in-hand around Manhattan. Dawn decided she needed to continue what they'd started in the bedroom. She teased him. "Just look at your reflection in the window."

"Who's that old man?" he asked, turning back to her and pecking her on the top of her head.

"I think he's my husband."

"Really? You're married to someone as old as him?"

"No, I'm sure he's younger."

"Do you know his name?"

"It begins with a 'p'."

"Could it be Peter?"

"That's my father's name."

"Maybe you should find out what his name is before you flirt with him."

"You think I'm flirting?"

"I do. And I like you for it."

Remembering their conversation after their first tryst, Dawn felt playful rekindling that time. So long ago, yet it seemed hardly any time at all had passed. A great nostalgia lurched her along the busy sidewalk. They were still in love. They were a lucky couple. What more could anyone want in this world but love?

The following Wednesday, the actual day of their anniversary, Dawn received two dozen red roses at work. Their delivery caused quite a stir in reception. Hilary signed for them as she always did for deliveries, then carried the massive bunch into Dawn's office. "I'll be back with a vase, if I can find one large enough."

Dawn watched her depart and couldn't help but wonder how the present of flowers made Hilary feel. Despite her upbeat mood, Hilary was going through a rough patch. She had found out that her partner was cheating on her. Her relationship with her former partner had ended the same way. Hilary was still a beautiful woman, always well dressed, and fit. She'd never had children which was probably just as well, Dawn thought.

The firm had marked their twenty-fifth anniversary earlier in the year. Dawn had a plaque on the wall thanking her for her years of service. As much as she'd enjoyed working with them, she began to wonder if she would remain. She wasn't a partner. Still, she was well paid, but maybe she shouldn't feel comfortable forever in the same place. Maybe she should be more ambitious.

Dawn read the card that came with the flowers. *"Dawn, I feel lucky to have fallen in love with you twenty-five years ago. You still matter to me, and I expect to spend another twenty-five years with you by my side."* Dawn put her open palm on the card. They did have a truly meaningful connection. With Paul she'd experienced a relationship that was secure and dependable. How lucky she was to have the stability of a marriage she didn't want to change.

In June of the following year, Billy graduated from high school. At his commencement, Dawn and Paul sat in the balcony with the other parents. They noted on the program how often their son's name appeared under the honour role: Bill Lewis-Wright, under a list of achievements: Bill Lewis-Wright, and under five awards: Bill Lewis-Wright. They watched proudly each time he was called on stage. The other graduate who was called as often was his good friend, Adam Kazama. One girl's name appeared many times, Nadya Perel.

Afterwards, they mingled in the crowded auditorium and congratulated the students asking them their plans for the fall. Nadya was going to McGill University in Montreal. Adam was going to Western University in London. Billy was staying home and taking an undergraduate degree in Science at the University of Toronto, his parents' *alma mater*. His long-term goal was to enroll in medicine. No one in their family was in medicine, not on Dawn's or Paul's side. Everyone seemed surprised by his choice, except Dawn. She remembered how he'd felt a need to protect the women in his life. When he was a toddler, he'd been traumatized by her emergency operation. Now her mother, Mary, his grandmother, had been diagnosed with stage four ovarian cancer. It was a cancer that was difficult to detect in its early stages because there was no screening test for it. It was a cancer that begins in the ovaries, but by stage four, it could have spread.

They said their goodbyes to the graduates and wished them well in their future studies. "Enjoy your party," Paul said. "Call a taxi or phone me to drive you home."

"Will do," Billy said.

Dawn threaded her fingers through Paul's hand. Unlike some teenagers in their neighbourhood Billy still talked to them. She felt reassured by this. So many other parents complained that their teenagers became mute in their company, grew sullen when they offered help, and sometimes were downright hostile. Even through Paul's ups and downs with his work he remained open with his son, never grew defensive about his career changes, and could be trusted to share confidences.

When Dawn and Paul got home after the commencement, they called Peter and learned that Mary had gone back into hospital. This was not unexpected, but still troubling. The next day, on Saturday, June twenty-sixth, they drove to Cobourg. Billy insisted on coming with them and slept the entire journey. Dawn thought about her maternal grandmother who had passed away late last year. Would her mother only outlive her own mother by one year? It seemed unfair.

At thehospital they found Mary asleep. On the advice of staff, they left to visit Peter. As soon as she entered the house, Dawn shed tears. She felt she'd been brave up to that point but couldn't shake the image of her frail mother in the hospital bed. There was a sour smell in the room that lingered in her nostrils. Sitting beside her Paul put his arm around her shoulders. It was heavy, but not a burden. His weight was a comfort. Her father brought her a box of Kleenex.

Peter told them what he knew. "The chemotherapy killed most of the cancer, but not all of it."

"For many women, ovarian cancer doesn't go away completely. For women over sixty-five, like Grandma, the prognosis is higher that the cancer will return."

Dawn looked over at her son. He had done the research. Her stomach sank. She'd accepted her grandmother's death. It had hardly filled her with sadness. It seemed a natural progression of time and Mary had said how grateful she was to have had her mother in her life for such a long stretch of time. "I'm too old to feel like an orphan," she'd said. Yet that was how many grown adults felt when losing a parent. That was how Dawn was beginning to feel.

"Did the doctor say where it had spread?"

Peter shook his head. "I didn't ask, Billy."

"The best we can do for her now is manage the pain."

Manage the pain, Dawn thought. How feeble that sounded. Billy had not delivered that line with any sense of authority. It came with empathy and compassion. Yet she felt a frisson of frustration with the situation. How had medicine reached this point after so much effort and money had gone into cancer research? Human life was so complicated. Surely a cure was on the horizon.

In the car on the way back to the hospital the next day Peter cried. "Sorry," he said.

"Don't be," Dawn said. She'd chosen to drive with him to keep him company. She could see at home that he was visibly shaken. They would say their goodbyes after the hospital visit. Now she felt guilty about leaving him alone.

Peter blinked. "Men are supposed to be brave."

"You are brave, Dad. You don't need to be tough."

"It's just not fair."

"I know."

"What has she done to deserve this pain?"

"Nothing. You can't think in terms of blame. She's not to blame."

In the car on the way back to Toronto Dawn shared what her father had said. "Who is to blame for cancer?" she said to no one in particular, to the interior air, to the larger world outside.

"Mostly lifestyle and heredity."

Turning around, Dawn faced her son in the backseat. "How could her lifestyle be to blame? She doesn't smoke or drink. She goes to church every Sunday."

"I know it doesn't make sense which is why it doesn't seem fair."

"But life isn't fair, is it, Billy?"

"No, Mom, it isn't."

At the beginning of October, Mary Wright passed away. Everyone sent flowers. They arrived at the house, at the store, at the funeral home and at the church. Dawn read the cards on the bouquets in the house. They were mostly from neighbours who had appreciated Mary's kind words when they lost loved ones, who remembered meals Mary had prepared when they were sick, and who knew her from the first day she'd moved into the house. Gwen told her about the bouquets at the store. They were mostly from customers. At the funeral home bouquets flanked them in the reception line and perfumed the air. Peter proudly introduced his grandson to everyone who then shook his hand. Explaining how his grandmother knew the person he was meeting, Peter said: "From church," "From the shop," "From the neighbourhood." When visitors stopped in front of Dawn, they reminded her who they were. She was humbled by their presence but surprised when one man introduced himself. "You may not remember me. I'm Christopher Mann."

"Yes, I do remember you," Dawn said.

"I didn't know if you would. I still frequent your dad's store."

"Do you? I must tell you that because of you I invested in gold."

Christopher looked confused.

"You don't remember the time you came into the store and told me what was happening to gold?"

Christopher blushed.

"You do remember?"

He sputtered.

"We were young once." Dawn smiled.

Christopher nodded and squeezed her hand.

The next day at the funeral service all the flowers were moved to fill the inside of the church. The effect was transforming: a rainbow of colours lightened the dark wood, a pleasing aroma hid the stale air, a festive ambience replaced the somber interior. Dawn thought she wouldn't cry but she did. She didn't know if she was crying for her mother or for the flowers. They were more than she ever expected. They were life-affirming. How had she missed that about her mother? How had she never admitted or told her how good she was? Now she longed to know her better. Why hadn't she given her mother more of her time?

After the service at the church, the family followed the hearse to the cemetery. Other mourners joined the procession snaking through town with their car headlights lit. At the graveside, Dawn and Billy joined Peter to throw a fistful of earth onto the casket. Afterwards, they assembled back at the church in the large room on the third floor where the ladies from the church who had known Mary all her adult life served tea, sandwiches, pickles, and sweets. Many approached Dawn to offer their condolences: "She died too young, but she lived a fulfilling life." "Your mother was the kindest person I know." "Mary had the good fortune of having a loyal husband and supportive family." "Your mother was always so proud of you, Dawn."

These sentiments touched Dawn more strongly than she would have anticipated. She'd never been close to her mother the way most daughters were, the way her cousins were with Aunt Muriel. To hear all these positives served to deepen Dawn's feeling that she had missed something. It was too late now for them, but Dawn told herself she could be consoled that her mother had had a good life here in the small town where she always knew she belonged. Dawn felt her mother's presence sweep around her as if she was still alive in her.

At the house, Dawn sat on the couch all evening while her family visited each other and made a meal that they ate buffet-style. Her thoughts returned to all the memories that others shared. At times she laughed with them. Isabel reminded the family how Billy had corrected them that time they'd gone to the beach before leaving the children for a week in the summer. "He said, they're not seagulls. They're herring gulls. And then he pointed to the smaller birds, saying they were terns."

"I have her spaghetti recipe," Muriel said. "She always made spaghetti on Saturday night."

"I'm going to miss her at the store," Gwen said.

Dawn looked over to her father. She wondered if he would keep the store, or give it up and, if he did, what would happen to Gwen. She knew he would stay in the house for as long as he could. She hoped he wouldn't feel too lonely. She knew she would. She knew if anything happened to Paul, she would give up the house. She would do what Morgan had done. She'd find a condo. She'd start again. In that way she was more like her mother-in-law than her parents. They were loyal to one another, to their life in their shared house, to the community and church. They were set in their ways. They didn't seek out adventure or challenges. They'd been content.

1993 was a buoyant year for cruises with record bookings, so Dawn decided that was what her family should do over the Christmas holidays. She wanted her family to spend more time with her father. Going on a cruise solved the problem of how to include him now that he was on his own. At first, he was reluctant, until Dawn described the trans-canal sailing through the Panama Canal. Then he got excited. He even said he could afford to pay his own way, but Dawn insisted the trip was a present. There was room on Carnival's newest ship, Sensation. It was advertised as a Fun Ship that carried over two thousand passengers. None of the thrilling features appealed to Peter or Billy. What attracted them was the chance to sail through the canal. They shared an ocean view room. Paul was mostly excited by the activities on offer, while Dawn liked the pool. They booked a balcony cabin. There were only twenty of them and they got the last one available. They could afford it. The economy was growing. Inflation was low. The stock market was booming. Paul was earning a decent income.

Before reaching the canal, they listened to a talk on the history of the building of the canal. It was attended by an older crowd with only a smattering of families with young children, mostly boys like Billy, eager to learn. The lecturer gave a slide presentation with black and white photos starting with the first diggings in May of 1904. He covered the progress of its construction over the next decade. The statistics were phenomenal with the number of workers and the costs.

On the day the ship crossed the Panama Canal, Peter and Billy stayed on deck to watch the captain from Panama

City steer them through the locks. Paul asked if it would be okay for him to join them.

Laughing at his eagerness, Dawn said she'd be fine on her own telling him that from the pool she could see as much as interested her. Under the sun she floated on her back relishing the outdoor experience, sensing her body soaking up the Vitamin D. So different from the routine discipline of doing laps indoors. Too often we give the best of ourselves to work, she thought. What do we bring home? The leftovers. A guilty twinge entered her heart. Turning she did a couple of laps. Was she guilty of being a reduced person at home? Holding onto the ledge in the deep end, Dawn lazily kicked her legs underwater. Like so many she could put achievement and products ahead of people. Yet she was critically aware that the quality of personal relationships determines the quality of life. She had that, despite all her neglect. Pushing against the edge she did the backstroke for a few lengths before leaving the pool. Dripping wet she crossed the cement floor to her lounge chair and picked up the heavy, cotton, pool towel. Such entitlement, she thought. Seated she stretched out her legs. They were still trim.

The crossing seemed a slow process, but it so excited the men Dawn couldn't help but be a little curious. They talked about it endlessly at dinner. She heard why they had to have a Panamanian steer the cruise ship, why the locks were named, and why they had to hold up in what was basically a water pen. At night they went on deck to watch the view of the night sky and the lights of the city.

Peter thanked his family for bringing him with them. "You know the idea of building a canal came centuries earlier with the Spanish conquest. Vasco de Balboa. And the first attempt was by the French."

"There hasn't been much talk about that history," Paul said. "Too political for a cruise ship dedicated to Fun."

"Political corruption, you mean," Peter said.

"It's the statistics on the losses from diseases that haunts me," Billy said. "Malaria. Yellow Fever."

"Spread by mosquitoes," Dawn said. "You're right, Billy. The human cost was huge. Still, I'm glad we got the opportunity to see it."

"Yes, we're very privileged. Your mother never wanted to take trips like this."

Dawn felt the weight of his sadness mixed with the excitement of this adventure. She'd done the right thing by bringing him along.

"How are you managing?" Paul asked. "Are you going to stay in the house?"

"Yes, I see no reason to leave."

"I must get that from you," Billy said. "Not wanting to leave home."

Dawn and Paul laughed.

"Gwen's the same," Peter said. "Some people are simply homebodies. Are you enjoying your studies, Billy?"

"Yes. I plan on staying at U. of T. for my medical studies. No reason to change like so many do. The hospitals are world class. Like Princess Margaret."

Dawn thought back to the Run For The Cure. They were still doing things together as a family. She trusted they would continue. Maybe they could include her father more? She missed her mother in ways she wouldn't have suspected. Grief was a strange beast. Her mother's illness was short-lived, but long enough to prepare them for her passing. Yet her death still came as a shock. Billy had told her he couldn't understand how the world had not found a cure, or at least, a fitter treatment that didn't leave patients weakened. "There has to be a better way than battling the disease by killing cells." His words stuck with her. Her son was a man of great empathy and vision. Maybe, one day, he would be part of the cure. Sometimes all it took was motivation rooted in experience.

On the last night before disembarking Dawn sat outside with her father. "How are you doing, Dad?"

"Ah, well, but I miss her."

Dawn reached over and touched his forearm. "Of course, you do."

"Mostly at night. It starts in the evenings, after the hustle and bustle of the day. That's when I find myself talking to her."

Dawn squeezed his arm and blinked tears away. "It must be lonely for you."

"She whispers into my heart. The dead don't die totally, not while there are those still alive to remember them."

"We all exist in the memory of others," Dawn said.

"Yes, we want the same person to be our best friend and trusted confidante."

And passionate lover, Dawn thought, but said aloud, "We think one person can give us what an entire village used to provide, but your community in town gives you that."

Turning to face her, he asked, "Did you want anything of your mother's?"

"Like what?" Dawn felt a little guilty. Should she have a *memento mori*?

"It's just that Gwen was asking. She's volunteered to clean out your mother's closet and drawers."

"Oh," Dawn said surprised. "Does she want my help?'

"No, no. Nothing like that. Gwen knows you are a busy career woman."

Too busy for her own mother, Dawn thought. She felt a twinge of guilt and a confusion of obligations. "I guess I hadn't thought about the practicalities of her possessions." Dawn started to wonder if her father was reluctant to part with Mary's things. Would Gwen see this role as a daughter's or a female duty?

"There isn't much. You know your mother. She wasn't one to splurge."

"No, she wasn't." In fact, Mary hated outward displays of consumption. Dawn wondered if Gwen felt closer to Mary than she did to her own mother. Maybe Muriel was too flamboyant for Gwen? "I think I would like some of her jewelry. Was she buried with her wedding ring?"

"Yes."

"Her pearls. I'd like her pearls to remember her by, and her birthstone. Her ring with her birthstone. That's all. Everything else can go to charity. Is that what Gwen will do?"

"Yes. I'll tell her."

"Dad, are you fine with Gwen taking over from Mom?"

"Yes, she's part of the fabric."

"But do you ever wonder if Gwen is missing out on life?"

"I used to. Your mother talked to her about it, but she said Gwen just rolled her eyes and said she was happy with her life."

"Well, I suppose that's all any of us can expect."

Barbara Simpson took the subway to Runnymede station and walked south through the streets of the area known as Swansea. The names and their historical context were too much for her. She'd asked Gordon about them. He was retired now, a professor emeritus living in a small condo in the city and spent the winters abroad, a different place every year, always at houses of former students or colleagues who were happy to have him come, and house sit. She'd spent New Year's with him in the Dordogne, eating duck and drinking French wines. They'd visited the caves. He'd told her that a Runnymede was a place in the meadow used to hold meetings, "It was where King John put his stamp on the Magna Carta."

Barbara knew where Paul had taken Dawn on their honeymoon. That he lived in Swansea near Runnymede station was no coincidence. It was fate. Why were the fates against her? She didn't confess this to Gordon because she knew he would chastise her for being irrational at best and possibly deranged. Since flying home the thought wormed its way into her psyche and caught hold of her every waking moment, sometimes even invading her dreams. She imagined battles with flashing swords and iron shields. She shared none of this with her mother. No one would empathize with her, not her family, not her friends, and certainly not her clients. They'd dismiss her as unfit, so she lived in lonely isolation with her madness. Finally, she resolved she had to face her demons. January had set record low temperatures and she couldn't bear going outdoors but finally the nights grew warmer. It was dark with no stars shining above her, only the pale light of streetlamps to guide her through the tangle of streets with names like Kennedy and Morningside and Ellis. Downhill then uphill she went until she found Grenadier Heights and walked up to where she stood in front of their house.

The curtains were open and indoor lights shone casting a yellow glow on the snow. Barbara could see movement. Was that Dawn who came into the front room? It was and Paul followed her. He hadn't changed. In all the time she'd been stalking them she hadn't seen him, only her and Billy and Megan. He came to the window and looked out directly at her, curious about the woman on his street in the night staring at his house. She held his gaze, bold and defiant. "I know what you've done," she said mouthing the words with exaggeration so he could read her lips. He turned and closed the curtain.

She remained glued to her spot. He had done what his ancestry had guided him in doing. He lived in Swansea on Grenadier near Runnymede station. No wonder he was so content with the witch that was his wife. She'd provided all of this for him. Barbara felt defeated. Her madness had driven her to do battle here and she'd lost. This defeat would remain her secret. Her obsession waned but her defeat caused her grief that visited every pour of her body and mind like a low- level disease.

Barbara turned, shivered, and retraced her steps.

On April first, 1995, Dawn turned fifty. "A half a century," she said to the crowd gathered at her home to celebrate with her. It was a Saturday night, and everyone invited R.S.V.P.'d to say they would come. She indicated 'no presents' in fancy print. Instead, she asked for donations to The Nature Conservancy of Canada, the foundation she now supported. She sat on the board. Her friends from The Young Naturalists had supported her nomination. They had also made her aware after she returned from the trip in 1993, that cruise ships were big polluters, especially of the oceans because they dumped plastic waste. That experience got her thinking about accountable accounting. She'd become a voice in the wilderness. At least, that's how she thought of herself.

Despite the size of the celebration, it was easy to organize. She hired The Cheese Boutique on Bloor Street to cater. It was a family business that started as a small cheese shop that she had patronized since moving to the neighbourhood. They even provided the servers who moved from her kitchen where they'd set up shop to the rooms indoors and outside with platters stacked with delectables. Of course, there was cheese.

Paul and Billy planned the entertainment, but Dawn asked that her opera singing intern, Christopher Cameron, be included and they agreed to let him go first. She'd heard him sing many times and, when she learned that he was retiring from opera, she invited him to join the firm as an employee under her. She introduced him while the men in her family handed out sheets. They had printed them from the original copy that Chris gave her, excusing his illegible handwriting by saying, "No one has worse handwriting than an accountant under pressure from Bay Street." She asked Chris to read aloud in his operatic singsong voice:

Creeping Credits	**And Dashing Debits**
	Now a debit, when you debt it With a corresponding credit, Should produce a zero balance in the end; But beware the creeping credit Who will wind up when you edit With a domineering debit for a friend!
For a debit has the habit Of escaping like a rabbit, And eloping to the credit's side of town; So when you go to edit credits The damn debit's gone and wed it, In your credit's edit's bed it's settled down.	
	When you dally with a debit, What a complicated web it Weaves, and soon your ledger looks a dreadful smudge; Don't delay, be quick and nab it, With eradicator dab it, And displace deleted debits with a fudge.
If you dub it double debit And not credit like you said it, And your debit dares to dash across the line, Then you'll have to use your talents To reverse the out-of-balance Just remember to invert the minus sign!	

Applause, laughter and cheering followed. He had a booming voice that didn't require a microphone, even outdoors. "Thank you, Chris. Sometimes we need to see the lighter side of our work. I want to welcome you all. It's been a special life to have so many successes, not just material, but with supportive family and friends. I have to get serious for a moment to tell you why I want your support with the Nature Conservancy. Our future on the planet is precarious. I've learned that from the volunteer work I've had the honour and privilege of doing. Accounting is simply a construct, a metaphysical construct. We can be more accountable in business by valuing the real cost of our human activity. Maybe I should have given you this talk before introducing Chris. Usually, you hear the serious then the lighthearted. But I deliberately chose this order because there is too much lip service being paid to our environment. We know but we don't act. Many of us here have children, grandchildren. Think of them and what kind of world you want to leave."

Applause followed her speech. Dawn felt relieved. Going public was a gamble. Look at how Prince Charles was treated for claiming the problem of global warming was something that "won't go away." She'd rehearsed her talk in front of Paul and got his approval, although he had said not to advise anyone to "Talk to the roses."

Asking Chris to use his booming voice once more Paul invited everyone to go inside to "Fill your plates. Don't all rush in at once, though. There's an order, oldest to youngest, and if you don't remember your age, Dawn has created a list that's posted on the dining room door."

More laughter followed. "Keeping count, are you?" someone yelled.

Two hours later, after dinner, Paul once again invited everyone outside. Once assembled, Billy gave a speech. "My mother wears many hats. She has been my mentor as well as caregiver ever since I can remember. She is loving, supportive, and loyal. For her, family comes first. First in line is my dad. He's number one in her life. I grew up hearing them talking things over and watching them kissing. These behaviours I remember from a very early age. They were a couple, but I was an extension of their family dynamic. So, I came second. Third comes the extended family: my grandparents, my aunts and uncles, my cousins. Fourth comes friends, a few very close friends: Karyn and Manfred top the list and we've been as close as any family to them. Jonathan and Anna are like my cousins. Her work friends: Hilary, Timothy, Ross. Her volunteer friends. My mother sat on the board of The Young Naturalists Foundation for years in support of me and my interests and in support of our future. Now she has asked you to support her in her new volunteer work. In case I'm painting her as perfect, let me just say she has a staggering ineptitude for learning foreign languages."

"*Si, si,*" Ernesto shouted. The crowd laughed.

Billy continued, "She is a liberated woman in the true sense. Yes, she would admit to being a feminist, and sadly that word seems loaded nowadays, but she is a trailblazer, a working mother, a professional, a breadwinner. She intimidates every girl I bring home. She doesn't do so stridently or deliberately. Some of those girlfriends are here tonight and that is testament to my mother's influence. Welcome guests of many generations. Welcome to our home. We're here to celebrate the best wife, mother, relative, and friend in the world. I love you, Mom. To Dawn," Billy said raising his glass.

"To Dawn."

When Dawn cut the cake, she took the opportunity to talk to every guest as she handed them a piece. Anna Freundlich stepped up to her with Adam Kazama by her side. "Have you two just met?" she asked.

"Yes. I've heard a lot about him from Billy over the years," Anna said.

"Me, too. I feel like I've known you forever." Adam looked into Anna's eyes as she handed him a piece of cake.

Dawn was pleased to see a budding romance. Then she greeted Teresa and Kelley, who said they would take four pieces. Next came Ross with his wife, Denise. She said she loved the view of the city from the backyard. Dawn was taken aback with the realization that she'd never had the couple to her home before. Her former professor, who was now retired from the University of Toronto, took one piece of cake and stood in front of her eating it wanting to chat and reminisce about old times. She listened while continuing to serve others. Clearly, he was alone. She caught sight of her father and asked Gwen Junior to take him a piece of cake. He didn't seem lonely, although he continued to live alone. She knew he missed her mother, but he seemed to have gotten on with life. Dawn considered that. He'd always been a good influence. Later she went over to her father and gave him a hug. It was something they'd started doing since her mother's passing. The three of them had never been a family who expressed their emotions, especially through physical touching. Dawn had missed that growing up. It was Paul who'd brought hugs into family life. She now knew the value of being tactile, of showing love by physical touch, of expressing love. Love had so many forms. Why hide its different faces? Her father's old face felt warm against her skull. Dawn turned her head and kissed the side of his. Her lips landed on his soft ear.

On a hot day in June Dawn took her coffee into the back garden. Fanning her dressing gown, she left her beverage on the table and walked across the grass. Kyle from the tree service company had warned them that the one tall Elm tree showed signs of stress. As she approached the magnificent Elm a wave of connection settled on her similar to what she'd felt when she'd first laid eyes on her son. How strange, she thought. It's a tree. Yet it wasn't any old tree. It was their one elm tree. It had survived the Dutch Elm disease during earlier waves of killing. "A highly invasive fungal disease," he'd said. "Infections are usually fatal, and the tree will probably die within a year or two."

Walking closer, Dawn stood under its branches and put her hand on its trunk. The air was cooler under its wide limbs. The bark was tough and rigid, a greyish hue. Looking up she could detect the problem immediately. Many of its leaves were withered. Pointy light green fingers with brown blotches. "You poor thing," she said aloud. Turning she leaned her back against its upright trunk. The tree reminded her of her husband: tall, lean, strong. "Maybe I won't tell him I've been talking to you," she said feeling the bark between her shoulders.

After her reverie Dawn walked uphill to the table and drank her coffee slowly, listening to the far-off noise of traffic that the trees muffled. They'd taken such good care of their trees thanks to Morgan's initial advice when they'd moved in. Trimmed dead branches. Cut down whole dead trees for firewood. The Elm could not even offer that. Its infected wood would need to be destroyed. Dawn sighed and returned indoors.

Billy was in the kitchen. "I saw you under the Elm."

"Yes, saying goodbye."

He took her empty cup. "So, you and Dad are having it cut down?"

"Yes, it's a loss. I'll miss that tree. It's so much a part of the landscape."

"The lungs of the earth," Billy said.

"Trees?"

"Yes, and our lungs work just like their branches."

"Do they? I remember you colouring the parts of the lung and other organs in that medical colouring book you had."

"The Anatomy Coloring Book. I still have it."

"You must show it to me."

When Paul returned from his run, they ate breakfast together. He was out of breath and Billy showed concern that he wasn't recovering quickly. "I'm getting old."

Billy and Dawn raised their eyebrows at each other. Then Billy excused himself and returned with the large, softcover book. Placing it on the table between his parents he opened it to page ninety-five then proceeded to describe the cross section. Pointing to the bottom of the page, he said, "And this is how certain diseases result in a reduction of lung capacity." Turning his head, he faced his dad. "You're okay now, Dad. Breathing normally."

Paul smiled. "Thanks for the reassurance. Just takes me a bit longer to recover."

At the end of June, the tree cutters arrived. The family returned from work to a quiet neighbourhood and an empty space. Billy came home with a print, "Study of an Elm Trunk," he said. "By John Constable."

"Oh, Billy, how thoughtful." Dawn gave her son a light kiss and held the print at a distance. "This will forever remind me of my last visit under the elm tree."

Paul's fiftieth birthday fell on a Sunday in September, 1995. He didn't want a fuss made, saying they'd celebrated royally for Dawn, and as far as he was concerned, that party had served them both. "But we didn't get to give you a toast," Morgan had said, and she insisted on marking the milestone by hosting a brunch. She levelled the playing field by offering to also make the gathering a celebration for Manfred who'd been appointed QC. "That really does make it a royal affair," she said. She served champagne and orange juice in fluted glasses.

Ernesto didn't know what QC meant. When told it referred to Queen's Counsel, he objected because he wasn't a royalist and considered the whole monarchy adoration archaic. "Waste of money," he said.

Morgan said, "Ernesto Gamez, put a sock in it." That was another phrase he didn't understand. "It's from the First World War," she shouted. They were in the kitchen and the family could hear them. Patti raised her eyebrows. "Glad it's only us here."

Dawn rolled her eyes at Paul. "What?" he asked. His captivating blue eyes could turn cold.

Ernesto objected even more loudly. "Silly war," he said. "Between meddling Europeans."

Finally, Morgan gave up, recognizing he came from an intellectual family. Ernesto had often sung the praises of his country because they did not have an army. Now he told them about his grandfather in Costa Rica who had joined the Foreign Legion to fight with the French during the First World War. "The war to end all wars."

"And it didn't," Morgan said.

"*El punto,*" Ernesto said.

"That's why we need to defend ourselves."

"*Yo no digo nada.*"

"Why don't they live together," Paul said, turning his attention to Dawn.

Dawn wondered if this was his delayed reply to her gesture. She felt badly, having been drawn into the negativity. Morgan always was more spirited than she was. Yet they continued to admire each other. Dawn also wondered about Patti. What had happened to her spirit? Morgan had a more active social life than her youngest daughter. Patti had spent the prime of her life raising the twins. She was a devoted mother. Her life centered around the girls. She worked tirelessly to fundraise at the school when they attended Howard Park and continued her involvement when they went to high school at Humberside Collegiate. Patti and Dawn often shared notes on their respective fundraising efforts. Yet here she was, still single. Maybe she should ask her cousins to offer some matchmaking advice.

The buzzer sounded and Morgan rang in Billy, who brought his girlfriend, Joelle Kwan, and his friend, Adam. When they entered the apartment, the twins hugged Joelle. Susie and Sam loved her. To them, she was exotic, and very smart. They both wanted to emulate her. Dawn hoped they wouldn't get hurt since Joelle had only been his girlfriend for a few months. Was there a future?

The buzzer rang again. The Freundlichs arrived. When Jonathan entered the room behind his parents and Anna, Dawn noticed the reaction of the twins. She had to admit Jonathan had grown into a striking young man. He was tall, much of his height in his legs just like Paul. His dark hair was combed in a classic flip, and he wore a suit jacket over an open collared white shirt. Dawn wondered if his mother had a say in his fashionable style.

Now they were ready for the toast, a drink that made Dawn dizzy. She sat down with Karyn. "I remember the first time we came here," Karyn said.

Dawn laughed. "Some things haven't changed," she said.

"Oh, I would say they have."

"How?"

"Just look at this crowd. It's practically a United Nations forum."

"Karyn, that's a bit exaggerated."

"You think so?"

"Yes."

"Well, you know me. Over the top. I still don't understand how Manfred can continue to be so regulated in his work."

"How do you mean?"

"This whole business of QC just goes to show that the law doesn't change. He talks about the standards, the old standards. Whereas I'm into change. Fusion. In design, in art, we respond to changing influences."

"Paul's impressed that he's been made QC. Paul knows he'll never be. In fact, remember that conversation we had years ago when he said he probably wouldn't get into law school if he had to apply today? There's more competition now. Manfred's always been very intelligent."

Karyn eyeballed Dawn. "As I am reminded every day. My parents are so proud of him."

Again, Dawn laughed. "Paul says I'm the one with the brains. I just think there are different intelligences. I keep thinking I should get out of my rut."

"You've had it good where you work."

"I know. It's served me very well while raising a family. Now I seem to spend much of my time doing volunteer work."

"How's that going?" Karyn asked.

Susie appeared and proffered a tray of small edibles. "Thanks," Dawn said, staring at her niece's midriff, which was bare and at eye-level. She was wearing a crop top. Dawn wondered if Susie was cold but didn't ask.

Karyn surveyed the choices before selecting a few nibbles, bite-sized quiche and cheese balls.

"I'm still excited by the work," Dawn said. "Though I think we need to change accounting. I've been thinking about that and now you've got me thinking. While accounting's not as rigid as the law; in fact, it's a metaphysical practice; but it's still a capitalist system. There's no reason we couldn't include other values in our accounting to reflect the true costs of doing business."

"That's deep," Karyn said. Sam stopped in front of them with another tray. "Isn't it nice having the young ones serving us," Karyn said to Dawn while reaching her hand into the tray.

Dawn smiled at her niece. She was the athletic one, played hockey and soccer. Sam was dressed like a cheerleader in a pleated, plaid miniskirt. Her tray looked heavy. It held the hot food with little plates. "Did your mom make these meatballs?"

"Yes, they're turkey."

"That's different."

"Anna made these," Karyn said.

"Joelle made meat sticks," Dawn said.

Sam nodded. "She'll be around soon."

Dawn looked over at Joelle who was wearing a slip dress that was shiny. Karyn and she were wearing denim jeans, stylish ones, expensive. Dawn thought about how anything goes in fashion nowadays. She felt she and Karyn were flaunting their age category by trying to look hip yet landed way wide of the mark, a standard set by the younger generation.

"So," Karyn said, turning to Dawn, "you were saying about doing business. I'm interested because of sourcing materials. So much is changing on that front."

"Actually, I've had some interesting conversations with Ernesto."

"He is an interesting guy."

"Yes. The Costa Ricans are much more conservation conscious than us."

"Oh, is that where he's from? Why did I think he came from Peru?"

"That's Paddington Bear."

Karyn laughed. "Now, you're being silly, Dawn."

"For instance, at one of their big gold mines, the workers were trained in new skills so they wouldn't be made redundant. It happens everywhere, the big companies with heavy machinery come in, dig up the land, and remove the gold that's easily accessible."

"You're still interested in gold?"

"Yes, I still have my stash. The price keeps fluctuating, but that's not what interests me most. I bought it in my youth, not thinking I was acting like a colonialist. I don't even know where my gold came from. I think it's important we hold mining companies more accountable for their practices. We should know where these materials are sourced before investing."

"That attitude can't make you popular at work?"

Dawn shook her head. "Yes, and no. Of course, too many companies just want to give the appearance of being fair. But, in the end, they have to answer to the stockholders."

"Yes. Yet it's a concern, isn't it?" Karyn chewed quietly then swallowed. "What do you think of what the twins are wearing?"

Dawn smirked. "You noticed. The question is, has Jonathan?"

"What?"

"I caught their reaction when you arrived."

Karyn sat up and surveyed the crowd. "You're right. They're huddled together. Aren't they the little flirts?"

"You have to admit your son has grown into a handsome man," Dawn said. "Did you have a hand in dressing him?"

"Good heavens, no. Sons don't listen to their mothers. I'm blessed that Anna takes my advice."

Dawn didn't point out that Billy still asked her advice. She looked over at Anna, who was dressed in a peasant skirt much like the one Patti was wearing. The only difference was that Anna wore a silk blouse that hung loosely over her shoulders while Patti's blouse was a solid-coloured cotton one that did not hang nicely. It seemed stiff by comparison. "I was thinking about Patti earlier. She'll be on her own next year."

"She never found someone?"

"No, not that we know of."

"That's sad," Karyn said.

Joelle came over. "Hi, Karyn."

"Hi Joelle. It's nice seeing you again."

"We had a great time at your cottage."

"I'm glad you did, and you got to meet Megan and Scott?"

"We did. We visited them and their children. Next year they're moving back to Canada."

"It's good they kept the house," Dawn said. "Of course, they can afford to buy anywhere, but it is a nice house, and it will be good to have them here, back home."

"How's the studying going?"

"Terrific. I'm thinking of applying to the University of Alberta for next year."

"Are you?" Dawn asked. Billy hadn't said anything about plans to move away. She looked over at her son. He was talking to Anna and Adam. Dawn wondered if this was the beginning of a changing domestic future.

"What are your long-term goals, Joelle?"

Joelle laughed. "To marry Billy."

Dawn blushed. A doctor who wanted to be the wife of a doctor. "I'm sure your parents have other goals for you?"

"They do. They've made many sacrifices to have their children educated."

"And all girls," Dawn said.

"Yes, but our families have always supported the education of women. Many of my relatives are in medicine."

"How many females are enrolled in your program?" Karyn asked. "In our day less than ten percent of medical students were female."

"Yes, the percentage is still low, or below fifty percent."

"We have no one in medicine in our families so it came as a surprise when Billy chose to be a doctor."

"I know. He told me when we first met. I don't think Billy wants to go to Alberta, so we'll have to endure a long-distance relationship for a couple of years."

Dawn breathed a sigh of relief. Karyn said she trusted they would survive. "So different from our day," Dawn said after Joelle left them.

"Communication is easier."

"That, too."

"I think you're right, Dawn. People are becoming more aware of our responsibility to our environment. Anna watches a lot of documentaries on TV."

"Does she? Like what?"

"You know. *The Nature of Things*. She's been watching it since she was a child,"

Karyn said.

"Yes, Billy too. But I don't want to concentrate on the environment in that way, cleaning things up. If we follow more accounting in the true sense, we won't create so much waste to have to clean up."

"You have a unique perspective, Dawn. I hope you can make it work for you."

"Thanks." The strength of friendship lightened Dawn, not in an enlightening or spiritual way, but still in a positive way. How lucky she was to have a friend who could so casually offer real support. The mark of a true friend was someone who could accept someone as they are, not as they wish them to be. Karyn didn't project her problems onto Dawn, any more than Dawn did onto Karyn. Despite their different backgrounds they accepted one another.

In the early morning of Sunday, August thirty-first, 1997, Paul woke Dawn. She stretched her arms over her head and looked up at him with half-closed eyes. "Have a good run?" she asked groggily, wondering why he'd disturbed her sleep-in. They'd returned from visiting Karyn and Manfred in Muskoka late Saturday to avoid holiday traffic. It was like him to keep up his routine of getting up early to run but unlike him to wake her.

"There's been an accident."

Dawn jolted upright. Immediately she thought of Billy and Joelle. They were staying at the house and had been out when Paul and she came home.

"Sorry," Paul said, seeing the fear in her eyes. "It's Princess Di."

"What about her?"

"She's been in a terrible accident in Paris. Shirley told me."

Shirley was their new neighbour. She'd moved in with her husband and teenage daughter over the summer. Dawn still felt confused. Why would Shirley come outside to tell him that?

As if reading her mind, Paul said, "They get the Sunday paper. It wasn't in the paper but it's all over the radio and TV."

"What happened? Is she injured?"

"Badly. She was in Paris with Dodi."

"Paris?" Dawn thought about the pictures in the tabloids of Diana on Dodi's yacht. Karyn had magazines at the cottage showing the couple holidaying in the French and

Italian Rivieras. It reminded Dawn of Jackie Kennedy Onassis. All that glamour. All that wealth. All that privilege.

"Yes. I'm going to shower now."

"Well, I may as well get up and make coffee. Listen to the news." Dawn decided not to go downstairs in her terry robe. Wanting to be semi-dressed for Billy and Joelle, she put on her velvet track pants and matching pullover that had the date lettered across the front in large block numbers. In the kitchen she turned on the radio. The coverage was of nothing but the accident. Diana, Dodi, and their driver, Henri Paul, were pronounced dead at the scene. The car had crashed in the Pont de l'Alma tunnel. It sounded horrific. There was much speculation about what caused the accident. Was the driver drunk? Were the paparazzi in pursuit of the couple? Was the Mercedes speeding?

Paul came into the kitchen and poured himself a coffee. "Well?"

"They're all dead: Diana, Dodi, and the driver."

"How awful."

In silence they continued to listen to the news coverage together. Then Morgan phoned "Have you heard?"

"Yes," Dawn said. "Paul heard from a neighbour when he was coming home from his morning jog. Do you want to come over for breakfast?"

"Thank you, Dawn. I would."

"Is she coming?" Paul asked.

"Yes. I thought she would like our company and to see Billy and Joelle."

"I'll cook."

When Morgan arrived, she hugged them both. "Doesn't it feel like you've lost someone in the family?"

"It does," Dawn said. "I wonder why."

"We seem to know more about their personal lives than we do about some of the members of our own immediate family."

"Too true."

"What do I smell? Bacon?"

"Yes, Paul's cooking," Dawn said.

Calling from the kitchen, Paul said, "Bacon and eggs."

"Can I help?" Morgan asked joining her son.

"Yes, you could toast the bread."

Dawn said, "I'll make more coffee."

As they were eating Joelle and Billy came into the kitchen.

"What's all this?" Billy asked.

"We've been listening to the news," Morgan said. "Princess Diana died in a car crash."

"That's terrible," Billy said.

Joelle inhaled and covered her mouth.

"Who was with her?"

"Dodi," Dawn said.

"The Egyptian boyfriend," Joelle said.

"And also, the driver's dead," Paul said.

"Apparently Diana was alive at the scene and was rushed to hospital, but they couldn't resuscitate her."

Later they learned that Diana had suffered severe chest wounds. "She had a tear in her pulmonary vein that caused internal bleeding. After several hours of operating, they couldn't get her heart to beat properly. Isn't that ironic?" Billy asked.

"What?" Dawn asked.

"Her former, recent boyfriend was the heart surgeon, Hasnat Khan."

"She should have stayed with him," Morgan said.

"Sorry, I don't follow royal gossip closely enough to remember all these love interests," Dawn said.

"It's just that he was her lover when she took up the cause of landmines," Joelle said. "You have to respect her for that. He was a doctor saving lives. He wasn't a royal or a playboy or a movie star."

Thinking that's how they knew, Dawn smiled and said, "A good guy like you two."

"It's a tragic death for a woman who suffered the ignominy of the royals," Morgan said. "Still in pursuit of a virgin. Utterly archaic. Those poor boys."

"Yes," Dawn said. "How sad for William and Harry."

Lifting her head Morgan turned to her grandson. "How was your party last night?" she asked.

"Good," Billy said.

"Tell me, who was there? Anyone we know?"

"Yes," Billy said, nodding to his grandmother, "the twins."

"What?"

Joelle laughed. "Those two are rivals. They're both after Jonathan."

"Were they flirting with him?" Dawn asked. She smiled at Paul.

"You're talking about my nieces," Paul said.

"And my granddaughters. How flirting?"

"They wanted to know if he had a serious girlfriend and if he was ever going to settle down," Joelle said.

"He's a bounder," Paul said, "according to his father."

"That's an old-fashioned word."

"This sounds like a Jane Austen novel," Morgan said.

"Some things never change," Dawn said.

"It was hilarious," Joelle said. "Jonathan said he likes a woman who knows her own mind."

"That settles it. Definitely, Jane Austen," Morgan said. "I'll have to have a talk with those girls."

"Well Jonathan is practically family," Paul said.

"Family connections are worth maintaining," Dawn said. Then she bit her lip, remembering how Morgan had initially cut ties with Patti and the twins. Did she sound like a morality officer? Victorian chastity was long dead among the royals and the general public.

"They were competing to show him what good people they are," Joelle said.

"You can be proud of them, Grandma," Billy said, wiping the egg yolk up with a piece of buttered toast.

"I'm sure you influenced Susie to study nursing," Morgan said. She shook her head as if to affirm her own insight.

"All that tutoring," Billy said. "Susie understood the sciences as well as math."

"What do you think of Sam studying film?" Morgan asked.

Joelle reached for another piece of toast. "Very modern. There's a future."

Morgan nodded. "I agree. And she's working at Toronto's film festival."

"Now called TIFF. That's Pam's doing, isn't it?" Paul asked.

"She's gearing up for it," Joelle said. "She was full of all the Oscar buzz. Especially around *The Sweet Hereafter.* Sam invited Jonathan to attend the gala with her."

"She did?"

"Yes. They were full of excitement about another Canadian title getting recognized."

"Last year *The English Patient* won the Oscar," Billy said.

"That's right. We should be proud," Paul said. "I'm Canadian."

Everyone laughed. "I'm glad you recognize it's more than hockey that makes us Canadian, Dad."

———————————

In November of 1997, a Canadian mining company that was opening a gold mine in Mexico contacted Dawn. "They're offering me a CFO position," she explained when talking it over with Paul.

"That sounds like a big opportunity for you, Dawn. You've been saying for years that you wanted to do something different."

"Yes, but I never sought out another job. I never went to the trouble." She didn't admit she'd been hampered by her lack of formal education. Those who held more senior positions than her had higher qualifications. Like Paul, they had advanced degrees. Dawn didn't want to point that out to her husband. "Now this has landed in my lap."

"It's a golden opportunity."

"Very funny, but, yes, and a big promotion," Dawn said, thinking how to best express what such a promotion could mean to them. "We've been very comfortable in our life together, as a couple and a family." Billy was still living at home and studying medicine at the same university where he did his undergraduate work. Joelle was studying in Alberta. Their long-distance relationship seemed to be working.

"And?" Paul asked.

Dawn looked directly into his eyes, those blue eyes that had knocked her for a loop when they'd first met were still bright and sparkly. They were happy eyes. They were a happy couple. "If I took this job, it would mean travel. In Mexico."

"Not always the safest place to travel."

They had taken family vacations to Mexico, to resorts, to all-inclusive resorts. They'd never gone off the beaten path. "The mine is in Sonora which is in the northwest close to the border with the states."

"Sounds like the middle of nowhere," Paul said.

"It is." Dawn hesitated. "We fly into Mexico City, take a connecting flight, then an armoured limousine drives us to the mining site."

"What?" Paul was bug eyed.

Dawn inhaled deeply and exhaled. She'd known he would react to this news. "It's airconditioned."

"Dawn, if that's your idea of humour, you get a failing grade. Why do they want a woman if it's not safe?"

Again, she inhaled. She knew he was being protective, not sexist. "They want me. I'm good advertising. These mines have a bad reputation for exploiting the environment and treating the indigenous population badly. They want to change that reputation."

"Well, aren't they?"

"Aren't they what?"

"Aren't they exploiting the country?" Paul asked. He sat forward, spread his legs, and put his elbows on his knees. They were sitting in the front room where they often sat in the evenings. It was cozy. Earlier in the year the room was lit by the setting sun. Now they had a fire going. Flickering light from the flames sent a warm wash over the carpet. Crackling wood burst through the silence between their words. Its calm challenged the potent atmosphere.

Dawn stayed comfortably enclosed in the arms of the wing chair. She wanted this job, but she didn't want to disrupt her stable family life.

"Do you want this job?"

Paul could always read her mind. "Yes, but it will mean changes. This is a good opportunity for me. Maybe I can make a difference? Then again, maybe I'm just a foil. Give me a quarter term and I'll know the true lay of the land."

Paul shook his head. "Then you should accept it. Don't worry about me. We still have Billy at home. He's good company. What are they offering?"

"I have an interview next Tuesday."

Paul studied her. "The eleventh?"

"Yes. At least I won't have to make up some excuse to take the day off work." Dawn still took Remembrance Day as a holiday. "Like I say, it's time to move on."

Billy was excited by his mother's prospects. "You've been headhunted," he said.

"I guess you could call it that."

"No guessing about it." He gave her a hug.

"Thanks for the reassurance. We'll skip Remembrance Day services this year. I think I should prepare for this interview."

On Tuesday, November eleventh, at three o'clock, Dawn entered the offices of Rio Nico Partnership on York Street. She met with the CEO, Jose Reyes, and the Manager, Stuart Morrow. Dawn was used to being in a boardroom with all males, but she was still nervous. These men were young. She could be their mother. "We're glad you're considering our offer," Jose said. They insisted on being on a first name basis.

"We like your experience," Stuart said. "We particularly like your reputation in the volunteer sector. I admit a conflict of interest."

Dawn smiled and relaxed. "Let me guess. You grew up reading *OWL* and *Chickadee*?"

Stuart laughed. Jose looked confused. Stuart explained. "My great aunt started the company that publishes those children's magazines."

"Sorry, foreign territory to me. I grew up in Mexico City," Jose said. "Do you speak any Spanish?"

"A smattering," Dawn said defensively. "I understand it better than I speak it. My son speaks it and so does my mother-in-law. Her partner, Ernesto Gamaz, is from Costa Rica."

"You will be travelling with me so I can translate."

"Thank you."

Stuart opened the file. "So, this is the contract we've drawn up."

Dawn opened it and followed along as he explained the terms. She was stunned, impressed, thrilled, but tempered her response. "I will talk this over with my husband. It means a change in my domestic life, but he is very supportive. I can give you an answer tomorrow."

"That would be terrific," Stuart said.

At home Dawn waited for Paul. He said he would leave work early. She made a pot of tea, then poured them a cup before sharing her news. Her salary would be three times what she was now earning, and much more than his. "There's more," she said, letting him digest the figure. "I know we don't need the money."

"That's not why you're taking the job, Dawn."

"No, I'm ending my professional career with a bang. My bonus comes in gold bullion. I can add to my stash and feel secure it is honestly gotten. I hope," she added.

"What's Jose Reyes like?"

"Young. Very handsome. Totally charming."

"Should I be jealous?"

"Yes," Dawn laughed. "I think I'm safe. My friends and family might be jealous. I'm decades older than Jose and Stuart, but not the secretary."

The next day she handed in her resignation effective in the new year. She got hugs of congratulations and nothing but well wishes from the partners. "You've done it," Hilary said. "You've broken the glass ceiling. I'm proud of you."

The partners were equally supportive. "I'm surprised we didn't lose you earlier," Ross said.

Timothy gave Dawn a big hug. "Don't lose contact. I want to hear from you and how it's going."

Dawn's eyes smarted. She fought back the tears. "It's been a hard decision. You've supported me throughout my entire career, when I was a newbie, then a working mother. When I challenged the corporate structure."

"Like other jealous women," Hilary said.

They laughed together. "I didn't always understand how much you did behind the scenes," Dawn said.

Timothy and Ross shrugged. "It's been our pleasure working with you," Ross said.

"There's still rampant misogyny," Hilary said.

"I know," Dawn said.

"You'll be fine," Timothy said. "We've always had your back. I'm sure Rio Nico will too."

Dawn strolled into the accounting office to tell Chris personally. She promised him that she and Hilary would continue to attend opera. Standing Chris came around the side of his desk to give her a hug. "It always surprises me who loves opera," he said, "but I'm not surprised you're moving up in the world."

On Friday Paul and Billy took her out to dinner to celebrate. Morgan and Ernesto joined them. Billy said exactly what Hilary had, "You've broken the glass ceiling. I'm proud of you, Mom."

"I didn't think that would be such a big deal."

"Of course, it is. A decade of feminism, demonstrating, getting the vote, and still it's a male dominated corporate world. You are a trailblazer," said Morgan.

They were at one of the Three Small Rooms, a restaurant in the Windsor Arms Hotel on St. Thomas Street. Usually, they didn't indulge in such high-end dining, but it seemed appropriate for the occasion, and Paul said he would pay while he still felt like one of the breadwinners in the family. Dawn was embarrassed by his comment, but he said it was made in jest.

"I looked into Jose Reyes," Ernesto said.

"Really?" Morgan asked drolly.

"Don't get your knickers in a knot," he said to Morgan. He'd become fond of learning English expressions to use on her. "He's very respected. He has a good reputation. He's honest. A family man."

"Well, that's good to hear," Paul said.

"Dad's jealous."

"No, he's not. I'm glad you told me that," Dawn said. "We're not going away this Christmas. I'm going to be travelling in January and Joelle is coming home."

"We'll do something special," Morgan said.

Dawn smiled. She was buoyed by their support. She hadn't known what to expect when she'd first received the job offer, but now she was a hero, like some blazing character in a comic strip.

That euphoria was tempered when she was introduced to the shareholders. In the annual report they sent before the meeting the company printed an introduction of her that read: "As we seek to reimagine solutions to the greatest problems of our times and harness the power of partnerships, we want to introduce to you our new CFO, Ms Dawn Wright, who comes to us with years of accounting experience in the mining industry. Partnership has been the font of our work since we first started which is why we refer to ourselves as Rio Nico Partnership. Sometimes our partnerships are among local communities or with foreign governments. We link with different sorts of expertise. Sometimes we bring them together to know how to power sustainable practices. Partnerships link those who can serve different needs. Dawn has an extensive background in environmental practices that benefit us and our partners."

While most shareholders heralded the foresight of the company, some objected that they understood the premier partnership was with them, the shareholders. There was a backlash that got ugly. Weren't accountants responsible for the 'bottom line', for 'maximizing the profit margin', for giving shareholders 'the maximum return'?

She was asked to share her vision of an ethical accounting system that recognized the true costs of taking from the earth. Dawn hadn't gotten far before she was heckled by a couple of men who called her "Aerie-fairy," and worse, "Dumb bitch."

Jose stood and asked the man to leave. The man did while shaking his fist and saying he was taking his "hard earned dollars" elsewhere. Only one other belligerent male followed him out the door. When gone, the others applauded Dawn. She blinked away the tears, not wanting to show any weakness in public, but she felt shaken to the core. She never shared the incident with family or friends. Later she would revisit that experience and question why she'd remained silent. Was she ashamed? Hurt? Embarrassed? Or was she finally aware that she was competing in the real world of male dominated capitalism? All the strife at Rupert & Green paled by comparison to such public humiliation. There her battles were in offices. There she represented the accounting department, an ephemeral calculating, not some higher goal of earthly accountability.

At the end of January Dawn returned home from Mexico in time for Chinese New Year. They were invited to celebrations with the Kwans. "Finally, we get to meet Joelle's parents," she'd said, alerting the firm of the dates when she had to return home.

She dumped the entire contents of her suitcase into the laundry hamper knowing she could trust Graciela to sort out her clothes. It didn't take much convincing from Paul and Billy to hire a domestic servant. "You mean you two want help when I'm away?" she'd asked when they'd complained about how hard it was to work and keep house and feed themselves.

"Everyone has a cleaning lady but us," Billy had said.

Dawn did use a housecleaning service that came every other week. One week they cleaned the two floors upstairs. The following visit they cleaned the main floor and basement. Graciela did not clean the *'casa'*. She did other chores one day a week. She did the laundry. She changed the beds. She shopped for groceries. She came from Mexico and lived with Jose Reyes' family. They'd sponsored her. Ernesto insisted on driving Graciela to the shops saying he liked to help and practice his Spanish. With Graciela he shopped for Morgan, too. The arrangement was mutually beneficial to all parties. "We're *familia*," Ernesto had said.

Graciela worried about Dawn when she travelled to Mexico saying the area where she went was *"muy malo"*. There'd been kidnappings in the Sonora region. Dawn did not explain that she travelled in a convoy. Her limousine was bulletproof. The vehicles in front and behind them weren't. Inside those cars were men with rifles and guns. Those details Dawn kept to herself. She didn't even tell Paul or Billy. Why worry them? In the limo Jose sat beside her and conducted business the entire way from Guadalajara. She did the same. She trusted his judgement. What choice did she have?

Days were short and it was dark when they left the house. Billy drove them to Dundas Street West and parked above ground. Paul and Dawn followed Billy to the restaurant that was half a flight of stairs above street level. He spoke Chinese to the maitre'd. They were used to hearing their son speak Chinese to Joelle. He was a quick learner of languages and was now fluent in French, Spanish, and Chinese, an asset given the multi-lingual patients he served.

It was crowded inside the restaurant, and they walked a zigzag course to keep up to Billy who escorted them to a large round table in the centre of the backroom.

Joelle stood up and greeted them with a wide smile. Billy introduced his parents to Joy, and Min. Joelle introduced them to her two sisters: Madeleine and Mina.

"Sit, sit," Min said indicating the empty seats between Joy and Joelle. Paul sat beside Joy and Billy sat beside Joelle. Dawn felt overwhelmed. The restaurant was noisy, crowded, and colourful, with red and gold decorations. There were no menus. The food arrived on huge platters that everyone passed around. Joelle would tell Billy what they were eating then Billy would tell her. "Dumplings," she said to Paul. "Spring rolls."

"Thanks, Dawn. I think I recognize these dishes."

Dawn laughed. She'd been caught up in the excitement of the moment. "This whole fish is served in a ginger shallot sauce," she said after serving him rice balls and noodles silently.

"Um," Paul said, "I like the smell of this."

"I'll warn you it's carp. You've probably never eaten carp," Billy said for Dawn's ears alone.

"No, I won't tell. Don't want to spoil your father's appetite."

"Steamed chicken," Dawn said, raising her eyebrows and turning to Paul. He loved crispy fried chicken.

"Sorry guys," Billy said leaning into his parents. "It's how they eat chicken at New Year's."

"Gross."

Dawn kicked Paul under the table.

"Hey, that's what Patti always did. Behave yourself, Dawn."

"Are you going to behave yourself?"

"I'm busy eating. What's next?"

"Healthy stuff," Dawn said. "Greens." There were four platters of different vegetables.

Min called for their attention. "Please let me explain the meaning of the lucky foods we eat. The dumplings bring wealth, the spring rolls also. The rice balls are for our family coming together. The fish wish you an increase in prosperity. When we are full, we will eat fruit."

Dawn turned to Min. "All very delicious."

"A hearty feast," Paul said.

Dawn smiled at Joy. Billy had warned her that she didn't speak English well. Where she worked, they spoke Chinese, so she hadn't felt a need to learn English the same way her father had. The waiter refilled their small cups with green tea. Billy had also warned them that the Kwans were tea totallers. Dawn studied the Kwans. They all had straight black hair, unlike her clan: Billy with blonde curls, Paul with wavy dark hair sprinkled with silver highlights, and hers a vibrant red, kept that way through colouring. She brandished a very expensive head of hair. Dawn liked how comfortable the members of the family were with one another. They talked, laughed, and shared. Dawn studied their faces. Joelle resembled Joy, while Madeleine and Mina took after their father. Her son amazed her. How had he come to be a cosmopolitan man while still a homebody?

With the fruit everyone was given a red envelope with a gold covered chocolate coin.

Dawn unwrapped the coin, and before putting it in her mouth, asked, "Billy said you're flying back to Edmonton tomorrow?"

"Yes," Joelle said. "Early flight."

"I guess it would be insulting to offer to pay," Paul said quietly.

"Yes." Dawn touched his knee under the table.

"We're very grateful for this opportunity to have met your family, Joelle," Paul said, squeezing his wife's fingers.

"We hope there will be many more celebrations together in the years ahead," Min said.

Barbara Simpson was diagnosed with Stage Four ovarian cancer. "The irony," Honor said to her nephew, Gordon. "Her whole life devoted to delivering babies. Never getting pregnant and having her own child. Now she faces an inoperable cancer."

"Is there nothing they can do?"

"No. Only keep her out of pain." She sipped her tea. The china was from her mother's set, handed down on her wedding day. Honor studied the pattern with the gilt gold edge. What good was all this heritage when she was losing her only daughter? Life wasn't fair. She knew that, in so many words. It stung her so fiercely she thought she might fling the fragile piece across the room, but, of course, she didn't. Honor Simpson had never given into anger. She'd bit her tongue for the sake of etiquette, manners, courtesy, stiff upper lip, good form, bah. Where had it gotten her? Death came to the lowliest and the richest. Why couldn't they do something about this cancer, this silent disease, this leveler? It seemed this type of cancer was becoming an epidemic. She got angry when she thought about the lack of a cure. Was this another slight against her sex?

Gordon shook his head. "Poor girl. I shall visit her."

"Yes, please do. She's always listened to you."

Honor placed an obituary in the paper:

Barbara Simpson, dearest daughter of Honor and the late Gordon Simpson, died from ovarian cancer on April fourteenth, 1998, at the age of fifty. Taken too soon. She devoted her life to helping others as a midwife. Service at eleven o'clock on Friday, April seventeenth. Visitations

Thursday evening from seven pm to nine pm, April sixteenth. Donations to cancer research at Princess Margaret.

They came in the hundreds: all her children and their mothers.

292

Dr. William Lewis-Wright was present at the handing over of the large donation cheque to Princess Margaret Hospital from Honor Simpson in honour of her daughter, Barbara Simpson. He had shown the hospital newsletter to his parents with the accompanying photo. "The same cancer as Grandma."

"What a shame," Paul had said. "We're getting old, but I didn't expect to hear about people from our generation dying."

"That's a very sizable donation," Dawn had said. She'd watched her husband to see his reaction, but mostly what she noted was that his spine had a slight curve. When had he lost his upright posture?

"That's just from the family. There were dozens of donations from mourners, mostly her patients."

"Really?" Dawn had shaken her head in astonishment. Clearly the woman had done something right.

"Even Patti. I'm not revealing anything that's not listed on the obituary page at the funeral home."

"Let's not tell Morgan," Dawn had said.

Billy had turned to his father. "Do you think Patti will?"

Paul had simply shrugged. Patti was in a new relationship. She'd waited until the twins had left home for university. Being an empty nester didn't suit her and having to leave the house in High Park when Megan and Scott returned to Canada forced her hand to make some changes. She now lived in Uxbridge, north of the city, with a man she'd met on a yoga retreat. Ron Morris was a public-school teacher who'd never had any children. "At least I don't have to be anyone's evil stepmother," she'd said.

While the men went about their business Dawn had looked more closely at the hospital newsletter. She was interested in how their foundation presented requests for appeals to support the hospital's needs in equipment, staffing, and care. "Remember I'm going out tonight to the theatre," she'd said leaving the table. Paul had asked her to say hello to Hilary. Billy had asked what they were seeing. "*Still the Night.* It's a musical that Chris Cameron recommended to us." Billy had been surprised by that suggestion, saying, "I thought Chris would recommend something like *Into the Woods.*"

"I remember watching the film with you," Paul had said. "It terrified you."

Dawn drove up to Bloor Street then made her way further north to Davenport Road. The Corner House restaurant was just east of the George Brown College campus. She parked on the street and entered the white stucco building where she was warmly greeted and escorted to their reserved table. "Hilary," she said, stretching her arms to hug her old friend. "This is a lovely place," Dawn said. "Thanks for arranging it."

"One of my mother's favourite haunts."

"I should have guessed. It is very formal with white linens. How is she?" Dawn dared to ask.

"Mostly bedridden, but somehow able to rise at the end of the day to be taken out for drinks and dinner."

Dawn smiled. "I have to tell you Billy brought home the Princess Margaret Hospital's foundation newsletter and guess who's made a sizable donation?"

"Honor Simpson. Old Money."

Dawn shook her head, not surprised at Hilary's guess. Hilary, who also came from Old Money, and really had no need for employment.

"My mother gets the newsletter too. Dr. William Lewis-Wright I was told, but still Billy at home?"

"Only under our roof." She opened the menu, asked for water, and ordered a glass of white wine. "How's it going at the firm?"

"Gang busters. Your replacement works long hours, is highly efficient and not nearly as much fun as you. And get this: he thinks maternity leave is nothing more than a corporate inconvenience."

"How did he get in the door?"

"Things have changed." Hilary held her friend's eye then looked down. "I think I'll have the filet."

"I'm having the fish special," Dawn said to the waiter handing him the printed menu. "We never cook fish at home," she said to Hilary, "but we always get take-out on Friday and sometimes that's fish and chips. Or falafals or pizza."

"Yes, I remember you and Paul did that from the start. Whereas I was always taken out for dinner on Friday nights."

"So, how's life treating you?" Dawn meant to skirt the personal at dinner. No point giving her friend indigestion, but since Hilary had disclosed her private memory, she asked.

"My personal life is on hold for now," Hilary said with a wave of her bejewelled hand, "but I am going away next month on a river cruise."

"Good." Dawn remembered how Hilary felt about her family's cruise. She supposed a river cruise was different.

"And how's Paul?"

Good question, Dawn thought. How to answer without complaining. She'd had experience with the negative feedback from nagging. Sighing, Dawn shrugged.

"I know he's not a go-getter like you, Dawn, but he is your loyal husband. And that's saying something."

"It is." In fact, it's everything, Dawn said in her head. No need to remind Hilary.

After dinner they exited the restaurant and turned the corner to walk down to Bridgeman Street then to the theatre. When seated Dawn opened the programme and asked, "This isn't a light-hearted musical, is it?"

"No, Chris said Theresa Tova is the daughter of Polish Jewish survivors of the Holocaust and very talented. Although not his usual opera fare, there's much music."

"No, although opera isn't light. Still, not what I expected."

After the show Hilary offered to drive Dawn to her car. "Please thank Chris for his recommendation. It was very powerful. And the female lead was outstanding."

"I thought so, too. Wonderful setting in the forest."

"I agree."

When Dawn arrived home the house was in darkness except for the kitchen at the back of the garage and the hall stairs. She quietly made her way to bed and was sound asleep when disturbed by Paul. "You have to help me," he said.

"What's the matter?"

"I think I'm having a heart attack."

"What?" Dawn jumped out of bed. Then she turned on the bedside light and looked down at Paul. He appeared to be his usual self. He wasn't pale but he was breathing heavily.

"Can you drive me to the hospital?"

"Yes," Dawn said checking the alarm clock. It was six-thirty. Billy always left early in the morning, out of the house by six o'clock. She was alone in the house with Paul. "What are you feeling?" she asked reaching over to touch his forehead. It was clammy.

"I have a shooting pain down my arm," Paul said, gasping.

Now aware that Paul was getting progressively worse, Dawn helped him out of bed and got him his clothes. She dressed quickly and led him downstairs and into the garage. Once he was in the car, she got behind the steering wheel then drove in the dark. There was commuter traffic along the Queensway which surprised her at this hour, but then realized that she was never on the road this early. Pulling into the emergency entrance at St. Joseph's she put the gear in park. Paul struggled with the car door, and she rushed around to his side to open it then helped him stand. As soon as they entered, they were greeted by an orderly who helped Paul into a wheelchair. "I'll park the car and come back," Dawn said.

When she returned, she found Paul in a bay on a stretcher hooked up to an IV. "What's happening?"

"They've stabilized me. I'm waiting for the specialist."

"How do you feel?"

"The pain's gone."

"Was it just down your arm?"

"No, on my chest too."

Dawn checked the time. It was after seven am. She pulled up a chair and waited.

"Guess I do have my dad's genes."

"Oh, Paul, but you're so fit."

"And I'm still alive. He was dead at my age."

Dawn felt stunned by the reality of it. Who would have guessed? "Maybe it was just a warning sign."

The heart specialist came at eight o'clock. "I'm Dr. Babiak," he said, then looked at the file he was holding. "Paul, you've had a heart attack. We'll admit you for further observation and tests."

Dawn blinked. The doctor was an elderly gentleman and very calm. "Should I stay with him?"

"You're his wife?" She nodded. "You can, or you can come back later after we've got him settled." Dr. Babiak departed.

Dawn looked at Paul with tears welling in her eyes.

"Go home, Dawn, and call my office."

"And Billy." She rose and bent over to kiss her husband. His skin felt cool and damp beneath her lips.

He squeezed her hand. "Thanks."

On the drive home Dawn was in a haze. What a sudden turn their lives had taken? One day they're living a normal life like all the other days of their life and in a blink of an eye they're facing a life and death emergency. What would have happened if she'd been away on business? Would Paul have phoned for help?

After contacting Paul's office, she called Rio Nico. They sympathized and asked her to let them know how Paul was later. "Don't rush back," Stuart said. Then she contacted Princess Margaret Hospital. While waiting for Billy she made a pot of coffee. The phone rang. "Billy?" she answered.

"Mom, what is it? They said it was an emergency."

"Yes, your dad's had a heart attack." She told him the details.

"You mean you drove him. Why didn't you call an ambulance?"

Why hadn't they? "I don't know. He asked me to drive him, and I did." She knew she sounded feeble. Were they that incompetent? She hadn't dial 911.

"Next time, call an ambulance."

Will there be a next time, Dawn wondered.

The upshot of Paul having a heart attack is that Paul gave up his practice. Everyone was shocked by the news; that is, everyone but Dawn. "His heart wasn't in his job," became her glib reply. After receiving a stent implant at St. Michael's Hospital, he was well but still seemed easily tired. One day she'd come home to find him in tears. He wasn't a crier. Neither was she. "What's this?" she'd asked.

"I'm a failure."

"No, don't say that." He was holding his head in his hands. Not knowing what to do to comfort him, Dawn had simply waited. Her mind was in turmoil, grinding thoughts of Paul's work history and revisiting images of him in pain at home and in hospital.

Over the following days they had long discussions about his condition, his work, and his lifestyle. Dawn second guessed that he may have been depressed for a long time, longer than he cared to admit, but typical of his positive outlook, kept it hidden. She concluded he'd suffered a delayed stress response to his heart attack after reading the book by Hans Selye that Billy had given him.

"A stressor is a biological agent," Billy had said. "It's a chemical response. We see it in many cancer patients."

"You don't want to work yourself to death, Paul."

"No, I don't."

When Paul had smiled at her in response, she was thrilled that she had his former self back. He was able to sell his practice and take early retirement. "The benefit of working for yourself," he'd said.

"It's enough for your pocket money."

"Including the hockey seats."

Dawn could only laugh.

Morgan had responded to her son's condition with tenderness. "I so hoped none of my children would suffer the way your father had. He regretted he hadn't taken better care of himself, that he would miss grandchildren, that he would leave me alone." She'd advised her daughters to go to their doctors and get tested.

"Tested for what?" Pam had asked.

"Your heart. Stress test. Your nephew says to get your cholesterol tested."

Patti was fine but Pam was prescribed a statin.

The family had some joyous news to lift their spirits. Billy was officially engaged, and the date of the wedding was set for Saturday, August twenty-ninth. He pointed out that the groom's family pays for the wedding in Chinese culture.

"You might have to cash in some of that gold, Dawn," Paul said.

"Or I might give you a few ounces as a wedding gift."

"Keep it," Billy said. "I've lived rent free all my adult life. You don't owe me anything."

"So, you're paying for the wedding," Paul said.

"I'm making the down payment on the house," Billy said.

Dawn shook her head. Her son was finally leaving home. Was it time to sell? House prices were steadily rising. There were bidding wars. Billy and Joelle found a place in the Annex that they purchased after losing out on two houses. It was on Brunswick Avenue. They favoured that area because it was easy to get to the hospitals on Avenue Road by transit or on foot.

What would Paul do with his time now? He found a cause with the Waterfront Regeneration Trust. They had opened three hundred and fifty kilometers of trail along the shoreline of Lake Ontario where Paul led cycling trips. One weekend Dawn joined him on a fundraiser at the foot of Ellis Avenue on the lakeshore. They cycled together downhill. She wondered how she would manage the return trip. Paul had a very high-end bicycle with multiple gears. He introduced her to one of the women who worked with the former mayor, David Crombie, who had facilitated the expansion of the park. "I really like the design of your logo," Dawn said, "with the bird, leaf, and fish. Very stylish."

"Would you like to buy a hat?" Suzanne asked, leading her to a table stacked with goods for sale.

"Yes, I would," Dawn said picking out two peaked caps in beige that had the blue and green images embroidered on the front, one large and the other small. It was a sunny day with a mild breeze coming off the lake. She placed the cap on her head and took the other to Paul.

"Let me show you the display," Paul said, leading her to a billboard with a map of the trail and a history of the work that went into realizing the project.

"I'm reassured by all of this," Dawn said. "People can come together to make something good for the environment and our lifestyle without thinking it has to be profitable." Recently she had been frustrated by her goals for accountable accounting. How to make people recognize a basic principle that all life is interconnected and dependent on the Earth for survival. How to replace the present economy of waste with a sustainable system. How to survive a collapse from climate crisis caused by global warming. She wanted to organize a fundraiser for the Nature Conservancy, but the challenge always was how to do so in a manner that befitted conservation. She could see from the timeline shown here on the board that nothing happened quickly. Everything took time. But how much time did they have? Getting that message across was difficult without raising alarm bells. Everyone was sentimental about their grandchildren, even Paul's late father, but how to spark their imaginations into recognizing that their grandchildren's future was at stake. Dawn decided she would raise this at the next board meeting. She would share what she'd observed today, use it as an example. Could they appeal to the public the way the Waterfront Regeneration Trust fund had? Maybe if she got Rio Nico on board. Yes, that's what she needed to do. Solicit some wealthy backers. Dawn squeezed Paul's hand.

"What?" Paul asked, looking down at her.

"I'm so glad you're part of this."

He placed his arm around her shoulders and squeezed her close.

———————

It is unusual for the mother-of-the-groom to get involved in wedding preparations, but Dawn did mostly with Paul's help. There were flowers to arrange and stationary to select. Both Billy and Joelle were too busy at the hospital to attend to details and Min and Joy had their attention divided between two daughters: Joelle and Madeleine, who was also engaged, so plans were underway for a double ceremony at Angus Glen Golf Club near their house in Markham. Dawn knew about the owner, Gordon Stollery, who was in mining. He'd taken over from his late father.

Graciela was thrilled by the upcoming nuptials but wanted to know if they would continue to need her help. "Yes," Dawn said. "For now. We haven't decided if we're going to stay in the house. We're so set in our ways here it's hard to make a decision."

Dawn and Paul put their heads together to draw up a list of family and friends to invite. They had to keep it under fifty.

"There's us," Paul said.

"That makes two," Dawn said, writing down their names at the top of the list. "My side of the family: Dad, Aunt Muriel, Uncle Joe, Isabel and Glen, Glen Junior and Gwen Junior, Gwen, Teresa and Karl, Keifer and Kelley, and her partner. What's his name?"

"Fabian."

"How could I forget that? That makes fifteen."

"And my family: Morgan and Ernesto, Pam and Trudy, Patti and Ron, Susie and Sam, and her boyfriend, Chuck, Megan, and Scott."

"That makes twenty-six."

"Friends: Manfred and Karyn, Anna and Adam."

"Isn't it nice they're still together," Dawn said looking up from her list making.

"Yes, it is. Jonathan."

"And he still hasn't found anyone?"

"But he might bring someone."

"You're right."

"Best put Jonathan and guest," Paul said.

"That makes thirty-two. Jose and Stuart and their wives." Dawn added their names.

"And Graciela."

"Yes, we must invite her."

"And our neighbours."

"Two more. That makes thirty-nine."

"Do you want to invite anyone from your old firm?"

"Yes, Hilary and her new friend, Chris and his wife, Ross and Denise, and Timothy," Dawn said writing.

"That makes forty-six."

"What about you?"

"Four more. Let me think about who to select from the waterfront trust." After tapping his head with the rubber tip of the pencil, Paul added two names, Suzanne and Spencer.

"And your old office?"

Paul added two more names.

"We did it. Billy and Joelle have their own list of friends and colleagues."

"How big is the venue?" Paul asked.

"It holds two hundred."

"Glad we're not footing the whole bill."

"I think we should pay for the bar," Dawn said.

"Since we're the ones who'll be drinking."

Dawn laughed. "That was easy. Now the hard part. Addressing all these invitations."

"Graciela and I can do that tomorrow, Dawn."

"While I visit my dressmaker." The next day Dawn made an appointment with Renata, who presented her with some sketches. "Mostly taken from Dolce & Gabbana," she said.

"You're a lifesaver," Dawn said, studying the images. She decided on a pattern that was sleeveless with a fitting waist. It had a long, slim skirt. The jacket wrapped around her waist with a tie at the side.

"Now for the material," Renata said. Leading Dawn to the stock of bolts of cloth Renata picked out a few floral patterns. "You don't want a solid colour. Big print but not bold."

"I like this floral print," Dawn said. "It's pinkish but more skin--coloured. And the flowers are big but open. Loose petals. Yes." She smiled up at Renata. "This will do nicely. "It's a little Oriental, and yet, conservative."

"Good choice."

Saturday, August twenty-ninth was a sunny day. Only close relatives attended the ceremony, the parents of both couples and siblings. Afterwards they took pictures in the gardens surrounding the golf course. Then trooped together inside to join the guests.

The meal was held in the Kennedy Room in the manor house where two buffet tables were set up. The two couples greeted everyone in line before taking their places. Isabel found Dawn and complimented her on her dress. "I have to tell you, you're helping to support me."

"I am?" Dawn laughed.

"Yes, the teachers' pension bought shares in your mining company."

"That's a good investment. You're going to be able to retire early, Isabel."

"Maybe in five years, if I'm lucky. Our pension board keeps a good eye on investments. Not only do companies have to be profitable, but they also have to practice fairly."

"Yes," Dawn said, bemused by Isabel's interpretation. "Healthy practices."

"Who said life wasn't fair?"

"Our children," Dawn said. Scanning the tables, she gave Isabel a quick hug. Dawn's gratitude for the presence of family was so strong it practically hurt.

The party lasted until midnight. Many of the guests stayed overnight and met up for breakfast the next morning, a meal that was included with their stay.

Dawn and Paul knocked on Peter's door. "Ready?" Dawn asked.

"Sure am."

"How are you feeling this morning, Dad?'

Peter locked his door and put the key in his pocket. "Slept like a baby. Were you up late?"

"Yes," Paul said, standing aside to let his father-in-law go ahead.

"That was a really fancy affair," Peter said. "Never been to such a big wedding like that one. My, my."

"Smart of Min to hold a double ceremony," Paul said.

"Yes," Peter said. "Good for Billy. She's a real catch. So's her sister."

Dawn walked slowly beside her father. His gait had become a bit wobbly. "It went off without a hitch." She smiled thinking how they were using such old-fashioned sayings: a real catch, without a hitch.

Peter nodded. "Nice seeing everyone. Hadn't seen most of those people since your fiftieth birthday party."

"Everyone came," Dawn said.

"That says something, eh?"

"Yes," Paul said, "no one declined the invite."

"There's Muriel and Joe," Peter said when they entered the dining room.

"Good morning," Joe said, pulling out a chair for his brother.

"I guess it's us old folks up first," Muriel said.

"Billy and Joelle can't sleep in too late. We're driving them to the airport before noon. They've packed their bags for their trip and we're taking their luggage from last night to their house."

"That must be a change for you," Muriel said. "Not having Billy at home."

"It is," Paul said, "but we've been so busy we haven't had time to miss him."

"Still, it's nice they bought a house."

"It is, Aunt Muriel."

"And it's a big house," Paul said. "Three stories."

"That sounds promising," Peter said.

"You can look forward to being a great-grandfather," Joe said.

"I can."

Dawn smiled. She did not feel any concern for the future in these circumstances. How a fun party, good company, and a bright future could lull a person's sensibilities.

Enjoy the day. Seize the moment. *Carpe diem.* Turning to Paul, she almost spoke the Latin phrase, then decided against it.

In October Dawn flew home from Mexico with Jose in first class. They always flew business class but were upgraded. "Are the flights to and from the country filling up because they are doing that much business?"

"Yes," Jose said. "There are large lithium deposits attracting investors."

"We have lithium deposits in Canada."

"*Si.*"

"And cobalt. And nickel."

"But in areas we may not want to extract."

"Damaging the environment."

"*Si.*" Jose turned to her. "Mexico experienced a drastic climate change in the fifteenth century."

"How?" Dawn asked.

"The area where we go in Sonora turned into a desert. People had to migrate to grow their crops."

"That was before the Spanish came."

"*Si,*" Jose said, "they came in the sixteenth century."

Dawn pondered that history. What could have caused the change if not the invading Spanish? Maybe farming although she doubted the indigenous population would be wasteful. Maybe the weather did simply take a turn for the worse.

She and Jose shared a limo dropping her off first. "Enjoy your weekend."

"Thanks," she said, then entered an empty house. Paul had taken the train to Cobourg to help her father who was finally moving out of his house, and she was driving down in the morning.

The drive on Saturday was stunningly beautiful with the changing fall colours. A total contrast from the bland landscape she visited in Mexico. Of course, not all of Mexico was desert, but she felt a visceral reaction to the contrast she was experiencing here along a highway corridor. The reds were particularly sharp which could only mean that the maple trees were at their height.

Dawn entered her old home. It struck her that the rooms were deserted, empty like a desert. The smell was familiar, old, and worn. It still held the lingering presence of her mother. The downstairs was bare. Walking into the kitchen, she found her father and Paul. "You're early."

"Yes, got up at the crack of dawn." She gave her father a hug. Paul stood and came over to her to give her a big bear hug. He held her tight. "I'm always happy to have you home safe."

"Sorry, I should have phoned last night."

"No matter. We were busy."

"And we ate at Joe and Muriel's," Peter said.

"You've certainly accomplished a lot," Dawn said sitting down.

"We've moved all his personal effects to the bungalow."

"How do you like it?"

"It's ideal."

Dawn turned to her father. "So, you think you're going to like it there, Dad?" After living on his own for five years, he had decided to scale down to one of the bungalow apartments that were built on church land behind St. Peter's Anglican Church. They were white frame and affordable.

"I feel at home there," Peter said.

"Perfect."

"Do you want some coffee? Toast?"

"Yes, please," Dawn said. She reached for Paul's hand and squeezed it. As far as she was concerned, her husband was a saint for doing what could have been her job. He'd helped with the closing of the house sale, with selling the furniture, with packing her father's personal belongings, with setting up Peter's new abode.

After breakfast they drove to the Cobourg Union Cemetery. In the car they were quiet until Dawn turned off Elgin Street onto the paved road and passed the sign. "It's nice they have so many evergreens here," Peter said from the backseat.

"It is," Paul said. "And the grass is still green."

"Most graves have flowers."

"Yes," Peter said.

"Should we have brought flowers?"

"I put a geranium plant beside her headstone last month. Replaced the summer flowers with them."

"Oh," Dawn said, alert to her father's habits with visiting her mother's grave.

"Park here," Peter said.

She did and they got out of the car. They were careful to close their doors without slamming them shut. Dawn marveled at how they all behaved as if they might disturb the dead. Just being respectful, she thought. Rest in peace. Sure enough, there was a large geranium pot hanging beside Mary's tombstone. It had sprigs of narrow green leaves and pale green stems added to the flowering plant. The petals were bright red, a different red from the maple trees, darker and more intense. Paul put his arms around her shoulders, and she held her father's hand. "It's hard to believe it's been five years," she said. Looking over at her father she saw how feeble he now seemed. Looking up at her husband she felt reassured that he still towered above her.

"It's gone like the wind," Peter said.

"Gone but not forgotten," Paul said.

Dawn silently read the inscription. Below Mary's dates was her father's name with his birthdate, waiting for the date of death to be added. She wondered how many years he would outlive his wife. Morgan had outlived her husband by decades. Dawn sighed in gratitude. She still had Paul.

The decision on what flower print to use as a fundraiser garnered great debate at the board meeting. It was proposed by Dawn Wright and duly-noted in the minutes. Her idea was that instead of buying flowers for Mother's Day which fell on Sunday, May ninth, 1999, the organization ask supporters to purchase a print of flowers. She presented a few ideas. One was a botanical print of birds of paradise. Another showed a field of poppies. The third was a close-up of red tulips with white daffodils bordering the front. All the artists had agreed to donate their artwork for the cause, and all had two hundred and fifty prints available for sale. Dawn had lined up a stationery company that would supply cardboard mailing tubes. The only expense would be the postage, and that cost could be included in the order. "Or we could invite people to come to the offices here in Don Mills to pick up their print, thus saving postage but also giving us the opportunity to get bodies inside the place to further promote our work," Dawn said.

Since most people, if buying flowers, would pick tulips and daffodils, the board agreed on the third print, and her proposal passed unanimously. Dawn was pleased with the decision and rounded up some volunteers to help her pack up the orders on Saturday, April twenty-fourth. Paul came with her to help.

They sold two hundred prints and all of them had to be rolled with tissue paper and carefully inserted in the tubes. Some buyers had selected a certain number believing that the ink on their print would be ideal in coloration. They parceled them first and stuck the address label on the outside. Then they divided them into the group that had to be mailed and the ones for pick-up. The staff volunteers took them downstairs to wait for the buyers. They chose to position themselves on the frontline to speak to the buyers about the conservancy.

"Isn't it great you have printers that spew out the address labels," Paul said.

"Yes," Dawn said remembering the days when all these tasks would have been done by hand. Paul always knew how to put a perspective on things.

"The staff has been super helpful," Bruce Meyers said. He was the chair of the board, and a great hiker and cyclist who had befriended Paul.

"Yes," Dawn said, "they got all these prepaid postage labels. We'd better not make a mistake about which ones get mailed or we'll be out."

Paul and Bruce laughed. "Ever the accountant," Paul said.

"Do you think we're making a difference?" Dawn asked.

"On awareness of climate issues?" Bruce asked.

"Yes."

"No."

Dawn looked hard at Bruce. "Why do you say that?"

"Well, think about it. The debate continues with scientists between them and the government and the corporate world. The latest prediction is we have until 2009 to reverse the damage caused by carbon emissions. How much headway have we made?"

"I don't like to hear that," Paul said.

"Nobody likes to hear it," Bruce said.

"Sometimes I think it's a failure of imagination," Dawn said. "I know I'm pushing all these practical accounting measures, but numbers don't sell. People think we're fooling them. Somehow tricking them."

"I'm afraid you're right, Dawn."

"The bottom line is they don't want to pay. They want cheap goods."

"Yet you work for a company that follows ethical mining practices."

"I do. They don't want investors who only want huge profits no matter what the cost. They've been successful because they've kicked those selfish bastards out of meetings."

Paul's eyes widened. He wasn't used to hearing his wife swear. Recovering, he said, "We can only hope that more investors will see the light."

"Hope springs eternal."

"Tell me how you two met?" Bruce asked.

Dawn smiled. "My version. Paul followed me with his eyes at a coffee shop on campus when we were both in third year at U. of T."

"I'll accept that," Paul said.

"Then what? Did he ask you out?"

"Yes. Sort of."

"What does that mean, Dawn?"

"He invited me home to meet his mother."

Bruce laughed.

"She approved," Paul said.

Dawn flashed her diamond. "His grandmother's."

"What attracted you to her, Paul?"

"Her auburn hair. Her brown eyes."

"And I liked his dark hair and blue eyes."

"She's my little red squirrel and I'm her big black one."

"How endearing," Bruce said.

Dawn smiled remembering the red squirrel chasing the black squirrel up the tree in Victoria Park in Cobourg. They'd never publicly acknowledged their terms of endearment for each other and here they were with Bruce divulging all. Dawn wondered about him. What had kept him single? He was a sweet man. Maybe she should introduce him to Gwen. Her cousin now worked at her father's car dealership, a job she took after Peter closed the store. Aunt Muriel couldn't convince her husband to retire.

One of the staff came upstairs and asked Dawn if she would join them at the front desk. Someone was asking whose idea the fundraiser was. Dawn grabbed a pile of cylinders for pick-up and followed her downstairs.

The plummeting temperatures during the month of December caused deep freezes that kept everyone indoors. Dawn was wishing she had an excuse to visit Mexico. Or Costa Rica. Why didn't they travel with Morgan and Ernesto to Costa Rica? They hadn't been invited. Was there a reason for that? She asked Paul.

"I don't know. I never thought about it."

"Think about it now. Why haven't we been invited there?"

"Do you want to go?"

"Yes," Dawn answered. "We've heard so much about the country from Ernesto I'm curious. We should investigate it."

"Mm," Paul said.

"Mm? What does that mean?"

"Maybe that's why we haven't been invited. Maybe they think you'd want to investigate the mining industry there."

"Don't be silly. Why would I do that?"

"Because that's what you do, Dawn."

"I also swim. I was thinking of the ocean. I haven't been swimming in warm water for a long time."

"You haven't even been swimming in the pool," Paul said.

"I know," Dawn said, defeated. "I've gotten out of my routine ever since I started my job as CFO."

"That's not healthy."

"You're right, Paul. I'm going to make a New Year's resolution to get back to swimming. Maybe we should sell the house and buy a condo in an apartment building with an indoor inground pool."

"Maybe. Or maybe we should join the Boulevard Club and you could go swimming there."

"And you could play squash."

Paul smiled. "Can't get anything past you."

"We'll think about that tonight when we're there." Dawn finished her cup of tea. "Time to get dressed." She had a new gown for the occasion, a bias-cut silk dress that fluttered around her ankles. The movement was what attracted her, not the price, but she figured she'd earned it and she was getting invited to more galas where she had to dress formally.

Paul wore a tux he'd purchased at Stollerys on sale. He drove figuring by the time they reached midnight he'd be sober enough to get behind the wheels of the car. He let Dawn off at the front door and parked the car. Dawn waited for him where she greeted the members and guests as they arrived which made her feel like the hostess. Arm in arm they made their way to the dining room that had a view over Lake Ontario where they met Karyn and Manfred. "Happy New Year."

"What do you think of all this hysteria around the end of the world predictions?" Karyn asked when seated.

"Just that. Hysteria," Paul said.

"Will we see the dawn of a new day?" Manfred asked.

"Will Dawn see the dawn of a new day?"

"Funny pun, Paul."

"Jonathan says the bug," Karyn said, "Y2K was probably caused by young people bored with life with nothing better to do than infect computer systems."

"If they all crash," Dawn said, "we'll be in trouble unless you've backed everything up on an external drive."

"We do, at the end of every day."

"So do we, Manfred," Dawn said.

"The repair bills could be enormous. Jonathan's in Germany."

"New girlfriend," Karyn said.

"Good for him," Paul said. "Must be nice to go where the wall once was and now has come down. The end of the Cold War."

"A decade of peace."

"Morgan and Ernesto are in Costa Rica," Dawn said. She looked over at Paul and smiled.

"Dawn wants to go to Costa Rica."

"Why not? I've never been to Central America."

"Have you ever been to Mexico, Karyn?" Dawn asked, thinking she hadn't.

"No, Florida. The Caribbean."

Dawn looked around the room remembering the recent wedding of Anna and Adam. "Have you benefited from your membership here?"

"We have," Manfred said.

"How's the swimming?"

"Great. Two pools. Indoors and out."

"Are you thinking of joining?" Karyn asked.

"Maybe. Or maybe we should sell the house and buy a condo."

"We've considered that."

The waiter came and took their drink orders. "We'll buy the champagne," Paul said.

After dinner they made their way to the lounge and took seats near the window. The party atmosphere was in full swing with hats, horns, and streamers. A musician played tunes on the grand piano. They sang and got loud and noisy then stood for the fireworks. Dawn loved fireworks. Over the years of watching the annual displays she marveled at the ingenuity of the size and changing colours and shapes. This evening's display bringing in a new millennium outshone anything from the twentieth century. Bursts of colour that hung against the dark sky changed from white sparks to red and purple falling stars. What seemed like small white balloons rose slowly then erupted into gigantic balls of yellow and orange fireworks. Colourful planets like Saturn's rings shattered into balls of fireworks that popped then drifted down.

Dawn leaned against Paul. She felt privileged to be with him and friends welcoming a new year and a new century. What lay ahead for them? What did the future hold? She wished beyond all reason that the world's environment would heal, that people would come together like they had in Germany, and that her family would grow.

"Happy New Year," Paul said, leaning down and kissing her.

Epilogue

In the twenty-first century gold prices continued to rise, as did Dawn's holdings. Real estate prices also rose continuously due to low interest rates and economic growth. Dawn and Paul sold their large home and property at the peak of the market and purchased a spacious condo on Toronto's waterfront. They started walking together along the lakeshore. Their condo had an inground pool. Paul hung up his bicycle then purchased an electric one.

In 2015 Dawn retired. Morgan died in her sleep in 2018. Shortly afterwards Peter was diagnosed with terminal cancer. He went into hospice care and died there.

Business did not embrace different accounting methods. New technology changed the lives of the entire global population and made a few fabulously wealthy. Oil production continued to be dominated by politics. Dawn and Paul bought a Tesla in 2010 and their new condo had a charging station. Climate change was mostly ignored, except by dedicated scientists who continued to make dire predictions until they decided they needed a more upbeat approach. Mass demonstrations became more frequent.

Billy and Joelle had three children. They purchased a hybrid car in 2018. A global pandemic shut down the world in 2020. A vaccine was created in record time. At the beginning of COVID health care workers were heroes, but as populations grew tired of the situation, they were maligned and burned out. A shortage of nurses and doctors continues.